Here's what critics are saying about
Spying in High Heels:

"A saucy combination of romance and suspense that is simply irresistible."
—*Chicago Tribune*

"Stylish...nonstop action...guaranteed to keep chick lit and mystery fans happy!"
—*Publishers' Weekly*, starred review

"Smart, funny and snappy, *SPYING IN HIGH HEELS* is the perfect beach read!"
—*Fresh Fiction*

"*SPYING IN HIGH HEELS* is a roller coaster ride full of fun and excitement!"
—*Romance Reviews Today*

"Gemma Halliday writes like a seasoned author leaving the reader hanging on to every word, every clue, every delicious scene of the book. It's a fun and intriguing mystery full of laughs and suspense." —*Once Upon A Romance*

"Fresh and witty little number that will appeal if you like sparkling, good stories with a splash of mystery. Full marks go to Ms. Halliday on what promises to be a very successful debut to a fabulous career."
—*Romance Junkies*

BOOKS BY GEMMA HALLIDAY

SPYING
IN
HIGH HEELS

a High Heels Mystery

GEMMA HALLIDAY

For Mary Ellen Halliday Thompson.
She never wore Manolos, Pradas, or Choos,
but with a style undeniable,
no one will ever fill her shoes.
We miss you, Grandma.

CHAPTER ONE

———

I was late.

And I don't mean the kind of late where I spent too much time doing my hair and was now stuck in traffic. I mean I was *late* late. The kind of late where the 99% effective warnings on the side of condom boxes flashed before my eyes as I white knuckled my way down the 405, silently screaming, why me? Why, oh why me? I'm a new millennium girl. I took copious notes in 6th grade Sex Ed. I carry just-in-case condoms in the zippered section of my purse. And, after that first singularly awkward experience in the back of Todd Hanson's '82 Chevy after junior prom, I have been meticulously careful. Me. I was late. And I was not taking it well.

"Dana?" Silence. "Dana, I need to talk to you." Silence. "I swear to God if you are screening me I am never speaking to you again."

I switched my cell phone to the other hand as I changed lanes, narrowly avoiding a collision with a pick-up that had "wash me" carved in opaque dust, before continuing my desperate pleas into my best friend's answering machine.

"Dana, please, please, please pick up? Please?" I paused. Nothing. "All right, I guess you really aren't there. But please, please, please call me back as soon as you get this message. I mean pronto. This is a serious code red, 9-1-1 emergency. I need to talk to you *now!*" I punctuated this last word by laying on my horn as a bald guy in a convertible cut me off then had the audacity to give *me* the finger. Welcome to L.A.

I flipped my phone shut, breaking a French tipped nail in the process, and counted to ten, trying to remember some of that calming yoga breathing from the one class Dana had dragged me to last month. Unfortunately, at the time I'd had my full attention focused on not falling flat on my face during a downward facing dog, and I think I was beginning to hyperventilate.

I merged onto the 10 freeway, glancing down at the digital readout on my dashboard clock, and realized with a twist of irony that I was now not only late, but late. As in not on time to meet my boyfriend, Richard Howe, for lunch. He'd made one o'clock reservations at Giani's and it was now twelve fifty-eight. I eased my suede ankle boot (which had maxed out my Macy's card, but was so worth it!) down just a little harder on the accelerator, after checking the rearview mirror to make sure the highway patrol was nowhere in sight. Not that I was speeding. Much. But considering the day I'd had so far, an encounter with the CHP was not on my list of to-do's.

As I checked for motorcycle cops, I also gave myself a quick once over in the mirror. Not bad considering I was having the freak out of my life. My ash blond hair was still tucked into a flattering half twist, a few flyaways but the messy look was in, right? I pulled out a tube of Raspberry Perfection lip-gloss and applied a thin swipe across my lips, ignoring the obscene gestures from the guy behind me. Hey, if a girl in a crisis doesn't have her lipstick, what does she have?

I'm proud to say I only got flipped off two more times before pulling my little red Jeep (top up today as a concession to my hair) into the parking garage on the corner of 7th and Grand. I fastened The Club securely on my steering wheel and prepared to hoof it the two blocks to my boyfriend's firm where I was supposed to meet him…I looked down at my watch…damn. Twelve minutes ago. Well, on the up side, as soon as I told him about being *late,* I had a feeling he'd forget all about my being late.

A conversation I was seriously dreading. In my mind it went something like this: Hi Richard, sorry I'm late, by the way I may be having your child. Insert cartoon sound of Richard hitting the door at roadrunner-like speeds. Ugh. There was just no good way to ease into information like that. We'd only been dating for a few months. We hadn't even made it to the shopping at Bed Bath & Beyond stage yet, and suddenly we had to have *this* conversation? I adjusted my bra strap as I walked, tucking it back under my tank top, trying like anything to present the appearance of a woman with it all together. And not a woman trying to remember which pregnancy test commercial touted early results with digital readouts.

Exactly fourteen minutes behind schedule I walked into the law offices of Dewy, Cheatum & Howe. In reality the firm was called Donaldson, Chesterton & Howe. But I couldn't resist the nickname. Considering the type of clientele they represented (the Chanel and Rolex crowd) it fit like an imported, calfskin glove.

Beyond the frosted front doors maroon carpeting yawned across the reception area, muffling the sound of my heels as I made my way to the front desk. The large oval of dark woods stretched along the back wall of the spacious room, flanked on either side by more frosted doors leading to the conference rooms and offices beyond. The faint clicking of keyboards and muffled conversations billed at three hundred dollars an hour filled the background.

"May I help you?" asked the Barbie doll behind the desk. Jasmine. Or as I liked to call her, Miss PP. As in plastic parts. Jasmine spent two thirds of her salary every month on cosmetic procedures. This week her lips were collagen swollen to Angelina Jolie standards. Last month it was new boobs, double D of course. As usual, her bleached blond hair was moussed within an inch of its life, giving her an extra two inches on her already annoying height of 5'6". I'm what could be referred to as a petite person, topping out at an impressive 5'1 ½" on a good day. I was lucky if I made the height requirement on half the rides at Six Flags.

"I'm here to see Richard," I informed Miss PP.

"Do you have an appointment with Mr. Howe?" Her blue eyes blinked (with difficulty due to the brow lift two months ago) in an innocent gesture that I knew was anything but. Jasmine's sole entertainment here at Dewy, Cheatum & Howe was wielding the power of entry to the sacred offices beyond the frosted doors.

I narrowed my eyes at her. "Yes. As a matter of fact I do."

"And you are?"

I tried not to roll my eyes. I'd met Richard here for lunch every Friday afternoon for the past five months. She knew who I was and by the tiny smile at the corner of her Angelina lips, she was enjoying this all too much.

"Maddie Springer. His *girlfriend*. I'm here for a lunch date."

"I'm sorry, Miss Springer, but you'll have to wait. He's with someone in the conference room right now."

"Why didn't you just say that in the first place?" I mumbled as I sat in one of the tan, leather chairs punctuating the waiting area. Jasmine didn't answer, smirking instead (which looked a lot like an Elvis lip curl in her new super-sized lips) as she opened what I'd guess was a game of solitaire on her computer and pretended to look busy. I picked up a copy of *Cosmo* from the end table and began flipping through the pages of drool worthy designer clothes I could never afford. Or fit into if I was actually pregnant. Oh God. What a depressing thought.

After what seemed like an eternity of listening to Jasmine's acrylic nails click against her keyboard, Richard walked into the reception area. Despite the anxiety building in my stomach, I couldn't help a little yummy sigh at the sight of him. Richard was six foot one and all lean muscle. He was a religious runner, doing 10k's for all the charities in his spare time. Muscular dystrophy, autism, even the breast cancer run last April. When we first started dating he tried to get me to run with him once. Just once. My idea of a cardio workout was elbowing my way through Nordstrom during the half-yearly super sale. Running was something I didn't do. Besides, I figured if the heels were high enough, walking the two blocks from my apartment to the corner Starbucks burned almost as many calories as running, right?

Today Richard's blonde hair was perfectly gelled into place in a casual wave, a la early Robert Redford. He was wearing a dark gray suit, paired with a white shirt and tasteful paisley printed tie. He looked downright delish and I resisted the urge to throw myself into his arms, unloading all my worries onto the shoulder of his wool suit.

Another man exited the offices with him, the two of them deep in conversation. I couldn't make out what they were saying, but whatever it was had Richard's sandy brows drawn together in a look of concern.

The other guy was dressed in Levis, worn with faded patches along the thighs and seat, and a navy blazer over a form fitting black T-shirt. His shoulders were broad and he had the sort of compact build that made you instantly think prizefighter. A white scar cut into his eyebrow, breaking up his tanned complexion. Dark hair, dark eyes, and the sort of hard look about him that usually went along with prison tattoos. I hoped Richard wasn't branching out into criminal defense.

I waited until they'd shook hands and the other guy had walked out of the lobby before approaching Richard.

"Hi honey," I said, standing on tiptoe to place a kiss on his cheek.

"Hi." He was still staring after the felon, his tone distracted as if I'd just interrupted him during football season.

"Who was that?"

"Nobody."

The way Richard was still staring after Mr. Nobody led me to believe that wasn't exactly true. However, I had bigger things to think about than Richard's latest client. Like being late.

"You're late."

"Huh?" I whirled around, panic rising like bile in my throat. Good God, could he tell already? Insanely I looked down to my abdomen as if it might have grown six inches in the last thirty seconds.

"We had reservations for one."

Oh. That late.

"Sorry, there was traffic on the 405. We'll just go somewhere else. How about the Cabo Cantina?"

Richard was still staring at the closed glass doors where Mr. Nobody had exited. I wondered again who the man was. He didn't look like Richard's typical clients and he certainly didn't give off that new car scent of another lawyer.

"I, uh, don't think I'm going to make lunch today after all. Something's kind of come up."

"Oh, that's too bad." Am I a totally bad person that I was actually a little relieved? At least we didn't have to have *that* conversation now. At least now I had a little time to come up with a better way of dropping the bombshell than, "Richard, we've got to buy stronger condoms." Hmm…I wondered if I could sue Trojan over this?

"Sorry, Maddie. I'll call you later, I promise."

"That's okay. I understand. I'll talk to you tonight then?"

"Sure. Tonight." He gave me a quick peck on the cheek before disappearing back through the frosted doors and into the bowels of Dewy, Cheatum & Howe. Jasmine looked up just long enough to give me an Elvis smirk before going back to her solitaire game.

* * *

I walked the two blocks back to my Jeep and left another message on Dana's answering machine. If she didn't pick up soon I was going to have to start taking résumés for a new girlfriend. I started my Jeep with a roar that echoed in the parking structure and instead of getting back on the freeway, made my way up Grand to Beverly Boulevard. I hit a drive-thru McDonald's and ordered a decadent Big Mac, large fries and a strawberry shake. This was not a day to be counting carbs.

I parked in the lot, enjoying my comfort food in the privacy and full blast air-conditioning of my Jeep. As I slurped the last of my shake, I wondered what to do now. I *should* go back to work, something I'd neglected ever since staring in horror at my calendar this morning. However, the thought of being creative right now didn't seem quite realistic.

As a little girl I'd always dreamed of being a fashion model, parading down a Milan runway in the latest designer creations as the world ooh'ed and ahh'ed. But by the eighth grade it was abundantly clear I was not going to achieve fashion model height. So, I settled for the next best thing, being a fashion designer. After four years at the Academy of Art College in San Francisco, I was ready to make my mark on the fashion scene. Only I hadn't counted on it being almost as hard to break into fashion as it was to break into modeling. After begging, pleading and promising to wash every fashion exec's car in the greater Los Angeles area, I finally landed a job. Designing children's shoes for Tot Trots. Okay, so it wasn't Milan, but it paid the bills. Most of the time.

The perks were I set my own hours, I worked from home, and I was happy to say that my work had been featured on the feet of fashionable tots everywhere, including the Barbie Jellies last spring and the SpongeBob slippers in the fall collection. Currently I was working on the Strawberry Shortcake high-tops—available in both iridescent pink and sparkling purple, thank you very much.

However, at the moment the idea of spending a day with tiny tot fashions didn't hold enormous appeal. Kiddie shoes made me think of kids, which made me think of babies, which led to thoughts about condoms that for no good reason at all sometimes broke and led to women being in my current position.

I looked down at my dash clock. One forty-five. Dana was probably getting to the gym right about now for her step-and-sculpt class. In addition to being my best friend, Dana was an aerobics instructor at the Sunset Gym. That is, in between auditions and bit movie roles. Like 90% of Los Angelinos, Dana wanted to be an actress. Though she swore as long as she didn't moonlight as a waitress, she could keep from becoming a cliché. I figured if I took the 101, I might be able to catch her between classes.

I set my shake down and put the car in gear, pulling up in front of the huge concrete and glass structure of the Sunset Gym in record time. I parked in the lot, declining the valet parking. Yes, in L.A. people actually avoided walking the two yards from the parking lot to the gym before doing their three-mile run. Go figure.

As I entered the gym, a tall guy with a buzz cut and Popeye arms stopped me at the front desk. He looked me up and down, taking in the two-inch boots, Ann Taylor skirt, and lack of Nike bag slung over my shoulder. I wasn't fooling him. We both knew I only used my membership for a swim in the pool on those hundred degree plus days.

After whipping out my ID card and satisfying the steroid gatekeeper, I entered the main floor, scanning past rows of exercycles for any sign of Dana. I spotted her at the front of a class by the windows, stepping and sculpting their little hearts out. I had a brief moment of guilt over my gazillion calorie lunch, but it didn't last long. Certainly not long enough for me to actually suit up and jump on a stepper.

Instead I grabbed a dog-eared copy of *Elle*, settling onto a bench along the wall to wait. It didn't take long for the gyrating steppers to finish, breaking into a self-congratulatory round of applause. The teacher of the step class came jogging toward me, her strawberry blonde ponytail swishing back and forth. A perfect size two, she looked like she'd just stepped off the pages of *Sports Illustrated*. And not the swimsuit edition, but the women-who-lift-and-the-men-who-love-them edition. I would hate her, except for the fact that Dana, a.k.a. aerobics queen, was my best friend.

"What's up?" she asked, looking down at my high heeled boots with a frown.

"I just ate," I said by way of defense.

Dana shot me a dubious look but let it go. Instead she began doing a little jogging in place thing as she talked. "So, I got your message. What's the big emergency?"

"I, uh…" I looked over my shoulder as if I almost shouldn't be saying it out loud. "I'm late."

"Okay, we'll talk fast. What's up?"

"No, no. Not late. *Late*."

Dana cocked her head to one side, taking this in before the meaning hit her. "Oh my God. You mean you missed your period?"

"No. I didn't *miss* anything yet. I'm just a little late."

"No wonder you're freaking out."

"I'm not freaking out. I'm…just a little late."

Dana shot me the yeah-right look she'd been using on me ever since we bonded over our love of New Kids on the Block in seventh grade. "Right. And that's why you left four messages on my machine this morning."

I cringed. Did I really leave four? "Okay fine. I'm freaking out. But just a little."

"Did you take a test yet?" she asked, switching to a jumping jacks routine.

"Like a pregnancy test?"

"No, an algebra test. Geez, anyone would think you've never been late before."

Truth was, I hadn't. And that's what was scaring me even more about my predicament. Ever since my monthly visitor began arriving, I'd been twenty-eight days like clockwork. Which is why I'd panicked and left a near stalker amount of messages on my best friend's machine. Hey, wait a minute, if she got my messages, how come she didn't call me back?

"Why didn't you call me back?"

Dana got that wicked smile on her face that said she was either dating someone new or about to give someone twenty push-ups.

"I wasn't exactly alone."

"Do I want to know who?"

"Sasha Aleksandrov," she said, switching to a little two-step footwork in place.

"Excuse me?"

Dana giggled. Yes, grown women with 1% body fat still giggle like middle-schoolers with braces when it comes to men. "He's a Russian body contortionist. Sasha's the bottom of the human pyramid in the Cirqué Fantastique."

I tried not to roll my eyes. Dana had an uncanny ability to pick guys who were destined for short-term relationships. "So where did you meet Mr. Pyramid Bottom?"

"Here. He came in with the Spanish trapeze artist to work out last week. I offered to show him how to use the Cybex machine. He doesn't have them in Russia."

"Of course not."

"And, we hit it off. He asked if I wanted to see him perform."

Considering the many meanings behind that statement, I'm betting Dana said yes. She never passed up an opportunity to see a muscular man "perform."

"That's it. I don't want to hear any more," I said, covering my ears. Dana giggled again.

"Okay, so how late are you?" she asked instead.

"Three days."

"And you called me before noon for that? Honey, three days is nothing."

"Dana, I've never been three days late before."

"Lucky for you, I've got an emergency preggers test at home. I have one more class then we'll go to my place and make a pitcher of margaritas while you pee on a stick. It'll be fun, okay?"

"No. No margaritas, Dana. I can't drink that stuff, I might be pregnant."

At this, Dana actually abandoned her aerobics, standing perfectly still. She stared at me, her pert little mouth hanging open. "You're not actually thinking of having a baby are you?"

Was I?

"No. I mean, I don't know. I don't know what I'll do if I…if…you know."

"We see a pink line?"

"Yeah."

"Fine. No margaritas for now. But you are so peeing tonight."

*   *   *

Luckily I convinced Dana that peeing on a stick was a solo mission and left her to her Kickboxing for Seniors class. I did stop by the drugstore and pick up a test, the most embarrassing purchase of my entire life including the first time I ever bought condoms and accidentally grabbed super ribbed for her pleasure. I also purchased a Big Gulp, so by the time I pulled into the driveway of my second-story studio in Santa Monica, I was ready to pee. Physically that was. Mentally, I was a wreck.

I locked my Jeep, climbed the wooden stairs to my apartment, and let myself in, dropping the drugstore package on the kitchen counter. Despite the fact I had to pee like a racehorse, I couldn't quite get up the courage to take the pregnancy test into the bathroom with me. Somehow now that I was faced with an entire array of IF's, that test had become scarier than a Wes Craven movie. I mean, what *if* it did turn pink? Did I really want a baby? I looked around my cozy (translation: dinky) studio apartment, filled to max capacity with a fold out-futon and my sketch table. Where the hell would I even put a baby?

I guessed I'd always assumed I'd have kids someday. But even though I was closing in on thirty (and I refuse to say just *how* closely) someday still seemed far, far into the future. When I was more settled, domestic. Married. Oh God, would Richard think I wanted him to marry me? Did I?

I think I was hyperventilating again.

I went to the bathroom, sans stick, then checked my answering machine. No messages. Namely, no Richard. I picked up the receiver and dialed his number, waiting as it rang on the other end. His machine kicked in and I left what I thought was a relatively breezy message, considering the circumstances.

I plopped myself down on the sofa and clicked on the TV, settling for *Seinfeld* reruns while I waited for Richard to return my call. By *Letterman*, I still hadn't heard from him. Which was annoying and also a little worrisome. He *had* said he'd call me tonight. And it wasn't like Richard to ignore my messages. I tried not to freak out, instead promising myself I'd take the pregnancy test just as soon as I heard from Richard.

A promise that would soon come back to haunt me.

CHAPTER TWO

———

Three days later, still no Aunt Flo. And still no Richard.

I was beginning to worry. About Richard, though the unopened pregnancy test on my kitchen counter didn't help matters. Richard had never ignored my calls like this. Usually he checked his messages every hour on the hour, returning mine with at the very least a text messaged smiley or "hi beautiful." Only I'd left about a gazillion messages and gotten no smileys back.

I left a second breezy message Saturday morning: Hi, how are you, guess you got too busy to call last night. At lunch I called his office, only to be bumped to voicemail. I held off calling again until almost five, when I then left another message on his voicemail, cell phone, home phone and emailed him a message full of my own smileys and "where are you?"s.

Dana intervened at that point, promising to tie my hands behind my back if I didn't give the man a little space. She was right. I was beginning to be bunny boiling scary. So, I didn't call all day Sunday until the time the perky newswomen on the Channel Two late report came on chatting about a burglary in Reseda and the day's record highs. Then I left three more messages. Still no answer.

This was really unlike Richard. And try as I might I couldn't shrug off the feeling that Richard's commitment radar had somehow picked up on my lateness and he'd headed for the hills.

So, Monday morning my over active-imagination and I woke up determined to track down the MIA boyfriend. I showered, dressed in my favorite jeans, green silk sleeveless top and strappy emerald slingbacks. After a quick turn under the blow dryer and a little requisite lip-gloss, I was ready to go. It was only ten when I parked in the garage down the street from Dewy, Cheatum & Howe, but already the sidewalk was beginning to haze from the heat. Nothing like a smog layer to add a little sizzle to your July.

Two blocks and three homeless guys later, I entered the cool, air-conditioned interior of Richard's building. Predictably, Jasmine was standing sentinel over the reception area.

"May I help you?" she asked, looking anything but helpful.

"I'm here to see Richard."

"Do you have an appointment?"

I swear that should be this woman's epitaph. Here lies Jasmine "do you have an appointment" Williams. May she rest in peace.

"No. But I'm sure he'll see me if you'll just let him know I'm here."

"And you are?"

I narrowed my eyes at her. "Maddie Springer. His *girlfriend*." I emphasized the word.

"I'm sorry, Miss Springer, but Mr. Howe isn't in. He's taking a few personal days. But, I'll leave a message that you stopped by." She seemed to take inordinate pleasure in the fact.

"Why didn't you just tell me he wasn't here in the first place?"

Jasmine's over-sized lips curled into a smile. At least I think it was a smile. Maybe a sneer. "You didn't ask."

I took a deep breath. Rationalizing that if I reached over the mahogany desk and scratched her eyes out I might ruin another manicure. "Fine. Did he say where he was going?"

"I'm sorry," she said with what was clearly a sneer this time, "but I'm not at liberty to divulge—"

"Never mind," I cut her off. I'd already given Jasmine way too much enjoyment today. Instead I spun around, digging my heels into the maroon carpet and stalked off toward the elevator, leaving Jasmine to her solitaire.

Clearly Richard wasn't at the office. Next stop – his condo.

Richard lived in a two-story condo in Burbank, nestled in a gated community of tall stucco buildings on Sunset Canyon. The condos were all painted a pale taupe that hid dirt and on high smog index days matched the exact color of the air. Richard's was the third structure on the right.

I parked across the street, thankfully finding a spot on the same block after circling only twice, and clubbed my steering wheel.

I keyed in the entry code on the electronic pad next to the iron gates and made my way through the mini garden courtyard, consisting of yucca trees, leafy green bushes and flowering agapanthus. I paused as I reached Richard's door, took a deep breath, and stuck my key in the lock.

I was halfway expecting Mafia thugs to jump out at me, or the place to look trashed as if Richard had been dragged away against his will, kicking and screaming, "Wait, just let me return my girlfriend's call first!"

I was disappointed. The condo looked exactly as it always did. Sleek, black leather sofas were set in the sunken living room, offset by chrome and glass end tables. The alcove kitchen to the right was clean, the green granite counters gleaming as morning sun filtered through the sliding glass doors to the second story balcony.

"Hello?" I called into the silence. But almost instinctively, I knew I wouldn't get an answer back. The house had the feel of disuse, the air slightly stale as if the windows hadn't been cracked in days. Which did nothing to reassure the anxiety building in my belly.

Richard wasn't here. He wasn't at the office. I was running out of places to look for him. Was it possible that he'd been called out of town suddenly? Maybe a family emergency? His mother lived alone in Palm Springs, maybe she was sick?

I crossed the room, angling down the narrow hallway that led to the marble tiled bathroom, Richard's bedroom, and the spare room Richard used as a home office. I opened the office door, gingerly peeking my head in first. No Richard. But the answering machine on his desk was blinking like mad. Feeling just the teeny-tiniest bit intrusive, I pressed the play button.

Would you believe all twelve messages were from me? Yikes. Quickly I erased all but one. There, that sounded more like a rational, sane girlfriend.

I took a quick look around the rest of the office. No plane tickets to the Bahamas, no telegrams saying, "Mom's sick, come now." I moved on to the bedroom, my heels echoing on the polished hardwood floor.

Like the rest of the house, the bedroom seemed untouched. The bed was made, the burgundy duvet unwrinkled. The dresser held only the usual bits of clutter: a tin of loose change, pair of old sunglasses, book of matches, packet of vitamins, and two Bic pens. Feeling a little like Colombo I checked the address on the matchbook. It was a club he'd taken me to last week. Drat. So much for my brilliant detective skills.

I opened the top drawer of his dresser. Rows of rolled up socks and Hanes briefs didn't provide any clue to his whereabouts either. I had a sinking feeling I was just snooping at this point. I searched through the drawer, grimacing as I found a pair of purple argyle dress socks. I opened another drawer. T-shirts and gym shorts. I shuffled them around a bit and came across a pair of neon blue spandex running shorts. Egad! Those had to go. I tossed them in the direction of the wastebasket, sure that Richard would thank me later.

I was just moving on to the pajama drawer when I heard a sound other than my own clucks of disapproval. The sound of the front door opening.

My first thought was that it was Richard and Obsessive Woman was caught red handed. Then I heard something else.

"Hello? Richard, are you in there?"

I froze. It was a man's voice, but not Richard's. Good Lord, what would I do if it was one of his friends? Sure, Richard had given me a key, but not so I could come in while he was gone and inspect his wardrobe. At the risk of forever being labeled "that crazy chick who went through your drawers," I quickly jumped into Richard's closet, securing the sliding paneled doors behind me. Just call me the obsessive chicken.

I heard the front door close, footsteps echoing through the condo. Cupboards opened and closed in the kitchen, leather squeaked against leather as I listened to him move cushions on Richard's sofa.

Footsteps clicked down the hall, then came to an abrupt stop, presumably at the door to Richard's office. They continued again, dimming as he entered the room. I opened the closet door just a crack and peeked out. I couldn't see anything. Ever so quietly, I tiptoed to the doorway of Richard's bedroom. I heard the message machine beep, then my voice filled the condo.

"Hi, Richard, it's me. Just wondering what you've been up to. I haven't heard from you in a while. Well, not a while really, but I thought you said you'd call me last night. Not that I was waiting or anything. But maybe you forgot. Or just got really busy. Which I *totally* understand, 'cause, duh, you've got lots of cases and stuff to think about. I mean, not that I think you *don't* think about me. I'm sure you do. But, you know, you just have a lot on your mind, so I can see why you forgot to call. So, um, anyway, call me when you can. 'K?"

Oh God, did I really sound like that? No wonder my boyfriend had gone AWOL.

I thought I heard the man chuckle as the machine beeped off Thank God I'd erased the rest of the messages.

I heard the sounds of desk drawers being opened and closed, papers being shuffled. I would swear it sounded like this guy sounded like he was going through Richard's stuff too. What kind of friend was he? I just hoped he found whatever he was looking for before he got to the bedroom.

No such luck.

Footsteps echoed again, drawing closer. I let out a little "eek" and I jumped back into the closet, quickly closing the sliding door as the footsteps grew louder, entering Richard's bedroom. I crouched on the floor wedging myself between a pile of winter sweaters and Richard's Bruno Magli loafers.

I heard the man opening dresser drawers, rummaging like I'd been doing just moments ago. What *was* this guy looking for? My curiosity got the better of me and I eased the closet door open a crack to take a peek at him.

I recognized him almost immediately. The solid frame hunched over Richard's dresser, the worn jeans, the dark hair. It was the same guy I'd seen with Richard the other day. Mr.

Nobody. He was in denim again, this time wearing a black T-shirt, sans jacket as a concession to the heat. The sleeves of his shirt were stretched taut over biceps that bulged like Nerf balls on his arm. I thought I caught the glimpse of a black tattoo just peeking out beneath the hem, but I couldn't quite make out what it was.

And then I saw it. A gun.

I froze, my eyes glued to the bit of gleaming metal shoved into the waistband of his jeans, the butt flat against his tight stomach. My breath came out in quick shallow gasps, my brain racing to come up with any good reason why a man with a gun should be searching through Richard's personal belongings.

Mr. Armed and Dangerous mumbled to himself again as he opened Richard's underwear drawer. I strained my ears to pick up what he was saying.

"Come on, come on…I know you left something…what the…?" He paused, holding up the pair of purple argyles. He shook his head, making a sound somewhere between a snort and a chuckle, before throwing them back in the drawer. Well, at least the bad man had good taste. I watched as he continued on to the next drawer. "…come on, come on…don't tell me the sonofabitch packed everything."

Wait—packed?

My eyes had adjusted to the dark and I looked around the closet at the rows of hanging suits, polos, and pressed slacks. Sure enough there were noticeable gaps. I felt my stomach clench up in a way that warned of morning sickness. Missing clothes, missing boyfriend. A man with a gun rummaging through Richard's underwear drawer. And me crouched in a pile of seasonal sweaters hoping like anything that the dizziness hazing my vision was just fear and not pregnancy hormones. This was not good. I didn't know what was going on here, but good it definitely was not.

And then things got worse.

Mr. Nobody stepped toward the closet doors. I bit my lip, hoping he would turn around. Nope. He headed straight toward me. I shut my eyes tightly, making myself as small as I could. I said a silent prayer, promising to attend church more often, give half my salary to the poor and really work in a soup kitchen this Thanksgiving instead of just telling my mother I was to avoid her dried out turkey.

I heard the wooden door slide on its tracks and eased one eye open, saying a silent thank you that he'd opened the other side of the closet and I was still in shadows. I held my breath, certain that my every inhale was as loud as a jackhammer in the silence.

Mr. Nobody looked at the clothes hanging in the closet. He squinted his dark eyes at them almost as if he were mentally counting.

"Damn." He breathed the word on an exhale, then turned around and stalked out of the room. His boots continued to echo all the way down the hall and out the door, which he shut behind him with a crash that sent my teeth chattering. Or maybe they were doing that all on their own. I realized I was shaking and wrapped a wool sweater around myself as I sat in the dark closet for a full two minutes before venturing back out into the room.

I don't know what Mr. Nobody would have done had he seen me there, but the gun poking out of his Levi's was not reassuring.

I slowly ducked my head out the bedroom door. No sign of the bad man. I tiptoed as quickly as I could down the hall, slinked out the front door and sprinted across the street to my car as if I were dodging gunfire. Once inside I locked the doors, removed the club, and revved up the engine, my hands still shaking as I adjusted the air conditioning controls.

I closed my eyes, taking deep breaths as I took stock. I was in one piece. Mr. Nobody hadn't seen me. No bullet holes and I hadn't wet myself. All was well.

Okay not *all* was well. Richard had obviously packed for a trip. That much was plain to both Mr. Nobody and me. A trip where? And why? Richard hadn't mentioned a trip, and by the way an armed man had broken into his place, I didn't envision it was a planned Club Med getaway. Was he hiding somewhere? Was he in trouble? Considering Richard thought claiming lunch with me as a deduction was unethical, I found it hard to believe

I wondered if I should call the police. But I wasn't entirely sure Mr. Nobody had actually committed a crime. Breaking into a man's house and going through his underwear drawer. In fact, I wasn't even entirely sure he *did* break in. Had I locked the door behind me? I'd been a little preoccupied to notice.

God, I hoped Richard was all right. What would I do if he wasn't? What about our potential unborn child? Again I felt that bout of possible morning sickness swell over me. I swear to God if Richard was just in the Bahamas, I was going to kill him.

Just then my purse rang. I jumped so far into the air I almost hit the roof of my car, adrenalin pumping through every limb of my body. I reached into my bag and flipped open my Motorola. My mother's number popped up on the caller ID. If it was anyone else, I would have ignored it. But knowing Mom, she'd send the National Guard looking for me if I didn't pick up by the fourth ring.

"Hello?"

"Maddie, you haven't forgotten have you?"

"Of course not." I racked my brain. Forgotten what?

"Good. Because we made reservations for five and Ralph's canceling his last appointment so he can join us."

Right. Ralph, a.k.a. Faux Dad, the owner of Fernando's, the hottest place on Rodeo, and my soon to be step-daddy. I still wasn't 110% convinced Faux Dad was straight, but I *loved* the discounted manicures.

Mom had hooked up with Ralph when, after twenty-five years as a single parent, Mom had discovered the wonders of internet dating and signed up for Match.com. Desperate to make a big re-entry into the dating scene, she'd gone to Fernando's for a full make-over, where Ralph chopped, styled, and colored her hair into a near masterpiece. After three months of flirtatious cut and colors, Mom was surprised to learn that not only was Ralph straight (allegedly), but his interest in her went way beyond her curly locks. Five months later they were planning a beautiful ceremony in Malibu, overlooking the ocean cliffs for a week from Saturday. I was to be the maid of honor and tonight Mom was laying official duty number three thousand on me. Planning her bachelorette party.

I debated fabricating an excuse to skip dinner. My hands were still shaking and, though my heart had slowed from NASCAR to L.A. freeway, I still had that jittery feeling in my chest like I was ready to fight or take flight any minute. However, knowing Mom (see National Guard reference) canceling dinner would lead to more questions than I currently had answers for. So I gave in.

"Right. No, I'll be there. Five thirty, right?"

"Five!" my mother yelled into the phone.

"Right." I looked down at my watch. Four forty-seven. Considering traffic on the 134 at this hour, I'd be cutting it close. "I was just getting in the car, Mom. I'll meet you there."

"Good. And don't be late."

I pretended not to hear that last comment. "You're breaking up, Mom. Sorry, gotta go."

* * *

At exactly five twenty-nine I pulled up to Garibaldi's restaurant in Studio City. I might have been on time had I not spent the entire drive over looking in my rearview mirror for any sign of Mr. Nobody lurking behind me. Thankfully, I saw none. But, paranoia lesson number one, that didn't mean he wasn't there.

I found a spot on the street and parallel parked between a Jag and a Dodge Dart on its last leg. Luckily I was wearing my ready-for-anything Spiga slingbacks, so the block and a half hardly even hurt my feet at the near sprint. Faux Dad was outside talking on his cell phone, a frown of concentration on his tanned face. Faux tan of course. When he hit Beverly Hills Ralph transformed himself from mid-western farm boy into Fernando, the European hair sculptor. He figured the chances of 90210's elite frequenting a salon called "Ralph's" were slim to none. Unfortunately, Ralph's family was Swiss German, so to keep up with faux Spanish roots he indulged in magic tan sprays twice a week.

Ralph's face broke into a smile when he saw me and he lifted a hand in greeting, gesturing inside.

The hostess, dressed in all black right down to her black eyeliner and gothic chic black lipstick, directed me to a linen sheathed table in the middle of the room where my mother sat, looking down at her watch and pursing her thin lips.

"Maddie, you're late."

I wished people would stop pointing that out.

I leaned down and gave her an air-kiss. "Sorry, Mom, there was traffic."

Mom rolled her eyes. While they were the same hazelish green as mine, hers were framed in that familiar pale blue eye-shadow she'd been wearing since before it became fashionable again. She had on a pair of black stirrup pants straight from 1986 and a sweater tank embroidered with a calico kitten on the front. I silently thanked the gods I hadn't inherited her fashion sense.

"You completely forgot, didn't you?" she said.

"I would have remembered."

"Right." Neither of us was truly convinced. "Anyway," she continued as I sat down, "I have a preliminary seating chart I want you to take a look at. And," she added, her eyes taking on an evil twinkle, "I found the perfect place for my bachelorette party."

Uh oh.

"Where?" I asked, truly fearing the answer.

"Beefcakes."

The fear was justified.

"Beefcakes?"

"It's full of..." Mom leaned in close, whispering. "Male strippers." She wiggled her eyebrows up and down in a way that made me queasy again.

"You sure you don't want to have a spa day with the girls instead?" I pleaded.

"Oh come on, Maddie. Lighten up. It'll be fun. Besides, I'm getting married, I'm not dead. I can still appreciate the male form in all its glory."

Yep. I was going to throw up.

"Oh, and we need a final count for the reception. I only ordered one tent for the buffet so I only pray it doesn't rain." Mom made a little sign of the cross.

"This is L.A., Mom. It never rains." Slight exaggeration on my part, but since Los Angelinos considered three inches a monsoon, we were probably pretty safe. Not to mention this was July. The weather gods wouldn't dare dump rain in the middle of tourist season. Charlton Heston would be after them with his shotgun.

"So," Mom asked, scanning the patrons behind me, "where's Richard."

That's what I'd like to know.

"He couldn't make it tonight," I answered instead. Hoping she'd leave it at that. I still wasn't sure what to think about Mr. Armed and Dangerous in Richard's apartment, but I knew I didn't yet have an edited-for-Mom version.

"Oh that's too bad," she said.

Luckily I was saved further comment on my boyfriend's dubious whereabouts as an aproned waiter brought three plates of salad to the table.

"What's this?" I asked, realizing I hadn't eaten since this morning and was suddenly famished.

"Ripe summer pears and crumbled gorgonzola over fresh baby greens," Mom quoted.

I took a bite. Delicious. Okay, so maybe I had to hear about the dreaded bachelorette party, but at least this beat the Hamburger Helper sitting in my kitchen cupboard.

I was stabbing a second pear and making little yummy sounds when Ralph finally joined us. He stooped down and deposited a kiss on my cheek before taking the seat beside me. "Sorry ladies, I had to take that. Perm emergency."

"Perm emergency?" Mom asked.

"I told Francine not to re-color her hair for forty-eight hours after her set, but did she listen to me? No. Now she looks like an auburn haired French Poodle. She's coming in tomorrow morning for damage control."

Mom and I both nodded appropriately.

"So," Mom said, folding her hands in front of her and sitting up straighter in her chair. "Now that you're both here, I have an announcement." She looked pointedly at me. "Guess who's pregnant?"

A ripe summer pear stuck in my throat.

There was no way she could possibly know, could she? Was I showing a belly already? Were my boobs swelling? Did I have that rosy pregnant glow? I knew I should have powdered in the car before coming in.

Luckily before I could blurt out that I was just a little late, Mom ended the guessing game. "Molly!"

I swallowed the pear, relief washing over me. Of course. My cousin, Molly. Or as she was known in our family, The Breeder. She'd already popped out three rug rats in four years. I think she was going for some sort of record. Which of course made my grandmother very happy. There's nothing an Irish Catholic family loves more than a prolific breeder.

"That's really great," I said with about as much enthusiasm as a lithium addict.

"Great? It's fabu!" Faux Dad shouted.

Okay, so I was 80% sure he was straight.

"Oh," he said, waving his hands in the air, "One of my clients does the most darling little baby baskets. She takes a bassinet and fills it with organic teddy bears and hand knitted little booties. Stuff so sweet it makes your teeth rot."

"Oh, that sounds perfect! We have to get her one of those," Mom gushed. "What do you say, Maddie? Want to go baby shopping with me?"

Actually I didn't. In fact this whole conversation was making me break out in hives. The more I thought about Molly and her three and a half little munchkins, hand knitted baby booties, and most of all the unopened pregnancy kit sitting on my kitchen counter I wanted to bolt out of the room and scream some choice obscenities at my boyfriend for buying defective condoms. Only I couldn't. Because I had no idea where Richard was and more likely than not I'd just be leaving more messages on his answering machine that Mr. Nobody would later play for his own personal amusement.

"Hey, aren't we missing someone?" Faux Dad asked, looking across the table at the empty seat. "Where's Richard?"

That, as I was about to find out, was the million dollar question.

CHAPTER THREE

———

Somehow I survived dinner even with Faux Dad getting all googly-eyed at the thought of a new baby and Mom getting all googly-eyed at the thought of shoving twenties in some young stud's G-string. I still wasn't sure which scenario made me more nauseated.

I took the 405 home, checking the entire way for signs of bad guys, and slowly climbed the flight of stairs to my studio apartment, where I promptly collapsed on my velvet upholstered futon. I didn't even glance in the direction of the EPT. Much. Instead, I called Richard's machine one more time for good measure. I didn't mention that I'd been there earlier or the man with the gun.

I flipped on *Seinfeld* and vegged out as Jerry and George tried to come up with a plot about nothing. I fell asleep fully clothed, trying to fight images of black tattoos, shiny silver 38 specials, and my mother holding a basinet full of pink baby booties.

The next morning I awoke with a renewed sense of purpose. It appeared I wasn't the only one looking for Richard, which meant I had to step up the search. I was his girlfriend, which theoretically meant I should have the edge, knowing him better than anyone. The trouble was Richard and I mostly just did couple stuff when we were together—dinner and a movie at the Dome, cruising the Venice boardwalk hand in hand, snuggling under the stars on symphony night at the Hollywood Bowl. Honestly, I didn't really know any of his friends, and now that I was thinking about it, I didn't really know what he did outside of "us" time either. It was a troubling thought.

So, I started with the short list of people in Richard's life I did know. Namely, his mother. The only problem was I didn't know her number, and didn't even know her first name to call information. Chances were good it was back at Richard's condo somewhere, but after the run in with Mr. Nobody that wasn't a place I was especially looking forward to visiting again.

That left Richard's office. I knew he kept a complete address book on his palm pilot and another on his computer at work. The only obstacle to getting that would be Jasmine. But I was confident I could come up with some way to get around her. The woman had the IQ of a squash.

So, I put on my kick butt clothes. Black DKNY cargos, ice blue baby T, and my prize black two-inch Jimmy Choos with the rhinestone details. I capped it all off with some thick, black eyeliner and I could have doubled for a Bond Girl.

I parked in the garage and by nine-fifteen I was standing in front of Jasmine's desk pleading my case.

"I think I left my cell phone in one of the conference rooms last time I was here. Can I go in and get it? Please? I'll just be a minute."

Predictably Jasmine was enjoying this, her penciled in eyebrows twitching with amusement. "I'm sorry. But I can't let you go in there."

"Please? I'd ask Richard, but I can't seem to get a hold of him. Really, I'll be super quick."

"I'm sorry, but only lawyers and clients are allowed back there," she said, pointing to the frosted doors. "We can't have just *anyone* roaming around."

"But I really need that phone," I whined. Jasmine shrugged her shoulders as if to say, tough luck, chickie.

I pouted, then faked a thoughtful face as I stared at the frosted doors. I paused, counted to three Mississippi, then opened my eyes wide as if I'd had a light bulb moment. "I know! Jasmine, you could go get it for me."

She looked doubtful, glancing at her computer screen. Before she could argue the importance of her solitaire game, I rushed on. "Oh please, Jasmine? I really, really need that phone. You'd be doing me such a huge favor. I'd really owe you one."

She bit her oversized lip and stared at me so long I thought maybe she'd forgotten the question. Finally she let out a long suffering sigh. "Fine. I'll go check. But stay right here."

I held up two fingers. "Scout's honor."

That was almost too easy.

I waited until she'd disappeared into one of the conference rooms before bolting through the frosted doors and fairly sprinting down the hall to Richard's office. I quickly slipped inside and closed the door after myself.

As expected, there was no sign of Richard. Though the scent of his Hilfiger aftershave still hung in the air. I inhaled deeply, suddenly all the more desperate to find him.

The office held three bookcases, filled with impressive looking volumes, and Richard's honey oak desk, situated in the center of the room. His desktop held an oversized, leather bound calendar, a computer monitor, a telephone with about a gazillion little extension buttons, a penholder, and a stack of bulging file folders. The message light on his phone was blinking double time. Not a good sign.

I gingerly sat down behind the desk, flicking the monitor on. Luckily, Richard hadn't logged out of the system the last time he'd been here, and it only took a couple minutes of clicking around until I found his address book with his mother's phone number in Palm Springs. I pulled a sticky pad out of the desk and wrote the number down, slipping it in my back pocket. I flipped the monitor off again and stood up. Mission accomplished. I was actually pretty good at this cloak and dagger stuff.

I pushed the chair back in, put away the sticky pad and was just about to leave when I caught sight of the stack of files again. Bulging with forbidden documents. I took a quick look over both shoulders in a totally unnecessary move that somehow made me feel safer. Nope. Nobody watching. Just me and the files. Alone.

I tried to resist…but I was only human.

I picked up the one on top, knowing that if Richard ever saw me looking at these he'd have a cow, then give me an endless lecture about client-attorney confidentiality. But this was an emergency. I was late. And there was no way I was going to take that damn test and deal with the results without him. He got me into this mess, he was damn well going to be there while I peed on the stick.

So, fully justified, I opened the first file.

Worthington v. Patterson. To my disappointment it contained one legal sized document after another that I could have sworn were written in a foreign language. The only words I understood were "the" and "party." So much for juicy stuff.

I dropped that one back in the pile, hoping that at least one of these included a blackmail demand, death threat, or secret cover up. I hated to think my snooping was just nosiness.

I picked up Elmer v. Wainsright.

"What are you doing?"

My head snapped up so fast I feared whiplash.

Standing in the doorway was none other than Mr. Nobody. My heart froze in my chest and I quickly checked his person for a gun. Fortunately I didn't see one. And considering how tightly his navy t-shirt and Levis were hugging the form in the doorway, there wasn't much chance of hiding it from view. He looked like he worked out. A lot. Dana would have been proud of him.

"Well?"

Well what? Oh, right. What was I doing here.

"Looking for Richard," I squeaked. Suddenly at the sight of him I'd turned into Minnie Mouse. I cleared my throat, trying to convince myself that this guy didn't scare me. We were in a lawyer's office for crying out loud. He couldn't very well kill me here. Right?

I took a step backward anyway. Better safe than sorry.

"What a coincidence," he replied, his voice much deeper and smoother than I'd imagined. "So am I. Any luck?"

I shook my head no, afraid I'd sound like a mouseketeer again if I spoke. This guy seriously flashed "danger" in big, bold neon. And it wasn't just the potentially concealed weapon. It was the hard set of his jaw, the steadiness of his dark eyes as they quickly swept the room, the white scar over his eyebrow that I'd bet my Spigas he hadn't gotten from a paper cut.

He walked slowly over to Richard's desk and glanced down at the file I'd been attempting to read. "Anything good in there?"

"I don't know. I don't speak attorney."

The corner of his mouth quirked up ever so slightly. "Cute."

"Thanks."

He leaned his back casually against the desk, crossing his arms over his chest. His biceps strained against the sleeves of his T-shirt, the tattoo on his right arm peeking out again. It looked like a panther. Dark and sleek. With razor sharp claws. "So, you want to tell me what you're really doing here?"

"Nuh-uh." I shook my head again.

He grinned. A slow, wicked grin that reached all the way to his dark eyes. It was the kind of grin that made women either cower in fear or want to rip his clothes off.

I licked my lips, my mouth suddenly filled with sand.

"Okay," he said, cocking his head to one side. "How about this. How about you tell me who you are then, huh?"

"Maddie."

"Maddie what?"

"Maddie Richard's girlfriend." I was reluctant to give him my last name as at the moment I couldn't remember if I'd been talked into a public listing by the phone company.

"His girlfriend? Really?" He raised one eyebrow at me.

"Yes. His girlfriend."

"Huh." He looked me up and down, his eyes doing a slow, thorough appraisal.

"What?"

"Nothing. I just didn't see him with someone so girly."

Hey! I planted my hands on my hips, throwing on my best tough chick voice. "This happens to be my Bond girl outfit. It is *not* girly."

"Easy, Bond girl." That slow, wolfish smile slid across his face again. "I didn't say I didn't like it."

Gulp.

"Oh." Dang it, I was going for tough chick again, but somehow in the wake of that I'll-huff-and-I'll-puff-and-I'll-blow-your-clothes-right-off smile, Minnie Mouse was back. "So, um, who exactly are *you*?"

"Detective Jack Ramirez. LAPD."

Ugh. Mental forehead slapping. That explained the gun. I silently hoped that snooping hadn't been upgraded to a misdemeanor.

As if he could read my mind, his lips quirked again. "Jasmine doesn't know you're here, does she?"

I did not dignify this with an answer. Which seemed to amuse him even more, his eye crinkling at the corners. However, he didn't comment, but instead changed his line of questioning. "When was the last time you saw Richard Howe?"

"Friday. We were supposed to have lunch together. What is this about anyway?"

"Did he cancel?"

"No, I was late." I cringed at the sound of the word echoing through my own head. "When I got here he was talking to you, then he..." I trailed off, remembering the way Richard had stared after Ramirez, then abruptly cancelled our lunch. It was clear even then he'd had something on his mind. And I didn't like the way that *something* had prompted Richard to pack his bags for parts unknown.

I swallowed hard, trying to change the subject. "How did you even get in here?" I asked, knowing that if Jasmine hadn't let me in there was no way she'd let a cop in.

He grinned. "I have a warrant."

Double ugh. Suddenly my theories of blackmail and secret cover-ups weren't sounding so far fetched. "Warrant?" I squeaked out. "As in, you have the right to remain silent?"

His smile widened, a dimple punctuating his left cheek. Clearly he was enjoying this. Personally I wasn't finding the predicament all that funny. My boyfriend was missing, there was a cop in his office with a warrant, and I had a pregnancy kit sitting on my kitchen counter waiting for another Big Gulp moment. This was not the stuff sitcoms were made of.

"It's a search warrant," he said. He sat down at Richard's desk, picked up the file I'd just been attempting to read, and began scanning its contents. His forehead creased in concentration. Apparently it meant something more to him than it had me. I tried to read over his shoulder, to see if words that made sense had suddenly materialized on the paper. Nope. Same foreign language.

"Searching for what?" I asked finally.

"Evidence." It was clear this guy wasn't going to win any public speaking awards.

If I wanted information, I was going to have to pry it out of him. I mentally greased up my crowbar. "Okay, I give up. What exactly is going on here?"

Ramirez looked up. He narrowed his eyes at me, as if trying to decide how much to share. "All right. Your *boyfriend*," he said emphasizing the word as if he didn't really believe it, "is wanted for questioning in connection with embezzlement charges we've brought against one of his clients. Devon Greenway." He paused. "You've heard of him."

I had, and apparently my expression betrayed it. Devon Greenway was one of Richard's biggest clients. I knew Richard had met with him often. In fact he'd canceled a dinner date with me just last Thursday to meet with him. However, if Richard was in trouble I wasn't going to be the one to nail his coffin.

"I may have heard the name."

Ramirez pinned me with a look that could pry pearls out of an oyster. Great, I had to pick now to become a terrible liar.

"Devon Greenway is the CEO of Newtone Technologies," he continued. "They're in the process of filing with the Securities and Exchange Commission for a place on the New York Stock Exchange. However, in the course of an independent audit of the company's finances, a minor discrepancy was noticed."

"How minor?"

"Twenty million dollars."

"Wow." I was *so* in the wrong business.

"No kidding. But before we could file charges, Greenway skipped town."

"And the cash?"

"Just as elusive. Originally the money was funneled from Newtone into a joint usage account, from which a series of checks were drawn made out to PetriCorp. On the surface everything looked legit until we realized that PetriCorp was only a business on paper. And guess who owns it."

"Devon Greenway?"

"Close. Under the business filing the owner of record is his wife, Celia. Filed under her maiden name, Wesley. Only PetriCorp's accounts are now empty, too. The paper trail ends with the person who set the accounts up in the first place."

A knot formed in my gut. "Richard?"

"Bingo." Ramirez sat back in the chair, crossing his arms over his chest again, watching me digest this information.

I tried not to look as shaken as I felt. "So, is Richard a suspect?"

Ramirez's face was unreadable. "He's a person of interest."

Uh oh. I'd watched enough episodes of *Law & Order* to know what that meant. Just one thing. I *really* had to find Richard now.

Before Ramirez did.

* * *

As soon as I could I hightailed it out of there. I didn't even wait for Jasmine to go on break before barging back through the frosted doors and jogging across the reception area to the tune of her calling "fraud" after me.

My head was spinning the entire two blocks back to the garage. Richard had blown me off and had dinner with Greenway last week. If what Ramirez said was true, it would have been the day before Richard took off for parts unknown. Suddenly I didn't want to know what had gone on at that meeting.

Not that I thought Richard was involved. Richard was a straight arrow. He couldn't even stand his tie being crooked. He would never be involved in something illegal. However, if he'd unwittingly helped Greenway, it was possible he knew more than was good for him, and if Greenway was as unscrupulous as he sounded, Richard might be in danger. And I didn't have the feeling he'd fare much better if Ramirez found him first. Any way you looked at it, my boyfriend was up poopoo creek.

I climbed the stairs to the second story of the parking structure and revved up my Jeep, pulling out onto Grand. I was contemplating my next move at a red light, when I saw Ramirez emerge from Richard's building and jump into a black SUV. Parked illegally. The perks of being the law. He started the SUV and pulled into traffic three cars ahead of me. As the light turned green I watched him weave through downtown, making a sharp right onto 8th. On instinct, I changed gears and followed him.

Did I know what I was doing? No. But it was abundantly clear that Richard hadn't just gone home to take care of his ailing mother. And I didn't have any better ideas.

Feeling very sly, I stayed two car lengths back as Ramirez got onto the 110 heading south. I followed him right through downtown, passing through Watts and Compton until we hit the 405. He was going a reasonably decent speed and I wished I had a less conspicuous car. While I loved my red Jeep, it didn't really blend into the background. I made a mental note to borrow Dana's tan Saturn if any more surveillance was needed.

The SUV continued south until we turned off at the 22, heading east toward the 5 and Orange County. It was getting late and I knew we'd hit traffic once we got to the 5. And I was starving. I reached across to my glove box, hoping for some protein bar Dana might have left in there. All I came up with was a packet of stale saltines and a stick of Doublemint. I ate the crackers, hoping Ramirez would pull into a Taco Bell soon.

No such luck. We merged onto the 5 and Ramirez moved into the left lane, settling in for a long drive. I groaned, making a mental note to always eat before tailing a cop.

Just when I'd decided I was on a wild goose chase and going to faint from hunger if I didn't have a Big Beefy DelDeluxe, Ramirez exited the freeway at Bear Street, toward the San Joaquin Corridor. My heart did a little jump as I realized he was taking me right into the heart of Orange County's premier shopping district. Maybe Ramirez wasn't such a bad guy after all.

As we neared the South Coast Plaza, Ramirez pulled away from the shopping district and into the residential. He moved through streets lined with two-story California Spanish villas and faux Tudors until he pulled up to a large, modern home, all glass on one side. I could tell it was designed by some famous architect or other by the angular lines of the structure, looming as if it was ready to topple in the next 6.3 earthquake.

The small yard was done in utilitarian bluegrass and decorative stone, which echoed the stark feeling of the glass structure.

Ramirez parked his SUV and got out, approaching the house. I parked across the street, slouching down in my seat in case he glanced behind him. Luckily, he didn't, because I'm sure my red Jeep stuck out like a sore thumb among the subdued Jags and BMWs lining the road.

Ramirez knocked on the front door, then waited. Then knocked again. Apparently no one was home. My shoulders sagged at the possibility that I'd just driven all that way on an empty stomach for a nobody's home.

Ramirez looked over both shoulders, as if someone might be watching him. Good cop instincts… I was impressed. I slouched down further in my seat, just my eyes and nose peaking over the rim of the driver side window. Apparently Ramirez was satisfied, as he proceeded to walk around the back of the house, disappearing through a painted, wooden gate.

I waited. Nothing.

Crap. If he was doing some fancy breaking and entering I couldn't see from this viewpoint. For all I knew he could have Richard in handcuffs back there. I opened the car door and slunk out, crouching as I ran cross the street. Then realized how ridiculous I must look. Gee, Maddie, that's not suspicious. I straightened up, throwing my shoulders back and walked around the side of the building as if I owned the place.

The backyard was much more lush than the front, the landscaping done in a mix of tropical birds of paradise, palms, and fat succulent bushes. Small levels had been carved out of the natural hillside, creating a barbecue area, a patioed terrace, and finally an Olympic sized swimming pool. Ramirez stood on the bottom level staring at the swimming pool. I couldn't see what he was looking at, so I quickly picked my way through foliage to the next level above him. I straightened up to get a better look.

Unfortunately, the uneven ground and my two-inch Choos made for a less than stellar combination. My foot slipped, my arms waving for balance that never came. I pitched forward and, before I could catch myself, let out a little scream.

Ramirez turned just in time to see me flailing like a lunatic, falling right toward him.

"Jesus..." he muttered, before collapsing with an "oof" as I landed on top of him.

I had to admit, landing on him sure beat the ground, though I'm not sure which was harder. His muscled chest didn't give way an inch. I wondered how many hours a day he spent at the gym.

"What the hell are you doing here?" he growled, his nose inches from mine.

I blinked hard, trying to ignore the rush of heat as his muscles wiggled beneath me. "I followed you."

"Hell, I knew that much. But I figured you'd stay in the car."

So much for my career as Maddie the fashionable stealth.

I pried myself off of him, awkwardly regaining my footing. Note to self: real Bond Girls don't wear Choos. "Sorry," I mumbled, sure I sounded as sheepish as I felt.

Ramirez grunted by way of response, standing up and dusting off the seat of his jeans. I tried not to stare. Much.

"I'll wear flats next time," I said instead.

"Smartass," he muttered. But he didn't go for his gun, now clipped conspicuously to his belt, which I interpreted as a good sign.

"So, whose house is this?" I asked.

Ramirez's eyes darkened, the line of his jaw tightening until I could see a little blue vein starting to bulge in his neck. "Hers." He gestured down to the pool.

I peeked over the edge of the hill at the sparkling blue water, shimmering in the late afternoon sun.

"Eek!"

My stomach clenched, the saltines threatening to make a repeat appearance as black spots danced before my eyes. The manicured landscape swayed in front of me and Ramirez's arm, suddenly at my waist, was the only thing keeping me from crumpling back down on the rocky ground.

In the pool was a tall, slim woman with clouds of flaming red hair.

Floating face down.

CHAPTER FOUR

———

Red and blue lights flashed through the palm fronds, reflecting off the surface of the swimming pool, which I was so not looking at again. Men in black T-shirts that read "CSI" on the back crawled over the hillside like little ants, stopping now and then to seal a piece of dirt or hair in a Ziploc baggie. Police radios crackled to life every five seconds, relaying indistinguishable messages to the uniformed cops standing guard beside the pool as they waited for the Medical Examiner. And I sat with my head down, trying really hard not to vomit.

"You all right?" Ramirez asked.

"I'm fine," I said. Only it came out as a muffled, "I five," as my head was still firmly placed between my knees in a semi fetal position in a teakwood deckchair. I'd been sitting here for what seemed like years, waiting for the backyard to stop spinning and those little black dots to stop dancing in front of my eyes. I had a vague memory of Ramirez carrying me across the yard and radioing for backup, but it was kind of blurry. Like a really bad dream I couldn't wait to wake up from.

"You'll be okay, just take a few deep breaths." Ramirez sat down beside me. Or rather, I heard him sit and felt the heat from his body beside me.

I peeked my head up, careful to look at Ramirez and *not* the swimming pool where I could hear the splashes of men fishing the poor woman out.

"She's dead, right?" I know, stupid question. But I had to ask. Somehow my mind really, really wanted her to be okay. For this all to be one big mistake or a really bad *Punk'd* episode.

"Very dead."

"Who is—" I paused, correcting myself. "*Was* she?"

Ramirez narrowed his dark eyes at me. I could see him mentally debating whether to treat me like a suspect, witness, or just some dumb blonde who couldn't balance in her new heels. Finally he opened his mouth to speak, apparently settling on the dumb blonde theory. "Celia Greenway."

I swallowed hard, trying to decide how best to phrase my next question. "So, uh, she didn't just slip into the pool, did she?"

Ramirez shook his head slowly.

"You sure?"

He nodded.

"It was…I mean, she…" Somehow I couldn't bring myself to actually say the word "murder" out loud. It seemed so John Grisham and so *not* anyone's real life. At least not anyone I knew. I designed children's shoes for crying out loud. I did not stumble upon dead bodies in posh Orange County swimming pools.

But, instead of tripping over my own psyche, I rephrased the question. "Someone did this to her then?"

He hesitated, taking in the crumpled position I'd been in for the past half hour.

I straightened my spine, trying to make the most of my meager height in a show of bravado I certainly didn't feel. "I can take it. I'm a tough chick." Yeah right. I forced my gaze to stay on him, not on the gurney now wheeling away the unfortunate Mrs. Greenway in a human hefty bag.

A half smile quirked the corner of his mouth and he gave in. "Okay. Yes, it looks like murder."

My stomach lurched again and I resisted the urge to stick my head between my knees.

Ramirez went on. "The official cause of death won't be pronounced until an autopsy can be done by the ME's office. But there were obvious ligature marks on the body. Her neck was black and blue."

"Strangled?"

Ramirez's gaze drifted to the swimming pool. "Looks like it."

As sorry as I felt for the poor woman, my mind immediately latched onto Richard, an unpleasant image of my boyfriend blue necked and face down in an OC pool invading my brain. I dropped the brave little soldier act and put my head between my legs again, taking deep breaths that smelled like my leather shoes, chlorine, and the cold sweat I felt trickling down my back.

"You sure you're okay?" Ramirez asked again.

"Yeah, fine." Which actually sounded like "yeffen."

"You're a really bad liar, you know it?"

"Duly noted."

"Well, since you're 'fine', maybe you wouldn't mind answering a few questions about your boyfriend now."

I froze, a horrible thought slinking through my brain. Ramirez couldn't possibly think Richard had anything to do with this. I mean, not with Celia's death. He couldn't. Could he?

"What kind of questions?" I would have loved a clue to what he was after. But as hard as I tried to read his stony expression, I came up blank. The man should have been cleaning up in Vegas with a poker face like that.

"Let's start with, where is Richard Howe?"

"I told you, I don't know. You think I'd be here if I knew?" My voice came out in a high whine I hadn't used since I'd lost my retainer in sixth grade. I sniffed back the tears I could feel welling behind my eyes. "I don't know where my boyfriend is."

Ramirez stared at me for a second. The real unasked question clear in his dark eyes as they narrowed in on me.

"Richard did *not* do this." I emphasized the point by shaking my head so violently those black dots threatened again. "He's not a killer. He's a lawyer. If he's pissed at someone, he sues them. He would never, *could* never, do this. You don't know Richard."

His cocked his head to one side. "Do you?"

I bit my lip. Good question. I thought I did. But obviously there were some aspects of my boyfriend's life he'd neglected to share with me.

Luckily I didn't have to come up with a clever answer as a guy in a CSI shirt walked up the hillside toward us. Only this guy looked nothing like the hunks on the CBS version. He was tall, skinny and bald as a cue ball. His nose hooked over like a beak and he had small, calculating eyes that I would venture to guess didn't miss much.

"Is she ready?" he asked, addressing Ramirez as if I were a piece of deck furniture.

Ramirez glanced at me. "I'm not sure."

"Ready for what?" I asked.

Neither paid any attention. Instead, CSI Guy set his black bag down by his feet. "I think I should do her before she gets any further contaminated."

"*Contaminated*?" I said.

Ramirez gave me another assessing glance. "Yeah, go ahead. She's ready."

"Ready for what?" My voice was threatening that Minnie Mouse quality again as my gaze ping-ponged back and forth between them.

Ramirez sighed, taking a patient tone one might use with a kindergartner. "They need to take samples of your hair, fingerprints, and shoe impressions. You've contaminated the crime scene by being here. They need to be able to rule you out as they process the evidence."

CSI Guy pulled out a small roller that looked suspiciously like the one I used on my black cashmere after visiting Mom and her army of tabby cats. His tiny eyes scrutinized me like I was one giant piece of evidence. Then, without so much as an introduction, he proceeded to run the roller over my blue baby T, down my sleeves, up my sides, and in places most guys didn't touch without dinner and a movie first.

Ramirez looked on and I could swear he was almost enjoying this.

"This isn't funny," I shot at him with as much dignity as I could muster while being groped by a lint roller.

"Nothing funny whatsoever." Only Ramirez's eyes crinkled at the corners as he said it.

I decided to change the subject. "Can I ask you a question?"

"Shoot."

"I assume this is Celia Greenway's house."

He nodded.

"Did you know she would be...I mean was..."

"Dead?"

I cringed. Somehow the word seemed so final. Like poor Celia Greenway would never again know the joy of a semi-annual clearance sale at Bloomies, the scent of new leather pumps, or the thrill of finding that one of a kind bag in the half-off bin. (Really, it's the little things that make life worth living.)

I tried to soften the image. "Swimming."

"No, I didn't. I just wanted to talk to her."

CSI Guy tucked the roller into a baggie, which he then deposited in what looked like a black fishing tackle box. He pulled out a pair of tweezers and eyed my hair.

"What?" I asked.

CSI Guy didn't answer, just circled me, scrutinizing my blonde highlights.

"What is he doing?" I ask Ramirez.

"He needs a hair sample. Preferably one with a skin tag for DNA analysis."

"DNA? I didn't say you could have my DNA. I don't want him touching my hair."

He narrowed his eyes. "Then you shouldn't have crashed my crime scene."

Touché.

I shut my mouth, not wanting to push my luck. If Ramirez wanted to I'm sure he could make my life very miserable. I knew I was trespassing, meddling, snooping and a whole host of other minor sins cops didn't look too fondly on. Besides, the way Ramirez had asked about Richard, I wasn't entirely sure that we were on the same side and it didn't seem wise to make enemies at this point. I had enough problems without Mr. Hardbody complicating things.

One of the uniforms called Ramirez down to the pool level, leaving me alone with CSI Guy, who continued circling my head for the perfect hair. After he chose a couple innocent little strands (*not* gently, I might add) he poured some plaster into two plastic trays and told me to step into them. I did, after making him promise on his mother's life that the plaster would wash off of my shoes. The death of Mrs. Greenway was tragedy enough for one day, we didn't have to compound it by adding the demise of $300 suede.

As the hook-nosed evidence collector worked, I dared to gaze back at the swimming pool again. With the body gone and the afternoon sun casting a shimmery light on the pool's smooth surface, the scene looked anything but sinister. In fact, if you dressed the CSI ants in chinos and Abercrombie, this would look like any other day in the OC.

Just goes to show you, looks can be deceiving.

I closed my eyes, letting the sun warm my face as I tried to wrap my thoughts around what I'd learned today.

Devon Greenway had embezzled twenty million dollars from his company. Celia and Richard were the only people who knew the details. Celia was dead and Richard was missing. I prayed Richard was only hiding out from Greenway and not...

Swimming.

"You finished?" Ramirez climbed back up the hill, addressing CSI Guy who was packing his plaster moldings into another black bag.

"I've got all I need," he answered, picking up his bags.

"Good."

CSI Guy gave me a curt nod, which I took as a "thanks for not squirming too much," and trekked back down the hill. Ramirez watched him go, then sat down beside me.

Close beside me.

A little too close. I wiggled away, the increase in pheromones nearly choking me.

Ramirez turned, his eyes darker than a double espresso as a half smile played at the corners of his mouth. "Do I make you nervous?"

What, me nervous? Nuh uh.

I nodded. I can be such a chicken.

Which of course caused his smile to grow into a full-fledged grin, complete with wolfish white teeth. "Good."

I looked away, preferring the sight of the swimming pool to the wicked gleam in Ramirez's eyes. I had a feeling it was the same gleam he got when he dragged someone off to jail.

Or into bed.

I didn't want to find out which. (Bok, bok.)

"So..." I said clearing my throat, "What now?"

Ramirez shifted closer. The scents of Downey and Right Guard hit me as Ramirez casually draped one arm around my shoulders.

"Now," he said, leaning in close. "I take you home."

Bok, ba-gawk!

*　*　*

Luckily, I convinced Ramirez I was okay to drive myself home. It *had* been a full hour since I'd been fetal. Not to mention that the idea of spending rush hour traffic back to Santa Monica beside Ramirez the Hormone Machine made the cab of his SUV seem about ten times too small. And last but not least, the idea of coming back to this place tomorrow to retrieve my Jeep didn't hold any appeal. In fact, I had a feeling I'd be staying out of Orange County altogether for a while. (Unless there was a sale at the Block.)

By the time I finally pulled up to my studio, it was dark and I was famished. I fixed myself a grilled cheese with tons of gooey cheddar and washed it down with a Diet Coke. After the day I'd had, I would have preferred a beer, but considering my persistent lateness I didn't think that was wise. Instead, I hit the play button on my answering machine, crossing my fingers there was something from Richard.

One message from my mom, telling me she'd booked Beefcakes for her bachelorette party. (Ugh!) One from Faux Dad, saying he'd picked up a basket of hand knitted baby items for Molly the Breeder. (Double ugh!) And one from Dana, asking if I'd seen a pink line yet. (There weren't enough ugh!'s in the world to express how this made me feel.)

Nothing from Richard.

I eyed the EPT still sitting on my kitchen counter and suddenly felt sick to my stomach. I felt like crying. I felt like my life had suddenly become an episode of *Law & Order: Special Blonde's Unit*. This week our fashionably, but oh-so-impractically, dressed blonde stumbles onto a dead body while searching for her embezzling boyfriend who flies the coop just as Maddie's monthly visitor refuses to make an appearance.

Not to mention the hunky lead of the series, Detective Jack Ramirez. He was danger with a capital "D." No, make that a capital, underlined *and* italicized, "D."

I grabbed another Diet Coke, trying to ignore the instant flush at the thought of Ramirez. Though in my defense, it was hard not to flush around a man like that.

I laid down on my futon and turned on the TV, telling myself these were not the kind of thoughts I should be thinking. I should not be fantasizing about rock hard abs, wicked brown eyes, and a smile that could melt the clothes off the Mona Lisa. What I should be thinking about was drinking a gallon of water, taking that EPT into the bathroom, and facing up to whatever reality those little pink lines threw at me like a big girl. And I would. I eyed the test. Someday very soon.

Instead, I flipped to Letterman and settled in as he ran the Top Ten Signs You've Been in the Heat Too Long. He only got to number five ("George Hamilton looks albino next to you.") before I fell asleep fully clothed.

And dreamed of Ramirez, doing laps in a sparkling blue swimming pool.

In the buff.

* * *

First thing the next morning, I retrieved the long forgotten phone number from my pants pocket and called Richard's mother. I didn't really expect to find him there now, but I figured I might as well cover all my bases. Unfortunately I was right. His mother hadn't heard from him since he'd called for her birthday three weeks ago. I then proceeded to call his cleaning lady, his gardener and his dry cleaner, asking if they'd seen Richard in the last few days. Nothing. He'd vanished off the face of the earth last Friday and no one had seen him since.

I made myself a cup of coffee and a chocolate frosted pop tart, which I ate at the kitchen counter as I went over my options. And really, when it came down to it, I didn't have any. Either I could track Richard down myself or I could let Ramirez do it and possibly lead my boyfriend away in handcuffs. Not that I really believed Richard was guilty of embezzlement. But I had a feeling his disappearing act wasn't doing much to convince Ramirez he was an innocent bystander in all this. Unless I wanted to visit Richard behind bars, I had to find him first.

I decided to start back at the beginning. The last place I'd seen Richard. His office.

Unfortunately, I knew it was going to require some serious maneuvering on my part to get past Jasmine again. My brilliant plan—wait until she went on break.

So, at exactly twelve-o-three, I had my little red Jeep parked across the street from the offices of Dewy, Cheatum & Howe as Jasmine wiggled her mini skirt covered behind out the doors and off to her lunch.

I jumped out of the Jeep, stuffed a couple quarters in the meter and sprinted across the street. In no time at all I was walking through the front doors and across the padded carpeting to the reception desk, manned by Jasmine's noontime replacement. Althea, a first year clerk with a pronounced overbite.

"Good morning, Althea," I said briskly, laying my little Kate Spade on the counter.

Althea mumbled an indistinguishable greeting while trying to avoid eye contact. She had on a blue-gray cardigan that was stretched out in places, giving her five-foot, 150 pound frame the shape of a ripe tomato. Her frizzy blonde hair (and not a Clairol Spun Gold, but natural dirty blonde) was scooped back on one side with a tortoiseshell barrette, and her big green eyes bugged out at me from behind thick lenses that made her look a little like Mr. Magoo.

"So," I continued, "I guess you've heard that Richard's on a little trip?"

Althea's face turned red. Apparently everyone knew Richard had flown the coop.

I leaned in confidentially. "Have the police been here?"

Althea nodded. "All day yesterday. They took out three boxes of files."

Damn. Ramirez was good. I wondered if I was wasting my time retracing first Richard's steps and now Ramirez's. I tried a different tactic.

"Althea, were you here when Richard left last Friday?"

"Uh-huh. I was in the copy room getting photos of the Johnson brief when he came in to use the shredder."

Shredder? My heart sped up.

"Uh, you didn't see what he was shredding, did you?"

"No. But the cops took the bag of shredded paper too."

Double damn. Ramirez was *really* good.

"Did he say anything to you as he left?" I asked, grasping at straws now.

"Just that I should make sure I gave the brief to Mr. Chesterton instead of him."

"Was it Richard's case?"

"Uh-huh. But he said it should go to Chesterton."

"Oh. Well, thanks, Althea. I'm, uh, just going to go grab something I think I might have left in Richard's office." I cringed. Against Jasmine that excuse wouldn't have stood a chance.

Thankfully, Althea was much more trusting. "Good luck. I'm not sure the cops left much."

I slipped through the frosted doors, the carpeted hallway muffling the sound of my heels as I mulled over what Althea had said. I was dying to know what Richard had been shredding. Maybe it was just some statement with a credit card number on it. Richard was diligent about shredding everything that even had his email address on it for fear of identity theft. But then again, it was curious timing. Ramirez had come to see him. He'd just cancelled lunch with me. He shreds documents, gives away his case to another partner, then goes home, packs his bags, and disappears.

For half a second my belief in Richard's innocence wavered. I had to admit, it didn't look good. It looked like the actions of a man who had something to hide.

I pushed that thought aside as I reached the door to Richard's office. With a backward glance over my shoulder to make sure Jasmine hadn't miraculously appeared behind me, I quickly slipped inside, closing the door with a quiet click.

My first thought was that a tornado had hit. The second was that Ramirez, although thorough, was a pig. Books were scattered haphazardly on the floor instead of alphabetically arranged in the bookcases. The wastebasket had been emptied and left on its side. File folders and papers littered the area around Richard's oak cabinets and the items on his desk were askew in a way that would have had Richard flying into an OCD-like fit of straightening.

I crossed the room, stepping over a file folder and two stacks of Westlaw books, and flipped on Richard's monitor. It hummed to life, but the screen remained blank. I looked under the desk and saw, to my disappointment, that the tower was gone. Rats. Ramirez was very thorough.

Well, when technology failed, there was always the good old standby, paper files. I groaned inwardly at the sight of files strewn over every conceivable surface. I started with the piles closest to the door, which turned out to contain copies of Richard's personal accounts payable for the past six months. Boring. Though, I noticed as I looked at the figures, Richard wasn't quite raking in what I thought he was. In fact, he had six overdue slips stamped with big red "delinquent" notices across the top. Great. Add that to the growing list of things Maddie didn't know about her boyfriend. He was a compulsive spender and didn't pay his bills on time. I suddenly felt guilty for prodding him into buying me those platinum dew drop earrings for my birthday. It was clear now that he couldn't afford them any more than I could afford a duplex in Beverley Hills.

I moved on to the next pile of files, teetering precariously beside the bookcase. Billable hours records. Dinners with clients, travel times, and phone records of every millisecond he'd spent on any given case, billed by the quarter hour at rates that made my head spin. But nothing to tell me where Richard might be now.

The pile leaning against the desk contained copies of employee files, no doubt distributed to each partner to keep tabs on the Altheas of the office. While I had a feeling they wouldn't yield anything helpful, I couldn't help my curiosity getting the better of me when I unearthed Jasmine's file. I opened it, peeking inside. Two complaints from other clerks about her personal long distance calls on the company phone, three commendations from the senior partner (who was older than dirt, bookoo rich, and in the middle of a messy divorce—suspiciously Jasmine's type if you asked me), and her salary statements for the past three months. I almost laughed out loud at the paltry sum Miss PP earned answering phones and guarding the frosted door. I honestly didn't think it was possible for anyone to exist in L.A. on a salary less than mine, but the statement proved me wrong. Poor Jasmine. I almost felt sorry for her. Almost, I reminded myself, thinking of how I'd had to sneak in here like a common criminal.

Speaking of which…I looked down at my watch and realized I'd been snoop—I mean, searching for evidence (there, that sounded much less nosey) for the last twenty minutes and Jasmine would be back from lunch soon.

Closing her file I rapidly began searching in earnest for anything that might lead me to Richard. Maybe I was having such lousy luck finding anything because I wasn't even really sure what it was I was looking for. Had there been any obvious clues, they certainly wouldn't be here now. Ramirez would have his CSI Guys scanning them for fibers and fingerprints back at Good Guy headquarters. No, my only hope is that Ramirez may have overlooked something that had meaning to me because of my intimate knowledge as Richard's girlfriend. Yes, I know the chances were slim, especially considering my knowledge wasn't turning out to be all that intimate after all. In fact, give him a couple days and Ramirez might know more about my boyfriend than I did. A thought which caused a bout of morning sickness to roll through my stomach again.

Ten minutes later I was frantically going through Richard's desk, pulling out letter openers, fountain pens, paper clips, rubber bands, and…hello, what was that? A shiny blue piece of foil protruded from under Richard's desk sized calendar. I lifted the calendar corner and pulled the foil out. Staring at it. *A condom wrapper*?

I froze, one hand gripped like a vice around an empty super ribbed Trojan packet and the other quickly balling into a fist at my side. Richard had a *condom wrapper* on his desk?

My brain went through a rapid search of possible reasons why this might be okay. It was left over from his associate days (read: pre-Maddie days)? He was representing the Trojan company in a lawsuit and had to inspect the product as possible evidence? Hormone crazed teenagers had broken in wanting to experience the thrill of sex in a lawyer's office?

Damn. None of these was even remotely plausible. I swallowed hard, trying to cleanse the sandpaper feeling that had suddenly formed in my mouth. My boyfriend used condoms at work. This was really not good. If I ever found Richard, I was going to kill him.

I was still staring at the offending Trojan wrapper when the telephone on the desk rang. On instinct, I picked it up.

"Hello?" Oh crap! I wasn't supposed to be here. I thought a really bad word and hoped it wasn't Jasmine checking in.

There was a pause on the other end, as if the person were as surprised I'd picked up the phone as I was. Then a tentative male voice said, "Give me Richard."

I gulped and hoped he didn't hear it. "Who may I ask is calling?"

Again with the pause. Only this time I heard him mumble a swear word under his breath, obviously not pleased with my interrogation and debating whether to answer or hang up on me. Finally he decided to go with option number one, and answered in a gruff voice. "Devon Greenway. Who the hell is this?"

CHAPTER FIVE

———

I froze, every muscle in my body suddenly tensing. Ohmigod. I was on the phone with a murderer!

A murderer that was looking for Richard. A knot formed in my stomach. There was no denying Richard was in this up to his eyeballs now. Only I didn't know exactly how. A part of me screamed that this was a good thing, look what happened to people who knew! They ended up face down in their million dollar swimming pools.

So, trying my darndest not to sound like a mouseketeer in front of the big bad embezzler slash murderer, I answered him.

"Maddie Springer."

"What're you, Richard's receptionist?"

I took personal offense to that, now knowing exactly how little his receptionist made.

"Noooo. I'm his girlfriend.

Silence. Then, "Richard never mentioned a girlfriend."

I fought down a stab of disappointment. Here I may be carrying his child and he'd never even *mentioned* me.

"You sure? Maddie Springer? Though sometimes he just refers to me as Pumpkin. That's his pet name for me. You sure he didn't mention a Pumpkin?"

I heard Greenway swallow an oath on the other end. Right. Irrelevant.

"Never mind. I guess it doesn't really matter. I just thought, you know, he might talk about me sometimes, just, maybe in casual conversation. I mean, not that you and he have a lot of casual conversations, I'm sure it's all just business and you don't have any sort of personal stake in each other's lives, so I guess really there would be no reason for Richard to mention me at all—"

Greenway cut me off. "Jesus, do you ever shut up?"

I swallowed hard. I did tend to talk a lot when I was nervous. And being on the phone with men who strangled their wives, then dumped them in their swimming pools made me *very* nervous. I took a deep breath and mumbled, "Sorry."

"Put Richard on," he demanded.

"Uh..." I looked around the police-ransacked office. "Richard's not here right now."

"Where the hell is he?"

Pal, I wish I knew.

On the one hand, disappointment welled inside of me as I realized this wasn't the great break in the Where's Waldo game my life had suddenly become. On the other, if Richard was hiding out from Greenway (as the dead wife now convinced me he was) he was doing a good job of it. I halfway hoped he stayed hidden. Something about Greenway's voice had the hairs on the back of my neck standing at attention. Like he'd almost enjoy strangling someone.

"Look, Richard's girlfriend, I don't have all day. Where is Richard?"

"I don't know," I answered truthfully. "He hasn't been here since Friday."

Greenway said a few colorful words, breathing heavily into the phone.

"Can I take a message?" I squeaked out, hoping if I kept him on the phone long enough my pulse might return to normal and I could think of something clever to say.

"You mean to tell me," he smirked through the receiver, "that prick took off? Without even telling his *girlfriend*?"

Even though I was pretty sure Greenway was being sarcastic with me now, but put like that Richard did sound like a prick.

I thought about not answering. I certainly didn't want to help Greenway get any closer to bumping off witness number two, a.k.a. The Prick. But, since I really *didn't* know where Richard was, I figured it could hardly hurt. "That's right. He didn't."

"Son of a bitch." And Greenway hung up.

I stood there for a full minute, staring at the receiver, willing my heart to stop pounding like a Latin conga drummer. I took a deep breath. Then another. And another. Then began to fear I was hyperventilating and sat down in Richard's leather desk chair to think.

If I were Ramirez, I could have traced the call. I'd probably have black and whites squealing up to wherever Greenway was right now, arresting him so my boyfriend could come out of hiding and I could pee on a stick. Unfortunately, I wasn't Ramirez. In fact, I wasn't turning out to be much good at this spy thing at all. I'd had the prime suspect in a murder investigation on the phone and I hadn't even thought to ask where he was! I thunked my head against the desk. I had no idea where to go from here.

I looked down at my watch. 12:28. Jasmine was due back from lunch any minute.

I pried myself out of the chair and willed my legs not to buckle under me. They didn't, which I took as a good sign, and I quickly slipped out the door, down the hall and into the reception area.

"You find what you needed?" Althea called to my retreating back.

"Yep. Great. Thanks!" I gave a half wave as I plowed through the front doors at Flo Jo speed. 12:29. I hit the down arrow on the first bank of elevators, nervously tapping my foot as I waited. "Come on, come on," I coaxed the elevator.

Finally it arrived and I slipped inside, just as the second bank of elevators to my left slid open and Jasmine exited. I put my head down and hoped she didn't look back.

She didn't, wiggling her size two behind to the reception desk with purpose as the elevator doors slid closed in front of me. Whew. Close one.

Two minutes later I was racing across the street to the safety of my little red Jeep. I hopped in, locked the doors, and flipped on the radio, letting Blink 182 fill the unnerving silence as I yoga breathed my pulse back to normal. Even though I knew Greenway wasn't going to reach through the phone and strangle me via AT&T, the conversation had left me with a serious case of the heebie jeebies. Until recently my biggest fear in life was spiders with hairy legs. The sudden jump into wife killer territory had me sweating and shivering all at the same time.

I tried to console myself with the thought that Greenway hadn't known where Richard was any more than I did. This was good. It meant the chances of finding Richard swimming were down considerably. (Something I was relieved to hear, because the more I thought about that condom wrapper the more *I* wanted to be the one to strangle him.)

So, what now?

I glanced across the street again, my eyes searching out the windows of Richard's office on the sixth floor. No sinister shadows, no cops to follow, no bad guys in black.

That's it, I needed reinforcements.

I grabbed my cell and punched in Dana's number. She answered with a groggy, "Hello?" on the fourth ring.

"It's me," I said. "You busy?"

Dana giggled. Then I heard a muffled male voice in the background.

I rolled my eyes. "Maybe the more appropriate question is, are you alone?"

Dana giggled again. "Not entirely. Why, what's up?"

"I'm kind of having a crisis here."

"Another one?"

Tell me about it. "Never mind, I can hear you're busy."

"No, no. Sasha was just leaving. He's got pyramid practice." She giggled again and I thought I might throw up. "Tell you what, I've got an audition later this afternoon, but you wanna meet me at Fernando's in, say, twenty minutes? I could use a pedi first anyway."

My day definitely screamed for a pedicure. "I'll be there in ten."

* * *

Fernando's was located in the center of Beverly Hills' Golden Triangle, at the corner of Brighton and Beverly Boulevard, just one block north of Rodeo. Faux Dad started his career as the great Fernando in a strip mall in Chatsworth, but through word of mouth, and a few fabulous mentions in the *L.A. Times*, Fernando had primped and permed his way out of the Valley and into the playground of the rich and Botoxed.

In addition to being a wizard with hair, Faux Dad also had an innate flair for interior decorating. (Okay, so I was 75% sure he wasn't gay.) Fernando's went through a yearly metamorphosis, keeping up with the "in" theme of the moment. This year the look was Modern Industrial. The walls were covered in a rusted finish with a metallic over-glaze, causing them to shimmer in the light coming through the all-glass front wall. Exposed copper pipes overhead and unframed modern art canvases on the walls added to the look, while a dozen blow dryers, rinse sinks and cutting stations hummed with activity down on the concrete floor. In Watts this would have been a warehouse, but on Rodeo, it was Warehouse Chic.

"Maddie, Dahling!" Marco, the receptionist, came at me with an air kiss on both cheeks. Marco was slim, Hispanic, and wore more eyeliner than Tammy Faye. "How are you?" he asked in an accent that was pure San Francisco.

"I've been better," I answered truthfully. "Is Ralph in?"

"*Fernando*," Marco reminded me, "is doing a color weave on Mrs. Spears." Then he added in a low whisper. "Britney's mother."

"Oh," I whispered back, suitably impressed. I looked to the back of the salon and saw Faux Dad weaving red extensions onto a fiftyish brunette in Chanel. He caught my eye and gave a little wave.

"So," I said, turning back to Marco, "I'm just having one of those days. Any way you can fit me in for a pedi?"

"For you, sweetie, anything." Marco grabbed his big black book off a desk that looked like it was made of aluminum siding. He flipped through the pages.

"Think you could fit Dana in too?"

Marco frowned.

"Pretty please?"

"Maddie, you gotta stop doing this, dahling. You throw me all off schedule."

I blinked my eyelashes at him. "Oh, pretty, pretty please with Brad Pitt on top."

"No fair, you know my weakness. Okay. Chia can do you both in fifteen. Why don't you go soak?"

"You're a doll, Marco."

Marco threw me a kiss. "Don't I know it!"

I made my way over to the line of pedicure chairs along the back wall and chose a vacant one, taking off my shoes and sinking my feet into the little bubble bath. The second I hit the warm water I felt myself begin to relax.

I closed my eyes, trying to calm the roller coaster of emotions I'd ridden today. I'd almost succeeded when Dana plopped into the chair beside me with a huff.

"Sorry I'm late. There was traffic on the 110."

I opened my eyes and blinked. Twice.

Sitting beside me was Morticia Adams. Or, more accurately, Morticia Adams meets Playboy Bunny. Dana was dressed in a black vinyl outfit, just barely covering her derrière and showing more cleavage than I even owned. Her own hair was covered in a black wig that was taller than my hair in 1985. Pale foundation, black eyeliner and deep burgundy lip liner completed the Halloween chic costume. Only it was July.

"Do I want to know?" I asked.

"What?" Dana looked down at herself. "I told you I have an audition later. It's for an Elvira look-a-like thing. Why, do I stick out?"

I looked around the salon. Actually, she didn't. Hey, this was L.A.

"So," she asked. "What's the pedi emergency?"

As quickly as I could, I filled her in on the events of the last two days. Ramirez in Richard's condo, the floating redhead, and finally my impromptu chat with Greenway. By the time I was finished our toenails were soaked, moisturized, and filed and Dana's jaw was permanently stuck in the open position.

"This is better than *The Sopranos*! You actually talked to a *murderer*? What did he sound like?"

"Kind of pissed, actually."

"Ohmigod. You could have been killed!"

Did I mention Dana has a flair for the dramatic?

"It was just a phone call, Dana." I didn't tell her about my own overly dramatic reaction to said call.

"So what did you do?"

"Nothing. He hung up."

Dana looked at me like I was the worst Nancy Drew ever.

"What do you mean, 'nothing'? Didn't you ask where he was?"

I slowly shook my head.

"Did you hear anything helpful in the background? Check the caller ID? At least star-sixty-nine him?"

I shook my head again. I was ashamed to admit I hadn't even thought of those. "Dumb, right?"

Dana was such a good friend, she didn't even answer that. Instead she drew her blackened eyebrows together in concentration. "You know, I dated this guy once who worked at the phone company. He said that some of these small companies keep a log of calls coming in or going out. You think maybe Richard's firm does that?"

I thought back to the blurb in Jasmine's file about her long distance calls. "Yes! They do. Ohmigod, Dana, you're brilliant."

Dana sat back in her chair, looking like she'd just solved a Rubik's cube.

Obviously Jasmine wasn't going to give out any company information to me, but I had a feeling if I waited until she went on break again tomorrow, I could probably convince Althea to look up the number. She'd seemed sympathetic enough to Richard's plight. And if that didn't work, I could always bribe her with a free manicure.

"This is so cool," Dana said, wiggling her primped toes. "It's just like that pilot I shot last spring, Diva Detectives. We're actually tracking down a murderer."

We?

"Whoa. What do you mean, 'we'?"

Dana feigned a hurt look, sticking out her over-lined lip. "Hey, there's no way I'm letting you go all Charlie's Angels without me."

While I appreciated the help, the light in Dana's eyes as she said "Charlie's Angels" had me immediately fearing feathered wigs and bellbottoms.

"It's not a game, Dana. I think Richard's really in trouble." And even as I said it, the whole idea of running down Greenway was beginning to sound a little crazy. What were we actually going to do if we found him? I mean, as Dana so exuberantly pointed out, he *was* a murderer. What if he had a weapon? What if he tried to shoot us? I didn't think I could face being shot at any more than I could face an EPT.

"Maybe I should just turn this all over to the police," I said. "I mean, they have all the resources. Not to mention experience with this sort of thing."

Dana narrowed her eyes at me. "And what do you think will be the first thing the cops do when they find Richard?"

I bit my lip. "Give him a ride home?"

"Ahhhnt." Dana made a buzzer sound. "Wrong answer. They're going to read him his rights and slap a pair of cuffs on him. Honey, they tore his office apart, they searched his home. They don't do that unless they're after a serious suspect. Don't you watch *C.O.P.S.*?"

My heart sank into a hollow pit in my stomach. I did. And she was right. The look in Ramirez's eyes as he'd questioned me yesterday had been clear enough. Richard was no longer considered just a witness.

"But Richard is *innocent*," I protested. Only it sounded oddly uncertain even to my own ears. "And there's more," I admitted.

"What 'more'?"

I leaned in close, half whispering to avoid Marco's gossip radar. "When I was going through Richard's office I kind of found something. Something that shouldn't be there."

Dana leaned in so close I could smell her morning nonfat decaf latte on her breath. "What?"

I swallowed hard. "A condom wrapper."

She blinked, looking at me as if still waiting for the punch line. "So?"

"So, Richard and I have never done it in his office. I mean, we've only done it in his bedroom. Or mine."

"Wait, you mean to tell me that you've never had sex with Richard outside of a *bed*?"

I'm no shrinking violet. I watch HBO, I have frank discussions with my gynecologist using anatomically correct language, and I've had enough sexual experiences that I have to take my socks off to count them all. But something about the way Dana was looking at me as if I'd just confessed I didn't know where second base was made my cheeks grow instantly hot.

"No," I said defensively. "Richard likes to be comfortable."

Dana made a disbelieving sound, something between a snort and a cough. "Comfortable and sex are two words that should never go together. Wild and sex, maybe. Passionate and sex. Even animal and sex—"

"Okay, I get the point." I think Mrs. Spears was beginning to stare.

"Wow. You live a sheltered life."

If my cheeks got any hotter, I'd erupt. So, Richard liked things comfortable. What was wrong with being comfortable? Comfortable was fine. No gear shifts in your back, no soap in your eyes. We might not be on the sexual safari that Dana was, but Richard and I were fine. And I swear my mind did not even flash for a second on Ramirez when she mentioned wild animal sex. Not one second.

"Dana, you're missing the point. That condom was not *mine*."

"Well, let's not jump to conclusions. Maybe it wasn't his, maybe it was one of his friends'."

Yeah right. That was the same excuse I'd used the one time I'd been dumb enough to try pot senior year of high school and my mom had caught me trying to air out my room before she got home from work. It was flimsy then and it didn't sound much better now.

But I was desperate.

"You think?"

"Sure. Or maybe he just emptied his pockets onto his desk after an overnight at your place."

Hey, that one didn't sound so bad. "Right. That's probably it."

"Of course it is. Richard's mad about you. It's not like he'd go bop his secretary or something."

Richard and Jasmine? That thought made me ill. I'd have to buy a gun and put myself out of my misery because I didn't want to live in a world where the likes of Miss PP could steal a boyfriend from the likes of me. Not that I'm a conceited person, but Jasmine was one step up from belly button lint.

"Right. You're right. I'm sure Richard will have a perfectly good explanation."

Once I found him.

* * *

After our toes were Fuchsia Fusion and Pinkberry Stain, Dana and I went for lunch at the Brown Bag Deli on Wilshire. There Elvira, Mistress of the Dark Eye-shadow, signed no less than three autographs for star happy tourist, with a hopeful, "I'm so getting this part." By the time we were both stuffed with kosher pickles and turkey sandwiches (hers with low fat mayo and sprouts. Mine with extra cheese and salty fries. Hey, I was possibly eating for two now, right?) it was getting late, and I realized I hadn't touched the Strawberry Shortcake hightops in days. I promised Dana I'd call her as soon as I saw Althea and dropped her at her audition before heading back to my studio.

I forced myself to finish the sparkly laces and Velcro closures for the Shortcake shoes, then ordered delivery from the Vietnamese place down the street. I was too tired to bother with dishes, so I ate my rice noodles with a plastic spork while standing at my kitchen counter. And trying to avoid eye contact with the little pink box that had become my obsession.

I knew I was being a wuss. Just take the damn test already. But if there had been too many IF's for comfort before, there were *way* too many now. *If* Richard was involved with Greenway. *If* he wasn't entirely innocent in this whole thing. *If* Ramirez—or heaven forbid Greenway—found Richard first.

If Richard didn't have a good reason for that condom wrapper.

So instead of opening the box like a normal, rational woman, I decided to go with the if-I-don't-look-at-it-it-doesn't-exist theory of matter and plopped down on the futon, turning the TV on instead. Denial is a girl's best friend.

But wouldn't you know it, the first channel I flipped to showed a perky reporter with a Tipper Gore bob doing a report from Celia Greenway's swimming pool. Ramirez appeared (dressed in butt hugging Levi's and a slick leather jacket—seriously hide-your-daughters sexy) and gave the reporter an update on the investigation. Basically repeating what he'd already told me. The coroner's office wasn't yet ready to release a statement and in the meantime it was being considered a "suspicious death." Suspicious was right.

The rice noodles squirmed in my belly as pictures flashed across the screen. A smiling, red haired Celia sitting on the beach. A press clipping of Devon Greenway, hair slicked back, dressed in a tuxedo as he shook hands with some politician. And another of the Newtone Technologies Corporation, now under investigation for fraud, misappropriation, embezzlement, and a whole host of other charges that made the reporter's plucked eyebrows knit together in practiced concern.

Thankfully there were no pictures of Richard.

Yet.

CHAPTER SIX

———

The next morning I woke up early, a bundle of nervous energy even before my requisite cup of coffee. All night long images of Ramirez, Greenway and, most importantly, Richard kept swirling through my head. Not to mention the permanently seared image of Richard's stray Trojan.

The more I thought about it, the more uncertain I became that Richard was merely an innocent bystander in all this. From the looks of his financial statements, he *had* needed money. And there *was* twenty million floating around unaccounted for. It was pretty tempting. And as much as I liked to think Richard was above temptation, I just wasn't sure.

I decided in the wake of my fitful night's sleep to treat myself to a double grande mocha-latte with decadent whipped cream for breakfast. (Sometimes a girl needs to splurge.) I slipped on a pair of low-slung, boot-cut jeans, a black Calvin tank, and silver patent leather sling backs that complemented my Pinkberry toenails. I grabbed my purse and pointed my Jeep in the direction of the nearest Starbucks.

Amazingly I found a parking place right in front and took my place in line, which, as usual, was about a million caffeine starved people long. It gave me way too much time to contemplate the bakery case. By the time I reached the pimply kid behind the counter, somehow a chocolate chip muffin and a blueberry croissant had been added to my order.

I found a quiet corner in the back and settled in to my breakfast of fat, sugar, and mass amounts of caffeine. By the time I'd polished off the croissant and was digging into the chocolate muffin (melt in your mouth delish, by the way!) I was beginning to feel like myself again.

Okay, maybe not totally like myself, as the biggest worry my *usual* self had to encounter was if the Spiderman rain boots were going to cover this month's rent. Now shoes seemed to be the last thing on my mind. Which was a sign my life was *really* falling apart.

I was just licking the muffin remains off my fingers when my purse rang. I pulled out my cell to see Mom's number lighting up my LCD screen.

"Hello?" I answered, still picking up the little stray muffin crumbs with my fingertip.

Mom sighed deeply into the phone. "You forgot, didn't you?"

Oh crap. Not again. "No, mom, of course I didn't forget." What now? I racked my little brain for what wedding related activity I'd spaced out this time. Flower selection? Cake testing? Please, God, don't let it be helping her pick out honeymoon lingerie. Yick.

"The dress fitting? Maddie you were supposed to be here at ten."

Mental forehead slap. The bridesmaid fitting. Mom's best friend, my cousin, Molly, and I all had the honor of being Mom's bridesmaids on her second trip to the altar. Mom had picked out vintage gowns for each of us that we'd been measured and pre-fitted for weeks ago, but today was the final unveiling. Mom had refused to show any of us the actual gowns, wanting it to be a "fun surprise." A phrase that inspired no end of fear in me.

Originally I had offered to design the dresses for her, after all I *did* have a degree in fashion, but Mom wanted a kitschy vintage theme. She insisted that this time around she wanted fun, something that had been seriously lacking from her first marriage.

On her first trip to the altar, Mom had gotten married in a stuffy church with stained glass windows (chosen by my Irish Catholic grandmother), with vows said in traditional Latin (insisted upon by my Irish Catholic grandmother) and an ancient priest to preside over the ceremony (picked out by my Irish Catholic grandmother—see a trend here?). Four years later Mom had found herself a single mother of a precocious three year old (yours truly) and Dad was on a plane to Vegas where I'm told he shacked up with a showgirl named Lola.

This time around Mom was doing the wedding *her* way. A civil ceremony presided over by a female justice of the peace on a cliff overlooking the Pacific. And vintage, "fun" gowns.

I put on a brave face.

"You *are* coming to the fitting, right?" I heard panic creeping into my mother's voice.

"Of course. I'm on my way now. I, uh, just got stuck in traffic." Yes, I know, I was going to hell for lying to my mom.

Mom sighed on the other end and I could almost see her rolling her eyes toward the sky as if asking for patience from somewhere above. "Just get here, okay, Madds?"

"I'm on my way," I said. Then added for good measure, "Seriously this time." I flipped the phone shut before she could respond and downed the rest of my coffee in one sugary gulp. I paused only long enough to touch up my lip-gloss before jumping into my Jeep and making a beeline for the 101.

Ten minutes later I was frantically circling Bebe's Bridal Salon, looking for a place to park. I rounded the block twice. Nothing. With a glance at my watch, I parked semi-legally with my tail end sticking into the red zone, hoping the fitting didn't take too long.

Mom was waiting in the lobby, her eyes blazing beneath vintage blue eye-shadow. Today she was wearing an ankle length denim skirt with sports socks and Keds. Topped off with a frilly button down blouse in a tiny floral print the color of refried beans. I suppressed a shudder and ignored that little voice of warning telling me I should have *insisted* on designing the dresses myself.

"Sorry I'm late." I kissed Mom on the cheek, which softened the fire in her eyes some. Not much, but some.

"I swear to God, Maddie, if you're late for the wedding, I'm disowning you."

"Mom!" I said in mock shock. "I'm hardly ever late." She narrowed her eyes at me.

"Okay. I'll set two alarm clocks."

I think I actually saw her suppress a smile that time.

"Come on, you. They've got your dress in the back."

I followed Mom as she led me to a fitting room in the back of the shop. Bebe's Bridal was small by Hollywood standards, with just three private fitting rooms in the back and a main showroom filled with six racks of long, flowing bridal gowns. I put blinders on as we passed by them. Not that I was one of those girls that has her dream wedding picked out by the age of five, but something about being surrounded by this much Happily Ever After couture had my female hormones squealing like a sixth grader. In fact, I spotted a Wang knock off on a passing rack that actually made my heart speed up.

Did I want this? A wedding? I mean, when I'd first realized I was late, all sorts of crazy thoughts had buzzed through my mind. Admittedly, some of them covered in white lace and gauzy wedding veils. But at the time I'd been envisioning the groom as a successful, predictable, if somewhat anal about folding his socks, lawyer. In the last 48 hours he'd morphed into a man on the run of dubious character. For the umpteenth time I wondered just how much Richard really did know about Devon Greenway. Or, even more disconcerting, what did he know about Celia's murder?

I shook my head, realizing my mother was talking to me.

"…and when I found this dress on the internet, I just knew it would be perfect for you."

Internet? Uh oh.

"Now," she continued, "I tried to pick different styles that would flatter everyone. Of course, we've had to let Molly's dress out a bit, but I'm sure yours will fit like a glove."

I smiled, trying not to let my trepidation show.

Mom settled me on a white sofa in front of a full-length mirror. Three curtained-off fitting rooms stood to the side. I could see bare feet peeking beneath the curtains of two of them.

"Dorothy? Molly? Maddie's here," Mom called to the curtains, then turned to me. "I'm going to grab your dress. I'll be right back. Don't go anywhere!"

Wouldn't dream of it.

One of the curtains opened, and my mother's best friend walked out. Or, more like waddled out. Dorothy Rosenblatt was in her sixties, had gone through six husbands, and shared a body type with the Pillsbury Doughboy. She was all of 4'11", topping out at around three hundred pounds. Though once she opened her mouth, people tended to forget about the outside. Mrs. Rosenblatt was what we in LA liked to refer to as "eccentric."

She and my mother met years ago when Mom went to Mrs. Rosenblatt for a psychic reading after a particularly depressing Valentine's Day alone. Mrs. Rosenblatt predicted Mom would meet a handsome black male and fall head over heels in love. Two weeks later a stray black lab showed up on our doorstep. Barney, as we named him, turned out to be the love of her life, and Mom and Mrs. Rosenblatt have been firm friends ever since.

Mrs. Rosenblatt was obviously already in her bridesmaid dress, a pale lavender gown shaped like a lampshade and covered in embroidered green daisies. (My trepidation kicked into overdrive.)

"Maddie, you made it," she said, clapping her hands in front of her. Her arms jiggled with Jell-O-like aftershocks from the force.

"Sorry I'm late," I leaned down to kiss her cheek.

"Wait!" she commanded. "Something's wrong."

For a second I had the horrible thought she'd somehow picked up on my *other* lateness. (Okay, I didn't totally buy into this whole psychic thing she had going on, but I was too chicken to totally discount it either.)

Mrs. Rosenblatt stood back and narrowed her eyes at me. "You're a purple," she finally said.

Huh? "I'm purple?"

"Your aura, Maddie. Oy, *bubbee*, it's streaked with purple flares. Is something on your mind?"

Hmm…my boyfriend is missing, possibly involved in embezzlement and murder. I watched the Los Angeles county coroner's office fish a woman out of her swimming pool, talked to a wife killer on the phone, and found a used condom wrapper at my boyfriend's office. Oh, and I may be pregnant. Nope, everything's peachy.

But, I decided to give her the condensed version.

"Nope, everything's peachy."

"Hmmm." The lines between Mrs. Rosenblatt's painted on eyebrows (Lucille Ball red) deepened. "Stay out of the rain. Rain is very bad for purples."

I tried not to roll my eyes. I'm not sure I totally succeeded. "It doesn't rain in L.A."

"Madds!" An overweight woman in solid lilac ruffles burst out from behind the other curtain and attacked me with air kisses. It took me a minute to realize she wasn't really overweight, just pregnant. Again.

"Hi, Molly. And, congratulations," I said, trying to navigate a hug around her already bulging belly.

Molly beamed from ear to ear, rubbing her tummy like a good luck Buddha. "Thanks. Stan and I are really excited. We're due in December. We had our first sonogram last week, you want to see the picture?" Molly didn't wait for me to answer before pulling a bulging wallet out of her purse. She flipped it open and a string of plastic encased baby photos unfolded.

"Isn't it darling?" Molly asked, shoving a fuzzy black and white photo of a deformed Muppet at me.

"Oh, yes, darling." I squinted, trying to figure out what I was looking at.

"Stan says he think it's going to be a boy this time, because we're carrying a little low."

We? I wondered how often her husband actually carried that belly around for her.

Mrs. Rosenblatt put a palm on Molly's stomach, rolling her eyes back in her head until she looked like a reject from *Dawn of the Dead*. "It will be a boy." She paused. "Or else a girl with a whole lotta *chutzpah*. You're gonna have to watch out for this one." Mrs. Rosenblatt wagged a fat finger at Molly.

"So," Molly said, nudging me in the ribs with her elbow. "Any wedding bells chiming in your future?"

I cringed at how very silent the bells in my life were at the moment.

"I have a boyfriend," I said by way of defense.

Mrs. Rosenblatt pressed a thick palm to my forehead and closed her eyes. "I see a wedding. And babies. Very soon, babies. Lots of them."

I felt faint.

"I'm back!" My mother emerged with something behind her back. She was smiling like the cat that ate the wedding canary. "Who wants to see Maddie's dress?"

This was met by excited squealing in stereo. (I'm sure I don't have to add, none of which came from me.)

"So…" Mom pulled a purple shower curtain out from behind her back. "Here it is. What do you think?"

Oh lord. It wasn't a shower curtain. It was a dress. *My* dress.

"Wow."

Mom did a pleased little nose scrunch, letting out a squeal of pleasure that only small dogs could hear. "I knew you'd love it."

The first mistake my mother made was taking my "wow" for one of awe and not horror. The second, and by far a much bigger mistake, was choosing the dress.

"Where did you say you got this?" I asked, horrified that I might have to be seen in public with this.

"Ebay. Can you believe it was only going for $29.99?"

I could believe it all right. "Wow," I said again.

"So, try it on."

I gulped, my skin suddenly clammy at the thought of having to touch *that*. "Oh wow."

Somehow in a whirlwind of ruffles and Molly squeals, my own jeans and tank came off and I became a vision in purple. And not lilac or lavender. This was Barney purple.

"Is this polyester?" I asked, feeling itchy already.

Mom moved around me, tucking, buttoning, adjusting. As if it would help. "Uh-huh. It should wash really well. That way you can wear the dress over and over."

I'm proud to say I did not laugh out loud at this.

"So, what do you think?" Mom asked.

I hesitated to even look at the mirror. But it was like a train wreck. I couldn't *not* look. I peeked one eye open, taking in my reflection as Mom stood back, clasping her hands together in front of her like she'd just created a masterpiece.

"Oh Madds. You look so lovely."

I faked a smile. Okay, actually it was more of a grimace than a smile, but I don't think Mom noticed. The dress (and I use this term loosely) featured a corseted waist that flared out into a bell shape at my hips. Which totally accented the fried food diet I'd been on the last few days. Yikes.

It was cut low in the front, high on the legs and reminded me vaguely of my high school prom dress. It was a style that screamed for crimped hair and jelly bracelets.

"Her wawas are falling out," Mrs. Rosenblatt commented.

I looked down. I did have a little cleavage.

"It's just a little tight." Mom stood back, scrutinizing my mid section. "Maddie, have you gained weight?"

I looked in horror from my stomach to Molly's bulging one.

"It's fine," I said quickly, sucking in. "It's just water weight. I ate a big breakfast. I haven't been to the gym lately." I know, it would have been more convincing if I'd picked just *one* excuse.

"You know what this dress needs?" Molly asked, narrowing her eyes at my reflection.

Hmmm…a Bic and a can of lighter fluid?

"Beads. All bridesmaids' gowns need beads."

I opened my mouth to protest, but I guess fashion shock must have made me too slow.

"I love it!" Mom squealed before I could say anything. "Maddie, stay here, we'll be right back."

All of them scurried out of the dressing room (with the exception of Mrs. Rosenblatt, who waddled out) in search of beads.

I stared at my image. Trying not to cringe. I reminded myself how many hours of labor my mother went through. It was just one day. I only had to wear it for one day, then I could shove it into the far recesses of my closet never to be seen again. I mean, how many people were even going to see me in it anyway?

"Cute," a deep voice said behind me.

Oh. Crap.

I spun around so fast I almost popped right out of my neckline…

And came face to face with Ramirez.

Volcanic amounts of heat hit my cheeks and I resisted the urge to cover myself and scream, "Look away!" Instead, I managed a more dignified, "Thanks."

"Purple's a good color on you." The corner of his mouth quirked up.

"It matches my aura." Oh great, that sounded intelligent.

Ramirez raised one black eyebrow at me.

"Actually, my aura's not solid purple. Just streaked with purple flares. Which means I have stuff on my mind. At least, that's what the psychic said. Which is good. It's better than having an empty mind, right? Besides, I think it's just water weight." Oh. My. God. Shut *up*, Maddie!

I took a breath, stopping myself before I completely turned into a caricature of The Ditzy Blonde. Instead I asked, "So, what are you doing here?"

Ramirez looked about as out of place in a bridal salon as Faux Dad at a 49er's Game. He was wearing those butt-hugging Levi's again, this time coupled with a white T-shirt that contrasted with his naturally tanned skin. Though white shirt or no, he still had that dark, dangerous look that had me warring between wanting to stand a little closer and backing against the far wall.

"A few things have come up in the course of our investigation," he said. "I need to ask you some more questions."

"Here? Right now?"

"Why not?"

"How did you even find me?"

He smiled. "Your jeep is parked illegally outside."

Ugh. I knew I shouldn't have parked in that red zone. "When did L.A. become such a small town?"

The smile widened, showing off that sexy dimple. "Since I started looking in my rearview mirror for little red Jeeps."

He had me there. I did have a tendency to follow him around. Damn, I hated how stalker that sounded.

Ramirez took a step into the room, leaning casually against the wall. Suddenly the room was way too small and I felt at a distinct disadvantage wearing The Purple People Eater. "You know, I'm not exactly dressed for an interrogation."

"You look fine to me." His eyes strayed down my frame...then slowly back up again.

Instinctively I covered my wawas.

"I've told you everything I know. Richard canceled lunch with me on Friday. I haven't seen him since."

"So, you haven't been to his office recently?"

I bit my lip. "Not really."

Ramirez narrowed his eyes at me. "Uh-huh. Want to explain that answer?"

"No," I answered truthfully.

His mouth threatened a smile again. "I didn't think so."

He paused, waiting for me to say something. Hoping maybe I would crack under the pressure. Which was entirely likely. His espresso brown eyes bored into me like a spotlight and I began to fidget. Instead of purple polyester I suddenly felt like I was wearing see-through undies.

Finally he spoke, changing the subject. "I've been looking through your boyfriend's financial records for the last few months," he said, crossing his arms over his chest. "He's a big spender."

"Richard's generous."

"He's in debt up to his eyeballs."

I gulped. I knew. But after saying I hadn't been in his office, I couldn't very well admit to having peeked at his financial records myself. So I said nothing.

"Yet," Ramirez continued, "he just keeps spending. Platinum earrings for Christmas, a new car, a cruise for his mother's birthday last—"

"Wait," I interrupted, suddenly confused. "Richard hasn't bought a new car. He's driven the same black beamer for as long as I've known him."

Ramirez put on his poker face again, his eyes steady on mine as if he could pry my every secret out with just one look.

"The car wasn't for himself," he said slowly. "It was for Amy. His wife."

CHAPTER SEVEN

———

Have you ever had one of those dreams where you're underwater and your lungs are bursting for air, but just as you make it to the surface something pushes you back down again? And you realize you may never be able to take a full breath? That's pretty much how I felt as I stared opened-mouthed at Ramirez, gasping for air as I tried to respond.

"His…his…*wife*?" Richard was so *not* married. It couldn't be true. It had to be wrong. They had to have the wrong Richard. There was no way my boyfriend would be married and not tell me. I knew Richard. Okay, fine, I'll admit it was turning out I didn't know *everything* about him. But I knew him well enough to know he couldn't be married to some bimbo named Amy.

"Look, there must be some kind of mistake. Richard is not married. I'm sorry, but your information is wrong."

Ramirez kept his poker face on, his only reaction a slight narrowing of his eyes. "You didn't know he was married?"

I spun around, my hands flying to my hips, my voice rising several octaves into a range I'm sure my Irish Catholic grandmother would deem inappropriate for a bridal salon. "Do I look like the kind of girl who dates married men?"

Ramirez looked me up and down. He was wise enough not to answer.

"Look, I don't know who this Amy is, but Richard isn't married," I protested again.

Ramirez dropped the poker face, the lines in his jaw softening. On anyone else it might have been pity. But I had a feeling Bad Cop didn't do pity.

"So, who is this Amy person?" I asked. Yes, I have a morbid sense of curiosity.

"You really want to know?"

No. "Yes."

He sighed, almost like he didn't want to tell me any more than I wanted to hear it. "Her maiden name is Amy Blakely. She lives in Anaheim, in a duplex owned by your boyfriend. She works as Cinderella at Disneyland."

I felt my eye begin to twitch. Richard was married to freaking *Cinderella?*

Ramirez continued. "Their marriage license was filed in Orange County just over two years ago."

"Maybe they got divorced? Maybe she's an *ex*-wife?" I asked. Only I was beginning to sound really desperate. Like a gambler playing her last chip. If only it landed on red this time, Richard would be single, Amy would be a figment of Ramirez's imagination and everything would be okay.

Ramirez shook his head. "We haven't found any record of a divorce. And considering Richard bought a new Z3 for his wife last month, I don't think we will."

A Z3? He bought Cinderella a freaking *Roadster?* I suddenly didn't feel so guilty about the platinum earrings. In fact, I wondered how much I could get for them on eBay. Maybe enough to buy a gun. Because I was gonna shoot the bastard.

"I take it she hasn't seen him lately either?" I asked.

"Doesn't look like it. Detectives are questioning Mrs. Howe right now."

Mrs. Howe. To think just minutes ago I'd been contemplating myself in that role. And it was already taken. So what was I, the understudy?

No, shooting was too quick and painless a death for Richard. Maybe a slow poisoning. I wondered if Mom knew where to find arsenic on the internet.

"I'm sorry," Ramirez said. He looked uncomfortable, as if he might have to deal with a hysterically crying woman.

And he just might. I was quickly going through all five stages of grief. I was past denial (Ramirez wouldn't make a mistake like this.) and was settling somewhere between anger (A freaking Z3!?) and bargaining (Lord, let her be an *ex*-wife and I swear I'll wear the Purple People Eater to my mother's wedding without complaint.).

I may have been able to overlook embezzling. I may have been able to pretend I didn't see that condom wrapper on his desk. I may even have been able to overlook the fact that he had killers looking for him. But a wife? That was where I drew the line.

Suddenly the image of Richard being led away in handcuffs didn't seem all that bad. In fact, I could really get behind the idea of him rotting in jail for, oh, let's say, the rest of his lying, cheating life. He deserved it. In fact, he deserved worse than that. He was married to Cinderella! He deserved the chair.

I might have spilled my guts to Ramirez right then. Told him about the call from Greenway, my suspicions of Richard's involvement, everything. But out of nowhere the image of Molly's sonogram and the deformed Muppet came flooding back to me. Okay, I'm pretty sure that behind all that fuzz was a baby. Growing inside her right now. I wondered…did I have one of those in me? My eyes slid down to my belly, sausaged into the Purple People Eater. I might. And if I did, it was Richard's Muppet. No matter what he'd done, did I really want the father of my child rotting in jail?

I closed my eyes, took a breath, and gulped back my anger, preparing to perform my very first selfless act in the name of motherhood.

"I wish I could help you, but I've told you everything I know." D'oh, d'oh, d'oh! Being selfless really sucked. Not nearly as satisfying as good old fashioned revenge.

Ramirez sighed again and I could see the disappointment in his eyes. "You sure about that?"

We both knew I wasn't. But I'd lied so much in the past few days, I figured one more wouldn't hurt. "Positive."

"Okay." He pulled a card out of his pocket and handed it to me. "Call me if you have any sudden memory sparks."

I took the card. But I think we both knew it was going into the deep dark recesses of my purse never to see the light of day again. "I'm sorry you wasted your time coming here."

Ramirez paused, did his one eyebrow thing again, then looked me up and down. Despite my anger and frustration, the naked appreciation in his eyes as they settled on my wawas created a heat somewhere in my granny panties region.

His eyes slid up to meet mine and I hoped he couldn't read the X-rated thoughts suddenly flooding my brain.

The corner of his mouth hitched up again. "Oh, I wouldn't say it was a *total* waste."

Damn. He was a good reader.

Before I could come up with a snappy comeback, Ramirez turned his back to me and walked out.

I staggered over to one of the white sofas and sat down. Or rather, tried to sit, as the gut pincher dress didn't allow for much bendage in the waist area. I closed my eyes and took in as many deep breaths as I dared without popping a seam. Only the deep breaths didn't do much good because the longer I sat there the more time I had to think. And the more I thought about what Ramirez had told me, the angrier I became. Richard had a wife. Oh God. That made me the other woman. Richard had turned me into a walking cliché!

* * *

As Mom, Molly, and Ms. Rosenblatt came back, tray of colorful beads in hand, I had one eye on the dress and one on the clock. I had to get to Dewy, Cheatum & Howe during Jasmine's break if I wanted to get any info about that phone call. And I *so* did want that information. In fact, I was on a mission now. I was going to smoke Richard out of hiding if it was the last thing I did. And once he showed his cheating little face, I was going to torture him until he sang soprano for the rest of his miserable little life.

Okay, fine, I wasn't *really* going to torture anyone. Truth was, I'd never even hit anyone before and I wasn't too keen on the sight of blood. Just watching those cosmetic surgery shows made me squeamish. So, in reality, torture was out. But it was a nice thought to keep me smiling while I waited for Mom to pick out the perfect beads and for Jasmine's break to start.

By 12:03 Mom had decided on a faux pearl beading for the Purple People Eater and I gracefully ducked out of Bebe's Bridal, praying there was no traffic on the 101. For once, the traffic gods were on my side, as there were no accidents and not a black and white in sight. I pulled up in front of Dewy, Cheatum & Howe just ten minutes before Jasmine was due back. I raced into the building, up the elevator, and came to a huffing stop at the front desk.

"Althea, thank God you're here," I said.

Althea looked at me, her eyes bulging behind her frames. "M-Me? Why?"

In her defense, I did come on a little strong. I took a breath and started again in a normal person's voice. (As opposed to a freaked out "other woman.")

"Listen, I have a tiny favor to ask."

Althea took a step away from the desk. "What kind of favor?" she asked slowly.

Uh oh. Maybe Althea was smarter than I gave her credit for.

"I know Richard got a call in his office yesterday and I was hoping you could check the call log and see if you could lift the number for me."

Althea bit her lip. "I don't know," she said slowly. "We're not really supposed to give out that information. Especially, with, you know..." She trailed off, her cheeks turning red. Apparently it was a little embarrassing to have an employer on the lam.

"You don't have to worry about that. I'm, uh, I'm actually working with the police to find Richard." A tiny fib. I was looking for Richard. The police were looking for Richard. It was kind of like we were working together.

Althea looked dubious. "Really?"

"Yep." I nodded so hard I felt my hair bobbing up and down.

"I...I don't know." Althea glanced down at the desk, avoiding eye contact. "Jasmine wouldn't like this."

I tried not to roll my eyes at the mention of Miss PP.

"Look, I really need that number." I leaned in closer with exaggerated importance. "I think Richard might be in danger."

Her eyes grew wide behind her thick frames. "Danger? What kind of danger?"

If it had been Jasmine asking, I'd have told her to go take a flying leap. But somehow I felt that with frizzy haired, cardigan wearing Althea, my secret was safe. I told her about the call from Greenway and my fear that Richard was hiding out from him. Or worse. Swimming.

Althea took it all in, her "O" of a mouth growing progressively wider. When I finished she did a few myopic blinks, staring at me as if this was the most exciting thing to happen to her since post-it started making colored pads.

"This is all so James Bond. But, are you sure we should be interfering? I mean, wouldn't this be better left up to the police?"

Yes it would. But as long as Richards's name was crawling up the list of Ramirez's suspects, I didn't have that option. So, I sweetened the deal. "I could get you in for a complimentary pedicure at Fernando's?

That did it.

"I'll be right back," she said, then disappeared behind the frosted doors in search of the phone records.

I stood at the front desk, anxiously tapping my nails on the mahogany surface. I glanced at the brass clock above Jasmine's desk. 12:23. I hoped Althea hurried.

Less than two minutes later she was back with a computer printout.

"Okay here are all the calls to Richard's office yesterday. There weren't many because, well, you know." She blushed like a beet again. "When did the call come in?"

I took the printout, scanning my finger down the page. I'd received the call from Greenway just before Jasmine came back from break yesterday. 12:27 a call was logged to Richard's office from an 818 area code. My heart was suddenly racing like the bus from *Speed*. It was a North Hollywood prefix. As of yesterday, Greenway was still in the area.

"I think maybe this one is it. Is there any way you can find out who owns the number?"

Althea clicked a few buttons on Jasmine's keyboard. "I can do a reverse look up." If I hadn't known better I'd say Althea was beginning to enjoy this. Her eyes were shining behind her thick frames, her fingers flying at lightning speed across the keyboard. "Got it."

I tried not to sound too excited. "Whose number is it?"

"It says the Moonlight Inn in North Hollywood. You really think Greenway is hiding out there?"

I could have kissed her. "God, I hope so. Thanks, Althea."

"Thanks for what?"

I froze. I knew that helium perky voice. Jasmine.

Althea knew it too. Her head snapped up, a deer in the headlights expression frozen on her face.

I sent serious psychic vibes across the desk at her. Say nothing. Play dumb!

Althea must have got them because she quickly closed the window on her computer screen, obliterating all evidence of our noontime caper. Not that I was actually threatened by Jasmine. On her steady diet of laxatives and vitamin water she weighed about as much as a toothpick. However, I had a feeling she'd take inordinate pleasure in tattling on me to Ramirez.

"Thanks for what?" Jasmine asked again. "What's going on here?"

I tried to put on my innocent face. I opened my mouth, hoping some great lie would come out, but Althea beat me to it.

"I said I'd forward Richard's bills to his accountant's office. She didn't want his accounts going delinquent."

I stood and stared. Wow, Althea wasn't half bad at this cloak and dagger stuff.

Jasmine narrowed her eyes at me. (Or at least tried. They didn't move so well after her lid lift last May.) I wasn't sure she was buying it, but what could she say?

"Well, thanks again," I said, turning and walking as fast as I could out the doors. I could feel Jasmine's cold stare at my back all the way to the elevator. It was unnerving, like she was putting some Barbie hex on me. I was glad when the elevator arrived and I quickly stepped inside, punching the lobby button.

As soon as I was clear of the building, I pulled out my cell and punched in Dana's number.

"Hello?" she answered.

"I've got the number. It's the Moonlight Inn in North Hollywood."

Dana squealed with excitement on the other end. I had to hold the phone away from my ear to keep from going deaf.

"So," she asked. "What now?"

"I'll pick you up in twenty minutes. Get your Angels clothes on."

* * *

Nineteen minutes later I pulled up to Dana's duplex in Studio City. It was a modest, stucco structure that she shared with four other aspiring actors slash personal trainers. Which meant it always smelled vaguely of costume makeup, gym socks and Rice-a-Roni (the struggling actor's treat).

I knocked on the door and was answered a couple beats later by No Neck Guy. I'd long ago given up trying to remember the names of Dana's roommates. Being an actor didn't exactly translate into steady income and they tended to come and go like nomads. There had been Bubbly Blonde, Guy with Bleached Teeth, Latin Dancer Guy, and my favorite, Italian Guy Who Can't Keep his Hands to Himself. (Yuck!) No Neck Guy worked at the Sunset Gym with Dana and reminded me of the Incredible Hulk without all the green dye.

"Is Dana in?" I asked.

No Neck shrugged, then bellowed through the house for Dana.

"Coming," she yelled from deep in the Actor's Duplex. No Neck Guy nodded at me, then disappeared up the stairs. No Neck was a man of few words.

Three seconds later Dana bounced through the doorway, doing a little skipping footwork thing. Though one glance at her outfit took my attention quickly away from her feet.

"What are you wearing?" I stared, torn between the urge to laugh and cry.

"You like?" she asked, twirling in her doorway for me. She wore a tiny pleather mini skirt in a bright blue, spandex halter top that was at least two sizes too small for her well endowed D chest (another reason I hated her), a long strand of fake pearls (I know they were fake because they were neon green.) and had capped the whole thing off with a jet black, pageboy wig. I won't even go into the make-up. I prayed she'd just come off the set of "Hookers for Hire."

Apparently I hadn't answered her yet, as Dana pouted her cherry red lips and put both hands on her exposed hips. "You don't like my spying outfit?"

"This isn't what Charlie's Angels wore."

"Well, duh! I was going for call girl."

"Okay, maybe this is a dumb question, but why are you dressed like a call girl?"

"See, here's what I was thinking. We're going need to get Greenway's room number. And if we just go ask the manager, he's going to tell us to get lost. But, looking like this…" She did another twirl and her pearls clacked against her boobs. "He'll think we're hookers."

"But I don't want to be a hooker." Not a phrase I ever thought I'd have to say.

Dana ignored me. "I've got it all worked out. I did this scene for my acting class once from *Pretty Woman*, so I totally know how to act like a hooker. We'll tell the manager that we're meeting a john and can't remember his room number. Don't worry, people expect hookers to be dumb."

I rolled my eyes.

"Anyway, he's not going to want us banging on every door in his place until we find our john, now is he? Trust me, if we're dressed like this, guys are gonna be a *lot* more helpful."

That I didn't doubt.

"Dana, I just spent the morning as Barney in drag. I am *not*—N-O-T—" I spelled out for her, "spending the evening dressed as a hooker."

Dana put her hands on her hips again. She tilted her head to one side. She narrowed her eyes. Then she pulled out the big guns. "You peed on that stick yet?"

I sighed and willed my eye not to twitch.

"Fine. I'll be a hooker."

Fifteen minutes later Dana was coaching me on hooker-speak (which apparently consisted of a lot of "yo baby"'s and "wa'sup dawg"'s) and pulling dress after increasingly tiny dress from her closet. Finally she settled on a neon pink, strapless spandex thing that looked small enough to be a size negative two. She added a long red wig that reached clear down to my butt and a pair of four-inch acrylic heels chunkier than a Snickers bar.

As she sat me down on her bed to put the finishing touches on my make-up I filled her in on Ramirez's latest news about Richard.

The great thing about really good friends is that they often get as upset as you, if not more, when your boyfriend does something really stupid. Like get married.

"That bastard. That cheating son of bitch. The motherfu—"

"My thoughts exactly." I cut her off before she got too colorful. She was, after all, in character.

"How could he be married? I mean, you've met his freaking mother!"

I'd been thinking the same thing. In fact my first irrational thought when Ramirez told me about Cinderella was, had all his family and friends been lying to me for the last five months? Had they all been briefed beforehand to keep Maddie in the dark? It was like I was a bad reality show contestant. Only there was no cash payoff with this hoax.

But even as I listened to Dana cuss him out, I couldn't help a teeny tiny part of me from hoping that maybe Richard had an explanation for all this. And that wasn't just the denial talking. I knew Richard. Okay, so there were a few aspects of his life I wasn't privy to, but deep down I knew the man. I knew he was no more capable of leading a double life than he was of growing seven inches and playing for the Lakers. This kind of deception just wasn't in his makeup. Somehow, I knew there was a logical explanation for all of this and I was having a hard time hating him as much as I should until I heard his side of the story. I just could not believe Richard was actually married.

Then again, I had a hard time envisioning him consorting with killers and yet, here we were.

"Okay, I'm done." Dana capped her lipstick and pulled back her closet door to reveal a full-length mirror. We stood side by side and Dana put one arm around my shoulder. "Oh, this is going to be so much fun!" she squealed.

Again with that "fun" thing. Why did everyone think dressing up in dangerously ugly clothing was fun?

The wig itched a little, the spandex was riding up on my thighs already, but I had to admit as I stared in the mirror for the final effect, it was a good disguise. I looked nothing like myself. Thank God.

"Honey, we look fabulous," Dana said. "Let's go."

* * *

I'm not ashamed to say I had a knot in my stomach the entire drive up the 405. Well, that and a wedgie from the incredibly tight and unforgiving spandex causing my granny underwear to bunch. I shifted in my seat, promising myself I'd do laundry tomorrow.

We decided to ride in my Jeep as Dana said it looked more hookerish than her car. I wasn't sure if I should be offended by that or not. As we crawled through rush hour traffic, I couldn't help looking in my rearview mirror every two seconds for signs of a black SUV. I was a little paranoid about Ramirez spotting my car now. As if having him see me in the Purple People Eater wasn't bad enough, catching me as the Happy Hooker would probably kill me of embarrassment on the spot. Not to mention put a serious crimp in our plans.

Speaking of which…

"So, what is this *Pretty Woman* plan of yours? I mean, do we just walk up and ask what room Greenway is in?"

"Don't worry," Dana said, flipping down the visor to check her makeup, "just leave the talking to me."

Why is it when someone says, "don't worry," it makes me worry even more?

"So," Dana asked, before I could question her further, "where exactly is this place?"

I consulted the directions I'd printed from Yahoo maps before leaving the Actor's Duplex.

"Lankershim and Vanowen in North Hollywood. We should be there in about twenty minutes."

Dana nodded, pulling out a tube of lipstick and lapsing into silence as she added another layer of Circus Clown Red.

We wove north up the 405 and through the hills, which were actually quite scenic, until we reached the 101 and started our descent into the Valley. As we neared the 134 split, I slowed down, exiting the freeway at Lankershim as we entered North Hollywood.

While Hollywood features famous landmarks, celebrity footprints, and glitzy tourist shops, North Hollywood's name is unfairly deceptive. North Hollywood is Hollywood's ugly stepsister. Homes have bars on the windows, '79 Oldsmobiles propped on cement blocks cover brown lawns and old toothless men of every conceivable race sit on front porches yelling things like, "That my damn garbage. Touch that and I'll break yo' arm."

As we passed toothless man number three (yelling about the damn dog going on the damn lawn) I instinctively locked my doors. It wasn't that I was afraid of North Hollywood. Hey, I grew up in L.A., it took a lot more than bars on a window to frighten me. But the way that toothless old man had been staring at me like he was counting his pennies had me worried about the kind of propositions two hookishly dressed young ladies might get in this neighborhood. I did a little yucky squirm in my seat at the thought.

"It should be up here on the right," Dana said, reading the addresses as we passed by a liquor store, a closeout furniture place and a Desi's Porn Palace.

My stomach began to feel queasy as we neared the address and I spotted a woman wearing my same spandex dress negotiating at the passenger side window of a dented caddy. Unlike Dana, I was no actress. Granted, I was exercising my truth bending skills quite a bit lately (lying sounded so tawdry), but I wasn't quite sure I could pull off "hooker with a mission."

Too late to turn back now.

"Here it is." Dana pointed to a run down motel on the right. Ten units on the bottom, ten on the top and a metal staircase running along the side. A small building in front served as an office and behind it I could see green Dumpsters overflowing with trash. The beige, stucco walls of the motel had seen one too many nights of gang tagging, being a tri-colored mass of symbols that meant nothing to me but could likely get one shot at in South Central. The windows predictably sported prison-like bars and the roof likely would have leaked buckets— if it ever rained in L.A. that is.

I pulled into a spot under a sickly looking palm. Dana got out and immediately adjusted her top. I followed suit, trying one last time, in vain I might add, to retrieve my grannies from my cranny.

"Dana, I don't know if I can do this." I glanced nervously at the front office. Or, as the sign read. _ront O__ice. It looked like someone had shot out the "F"'s.

Dana looked in the side mirror, adjusting her wig. "Relax, it'll be fine. Just leave the talking to me. I'm a sweet-talking expert." Dana gave me a wink.

I took a deep breath. Okay. I could do this. Maddie Springer, Happy Hooker Extraordinaire.

CHAPTER EIGHT

———

The first time I ever saw Dana was on the blacktop at John Adams Middle School. She was wearing pink stirrup pants, a Madonna cut black, mesh shirt, and way more make-up than any other seventh grader I knew. She was standing with Alan Miller, our pre-teen equivalent of Donnie Wahlberg, and flirting. And not in the giggle, giggle, hair-flip way other girls I knew did. Dana had moves that made Alan's pants look like a little pup tent. She did the eyelash batting, the hip jutting, the shoulder thrusting, and what was later to become known as her signature move, the Lean and Shake.

Over the years the Lean and Shake has been perfected to the highly effective form I was now witnessing as Dana leaned her elbows on the stained Formica counter of the Moonlight Inn, her boobs threatening to spill from her halter, her round bottom doing a little shake, shake, shake in the air behind her.

And it was no less effective now. The night manager (a short, bald guy with mustard stains on his Metallica T-shirt) stared at Dana with a glazed expression and I could swear I saw something move in his pants. Ew! I quickly looked away.

"So, you can see our predicament," Dana said, her voice sugary enough to create instant cavities.

Metallica licked his thin, chapped lips. "Dude," he said, talking to Dana's cleavage, "I'd, like, really love to help you. What was the guy's name?"

"Mr. Smith." Dana winked.

"Ah." Metallica nodded. "So it's one of *those* kinds of dates, huh?" He wiggled his sparse eyebrows up and down.

I had a feeling the Moonlight Inn saw quite a few of *those* kind of dates. As ratty as the outside was, the interior of the office was even worse. The floor was covered in peeling vinyl that cracked under my heels and hadn't been washed since sometime in the Reagan years. The walls were a dingy gray showing water damage and mold from faulty plumbing. Two dim, fluorescent lights buzzed above us and the air had a thick, uncirculated smell of burnt food and unwashed bodies.

"Alls I know," Dana said, continuing her rump shake, "is Spike, that's my manager, told me to meet Mr. Smith here. And now I can't remember the room number." Dana pouted her lower lip out. "Spike's gonna be so pissed if I come back empty handed. Ya' know?"

Wow, Dana did a really good dumb blonde voice. It was somewhere between Betty Boop and Marilyn Monroe. Totally nine hundred number fake, but Metallica was eating it up. Nothing a metal head loves more than a dumb blonde in a halter top. I could see sweat beading on his upper lip as Dana poured on the charm.

"So, I was thinkin', maybe I could just kinda describe my Mr. Smith to you and maybe you could tell me what room number he's in?"

"We'd really appreciate it," I chimed in, licking my lips and making a kissy face. Okay, so I'm not the flirting expert Dana is. In fact, I felt really ridiculous in this whole getup and totally not sexy at all. Satin lingerie from Victoria's Secret is sexy. Neon spandex is just wrong.

Luckily, Metallica didn't seem to share my thoughts. He continued to eye Dana like a kid in a candy store.

"I don't know," he said, "We get an awful lot of dudes coming through here. I'm not sure I'd remember one from the other."

"Oh, I bet you have an excellent memory." Dana laid her hand on Metallica's arm and I thought he might start hyperventilating.

"The guy we're after probably checked in on Friday, alone," I added. "He's got dark hair that he wears slicked back from his face and probably keeps a real low profile. He was last seen wearing a leather bomber jacket, black pants, and a red button down shirt." I'd learned that much from the ten o'clock news last night.

Metallica tore his gaze from Dana's chest to quirk an eyebrow up at me. "How do you know so much about this guy?"

I swallowed. Dana shot me a look that said I should have let her do the talking.

"We've dated him before," she quickly covered.

"Cool." I'm not sure Metallica believed her. Then again, he didn't much seem to care as long as Dana kept crooning to him. I had to hand it to her. She was proving to be a hell of an actress. I hoped she got that Elvira gig.

I, on the other hand, didn't know how much longer I could keep this up. A cockroach crawled across the floor, scuttling under the counter and I suddenly got that creep crawly feeling on my skin. The sooner we got out of here the better. "So, is he here or not?" I asked.

"I don't know," Metallica hedged. He took a step back, looking from Dana to me. "You know, it seems kind of greedy a dude getting *both* you girls."

Uh oh.

"Hows about I tell one of you what room he's in and the other stays here and keeps me company."

Ew, ew, ew! I pasted a fake smile on my face, willing myself not to barf.

Even Dana looked like she'd just about had her fill of this guy.

"Oh, that's quite an offer," she said through a fake smile of her own. "But, see, I'm not so sure you could afford us. We're high class ladies, if ya' know what I mean."

Metallica smiled, showing off the gaps between his teeth. They reminded me of a jack-o-lantern, a cross between really goofy looking and kind of creepy.

"Well, how about you just do me a little favor for free then. I might remember all sorts of stuff for a little favor."

Gag.

Dana sighed. She leaned over the counter until her cleavage rivaled the Grand Canyon. She ran her tongue slowly over her lower lip. She slid a manicure hand up Metallica's shirt. His forehead beaded with sweat and his breath came out in quick gasps. I didn't dare look, but I was pretty sure his pants were in pup tent territory.

Dana slowly slid her hand up his chest until she reached his collar…then she grabbed a handful of T-shirt and yanked him off the ground.

"Listen you little turd," she breathed, her nose inches from his. "We need the room number, and you're going to give it to us."

Metallica suddenly turned white, his feet dangling off the ground as his eyes bugged out. "Jesus, okay. Just, put me down lady."

I stifled a laugh. Don't piss off the Aerobics Queen.

Dana's sweet smile returned as she put him back down. But she kept her fingers wrapped around his collar. I had the fleeting thought she'd need some antibacterial cleanser for her hands after this.

"That's more like it. Now, where is our friend staying?"

Metallica looked from me to Dana, the pup tent suddenly more like a wet noodle. "Room two-ten," he finally spit out. "Second floor. Jesus, lady."

Dana let go of his shirt, patting him on the cheek. "Thanks a ton, *dude*."

I couldn't help it. I laughed out loud at the stunned expression on Metallica's face as Dana shook, shook, shook her way out the door.

I followed closely behind her. "Whatever happened to sweet talking him?" I asked.

"The cockroaches were making me antsy."

I couldn't argue with that one.

"So, now we know where Greenway is. Let's go call Ramirez," Dana said.

Right. We should call Ramirez. I mean, he was the cop, after all.

But something held me back. Maybe it was the ditzy blonde syndrome that struck me every time I encountered Ramirez. Or maybe just the way he'd smirked a little too much at the sight of me in the Purple People Eater. But I really didn't want to look stupid in front of him again. If we called him now and it turned out Greenway wasn't in that room, I was going to look like a total flake.

"Maybe we should make sure he's here first," I said.

Dana looked at me as if I'd just suggested we go service Metallica. "Are you kidding? You want to go knock on the door and just ask, 'Hey, you're the guy who killed his wife, right?'"

Put like that, it didn't sound like such a hot plan. "No. Yes. I mean, what if Ramirez sends a swat team out and the room is empty. What if Greenway went across the street for a cup of coffee? If he sees the place swarming with cops, he'll be long gone again."

Dana chewed her lip for a beat. "Okay, fine. We'll knock on the door and see if he's home. But, for the love of God, leave the talking to me this time."

Right. No problem there. I wasn't exactly *dying* to speak to Greenway again. I cringed. Ouch, bad choice of words.

Dana and I clanked up the metal staircase to the second floor. The walls of the Moonlight Inn were thin and I could hear the sounds of "favors" being given out all over the place. "Oh baby," seemed to resonate in stereo from behind the thin wooden doors, mixed with a steady bass rhythm from warring rap and heavy metal stations playing at top volume.

And I'm not ashamed to say my heart was beating almost as loudly as the guitar riffs. Being on the phone with Greenway had been unnerving enough, but my teeth were starting to chatter at the thought of a face to face encounter. Our pace slowed as we neared two-ten. On the other side of that door was a murderer. I suddenly felt very vulnerable. And, I realized, thinking about Ramirez's big black gun, very unarmed.

Dana and I paused outside the door. The room had one window facing the parking lot. It was covered from the inside with a faded green curtain and, from the absence of light peeking between the ratty fabric, it looked like no one was home.

"Maybe he isn't here?" I whispered.

"Maybe he's sleeping."

"Maybe we shouldn't wake him up."

"Hey, this was your idea," Dana whispered.

I know. And it sounded good downstairs. But close up, I was having second thoughts. Before I could act on my newfound chickenhood, Dana rapped her knuckles against the wooden door. I bit my lip, resisting the urge to run and hide.

Nothing.

Dana knocked again, this time yelling, "Hello?"

Nothing. I heaved a sigh of relief strong enough to ruffle my fake bangs.

Then I heard it. A gun shot.

It cracked like thunder on the other side of the door, rendering both Dana and me paralyzed for one awful second.

If this were the movies, we would have rammed our shoulders into the door, busting it open and tackled the perp without breaking a nail. But, since neither of us was under contract with Warner Brothers, we did what all Los Angelinos are trained to do when confronted with real live gunfire. Run.

Dana and I turned as one, diving to the right amidst high pitched, "ohmigod"'s. We clacked back down the stairs as quickly as our insanely high heels would allow and made a mad dash for my Jeep, parked across the lot. Dana hiked her dress up and was charging with quarter back determination toward the car. I was a short step behind her, my arms flailing like a crazy woman for balance as we sprinted across the black top.

Metallica poked his head out of the office doors. "What was that? What the hell did you crazy ho's do?"

"Nothing," Dana yelled, reaching my Jeep.

"I heard a gun."

"No you didn't," I said. I know, world's lamest comeback. But at the moment speed was more my goal than wit.

We climbed in and were just pulling out of the driveway when I swear I heard a second gunshot. I didn't stop to make sure, instead pulling down Vanowen, going two blocks before circling back around toward the freeway.

I was still reeling from the adrenalin high when Dana voiced the obvious.

"We just got shot at. Can you believe someone just shot at us?"

No I couldn't. This was so not my life. Somehow I'd been transferred into Lucy Liu's body, I was sure of it.

"Do you think it was Greenway?" I asked.

"Uh…duh! Do you know any other homicidal maniacs that would shoot at us?"

Good point.

"So, do we call Ramirez now?" Dana asked.

I couldn't help it. The smart-aleck in me reared its ugly head. "Uh…duh!"

I pulled into the parking lot of a Denny's at Van Nuys and Oxford and reached into my little bag for the card Ramirez had given me. I'm not ashamed to say my hands were still shaking as I dialed the number on my cell phone. I let Dana do the talking on the off chance Ramirez recognized my voice. I knew he'd want to ask me all kinds of annoying questions like, how did I know where Greenway was staying? How did I get his room number? Why did he shoot at me? Questions I would much rather avoid altogether. So, Dana put on her Betty Boop hooker voice again and left the anonymous tip with the desk sergeant who answered the phone.

"I don't know about you," Dana said when she hung up. "But I could use a stiff drink."

"Me too." Only I couldn't drink. Not until I knew if that line was pink or blue.

"Want to start happy hour early?"

Honestly, all I wanted to do was go home and take about ten showers to wash the creep off me, but considering I was the one who'd dragged Dana out to North Hollywood in the first place, not to mention got her shot at, I felt like I owed her.

"Sure. You have someplace in mind?"

Dana flipped down the visor and began touching up her makeup again. "I know a guy who bartends at Mulligans. It's just a couple blocks over on Van Nuys."

I pulled out of the Denny's and drove down Van Nuys, following her directions until we pulled up to a brick building with a blue neon sign above the door, blinking the word "Mulligans." A steady stream of people in business casual attire filtered through the door. I looked down at my spandex. Silently making bets on how many propositions I'd get before the day was out.

The lot was packed, so I found a place on the street and after reluctantly feeding the meter, Dana and I emerged into the dimly lit interior of Mulligans. I immediately recoiled as the sounds of bad karaoke echoed from a small stage in the corner where a pudgy, middle aged man was belting out a Shania Twain song.

Dana immediately ordered two vodka martinis with extra olives from her bartending friend, a Bruce Lee look alike dressed all in black. If any day of my life ever called for a martini, today was it. However, counting selfless act number two, I promptly changed my order to a Diet Coke. Once they arrived, Dana only had time to munch one olive before Bruce Lee grabbed her hand and dragged her over to the karaoke machine for a duet of American Pie.

I sat at the bar by myself and sipped my Diet Coke. Generally, I'm not much one for the happy hour crowd. I prefer places where you can actually hear your friends talk, like Starbucks or Nordstrom. For me a night on the town consisted of dinner and a Julia Roberts movie at Citywalk. But something about the loud, crowded, anonymity of Mulligans was oddly soothing at the moment. Like a huge, badly sung escape from my real life.

My hands were only slightly shaking as I took another sip of my Diet Coke. It really was a poor substitute for a martini.

I was dying to know what was going on back at the motel. Had Ramirez gotten the tip? Was he arresting Greenway right now? I wondered if there was a big shoot out with the cops when they arrived. God, I hoped nobody got hurt. Well, I guess I wouldn't mind Metallica taking one in the ass, but I really didn't want anyone to get killed. Least of all me, which is why even though I was dying of curiosity, I made myself stay right where I was and sip my Diet Coke. I'd give it two hours, then I'd call Ramirez's number again and nonchalantly ask if there'd been any new developments. I would, of course, leave out the part where I gloated about finding Greenway when the whole police force couldn't. Ha, who's girly now?

Dana jostled up beside me, diving for her drink again and took a long sip. "Ohmigod. I forgot what an awesome singer Liao is." She drained her glass and crunched down hard on an olive. "Come up with us. We're gonna do 'I've Got You Babe' next."

"No thanks. I'm not really in a karaoke mood."

Dana cocked her bobbed wig to one side. "Hey,are you okay?"

No, I was not okay. I'd just been shot at!

But Dana had been nice enough to come all the way to the Valley with me, even though I'd almost gotten her killed, so there was no reason to ruin her evening with Bruce Lee.

"I'll be fine," I said. Eventually.

"You sure?"

I fake smiled. "Yeah. Fine. Really."

"Okay. Well, in that case, you wouldn't mind driving home alone would you? See, Liao's house sitting for this guy in the hills and he says he's got a hot tub that looks out over the Hollywood sign."

I looked down at her outfit. I hoped the invitation didn't have anything to do with the mini skirt. Then again, knowing Dana, she probably hoped it did.

"Yeah, go. I'm fine."

"Cool. I'll call you tomorrow and we'll read all about the arrest over bagels." She gave me co-conspirital wink before disappearing back into the ever-growing mob of happy hour patrons.

Right. The arrest. I just hoped there was one. Again I got that itch to see what was going on at the motel. Was Greenway in custody? If he was, I was sure Perky Reporter Woman would be singing all about it on the evening edition. If Richard saw news of the all clear, he might even be back in his condo tonight. I took another sip of my Diet Coke, wondering just how I felt about that.

Now that Cinderella was in the picture, I wasn't a hundred percent sure I knew how things stood between Richard and me anymore. I mean, of course I was pissed at him, he was married to a freaking Disney princess. But, as I'd learned from Mrs. Rosenblatt's parade of husbands, there were all kinds of married. Maybe they were separated, estranged. So what then?

And, to make matters worse, I couldn't stop thinking about that heated panty thing that Ramirez seemed to inspire in me, which I'm sure was just a bad case of not getting laid in awhile, but was a little unnerving all the same.

I took another sip of my Diet Coke, really wishing it had a higher vodka content. Which was a sad commentary on my life. Fashion designer wanna-be yearns to get drunk after being shot at by her lying, cheating ex-boyfriend's murderous client.

While thinking really unwholesome thoughts about annoying, yet oh-so-sexy, homicide detective.

"Excuse me," a voice said behind me, catching the attention of Liao's replacement behind the bar. "I'll have a Coors."

I froze.

Have you ever noticed that some people have a tendency to show up just when you're thinking of them? Mrs. Rosenblatt would undoubtedly say it was the cosmic thread that bound us all together. Personally, I think it's just dumb luck. And my luck seemed to be really bad tonight.

I resisted the urge to slink away into the dancing crowd (Because he'd probably find me anyway, after all he *was* a cop.) and turned around to face him.

"Well," Ramirez said, a sly grin creasing his features, "Fancy meeting you here."

CHAPTER NINE

———

All I could do was stare. Damn, did this guy have a homing device or what?

Ramirez just smiled, casually depositing himself onto the stool beside me as the bartender slid him a bottle of Coors.

"Love the outfit," he said.

"Thanks." I tugged at the hem of my dress, suddenly very aware of my bunching grannies again.

His smiled widened, showing off that too-sexy dimple. "Something about a woman in spandex gets me all hot and bothered."

"You're mocking me aren't you?"

"Just a little."

"It's supposed to be a disguise."

"From whom?"

I paused. "No one."

"Hmm." He studied me, his hands idly picking up a swizzle straw from the bar and drawing little circles with it.

"What?" I asked.

"The wig is a nice touch."

"Real classy huh?"

"I think I prefer you as a blonde."

I hated that somewhere inside me a pleased little voice screamed, "He likes your hair!"

"So, what are you doing here?" I asked, squelching the little voice.

"Working." He fixed me the kind of stare Superman used when switching on his X-ray vision. "What are *you* doing here?"

I bit my lip. I wasn't sure how much to spill. Worse, I'd told so many versions of the truth lately, I wasn't entirely sure which version I'd last given Ramirez. But considering Greenway was likely on his way to County right now and Richard would be home soon, I figured I didn't have much to lose.

"I was looking for Greenway but I got shot at, so I needed a drink."

Ramirez looked down at my Diet Coke and raised an eyebrow. Luckily he didn't say anything. I wasn't sure I could explain *that* on top of everything else.

"Okay," he said, shaking his head. "Because I like you and I've haven't got time to do all the paperwork, I'm going to pretend I didn't hear that shooting thing."

Did he just say he liked me? Damn, that little voice was perking up again.

"Look, Maddie," he continued, "this is a homicide. Bad men with big guns. This is not children's shoes. Don't you think maybe it's time you went home and let the big boys handle this?"

He had a point. I wasn't thrilled about the guys with guns. And getting shot at again was way, way low on my list of to-do's. I'd neglected the Strawberry Shortcake shoes, I'd dragged my best friend into the Valley, I'd very nearly gotten Althea fired, and I was in neon spandex of all things. And in all honesty, I had planned on finishing my drink, going straight home, and gluing my butt to my futon as I watched for any sign of Greenway's arrest on the news.

But the way Ramirez said "big boys" made my spine straighten, my jaw clench, and my eyes narrow into cat-like slits as I flipped my fake hair over one shoulder.

"Listen, 'big boy', I may have ovaries, but I'm not going to just sit at home and knit while Richard is out there being hunted down by a killer. Even if he is married to Cinderella."

'Kay—not a good idea to spout off to a cop. Ramirez stared at me, pinning me with his best Bad Cop face. I said a silent prayer that he didn't reach for his cuffs. On any day, spending a night in a county cell wasn't my idea of a good time. And dressed like this, it would probably rank below wearing the Purple People Eater down a Milan runway on the fun scale.

Just as I was about to throw myself on the mercy of the law, Ramirez's eyes crinkled at the corners. His lip jerked up.

And then he laughed out loud.

It should have pissed me off, but instead I found my fighting stance fading. Man, he had a great laugh. It was rich and full and totally transformed his face. For a second I got a glimpse of the cover model he could have been in another life.

"Fine," he said, finally recovering. "I'll make you a deal." He leaned in close enough that I could smell his brand of soap. Ivory. I inhaled. I'd always liked that brand.

"What kind of deal?"

His eyes locked on mine and in a voice that was way too intimate said, "You show me yours and I'll show you mine."

Yikes. I hoped he was talking about the case. Okay, well I mostly hoped he was talking about the case. There was one teeny tiny little corner of my brain that flashed on Dana's "animal sex" phrase again.

"What do you want to know?" I squeaked out.

His gaze didn't waver. "Everything."

That covered a lot of ground. I decided to go for the cliff notes version. "Okay. I was at Richard's office yesterday and a call came in from Greenway. I traced the call to the Moonlight Inn and my best friend, Dana, and I dressed as hookers to try to get Greenway's room number out of the night clerk. Only when we go to the room, someone shot at us, so we bolted."

Both Ramirez's eyebrows headed north this time.

"You traced the call?"

"Okay, I didn't so much trace it as I bribed his receptionist with a manicure to look up the number for me."

"Jesus." He rolled his eyes.

"What?"

"You really are girly."

I narrowed my eyes at him. "Hey, it worked didn't it? I showed you mine, now show me yours. What are *you* doing here?"

Ramirez took another sip of his beer and looked at me. I feared he might renege on his deal.

"Okay. Someone called in an anonymous tip that Devon Greenway was staying at the Moonlight in North Hollywood.

We traced the call to your cell number. And I mean traced, as in using technology, not manicures."

My turn to roll my eyes.

"So, I sent a couple uniforms to check it out. Imagine my surprise when on my way there, I spot your red Jeep parked on the street."

I ignored the sarcasm. "So, did they arrest Greenway?"

"No."

"What do you mean 'no?!'" My voice took on that high, screechy quality again as panic grabbed me by the hair and whipped my head around the room. Suddenly the safe anonymity of Mulligans felt very much like a room full of strangers. Any one of which could be wielding a gun.

"I mean the motel room was empty. No one was there."

For the second time in as many days I willed myself not to hyperventilate. I wrapped my shaking hands around my glass and downed the last of my Diet Coke. Too quickly. It went down the wrong pipe and I started to choke, quick unproductive coughs that sounded like a hyena in heat. Ramirez smacked me on the back, bringing tears to my eyes as I finally got a hold of myself.

Ramirez just shook his head at me, a little half smirk on his lips as he took another sip of his Coors.

"He was there," I said. "I swear he was there. He called from there yesterday. You can check the call log at Richard's office. We had a long conversation about how Richard calls me pumpkin."

"Pumpkin?" Ramirez smirked again.

"It's his pet name. I didn't pick it out."

"And pumpkin was the best he could do?"

"It's cute!" In all honesty, I'd never really liked pumpkin. It always reminded me of something my grandfather would call me. But I wasn't going to admit that to Ramirez.

"You're more like a *fregadita*, if you ask me."

"A what?"

Ramirez smiled. "You figure it out."

I think I hated him.

"You're sure Greenway's not at the motel?"

"If he was, he's gone now. And if he's smart he's on a plane to the Caribbean. I've got a couple CSI going over the motel now just in case he left a calling card."

I bet my hook-nosed CSI Guy was having a field day lint rolling Metallica.

"You think they'll find anything?"

Ramirez shrugged. "My guess? He's long gone."

Great. Back to square one. Only now I felt this irrational need to look over my shoulder every three seconds for angry gunmen. And Richard was still out there somewhere. Still hiding. Still not returning my calls. Still married to Cinderella.

I seriously needed something stronger than Coke.

"So," Ramirez said, draining his Coors, "now that we're on the same page, it's time for you to go home."

"Will you tell me if they find anything at the motel?"

Ramirez's expression was suddenly serious. "Look, this is a murder investigation. It's not shoe shopping. Go home."

"But—" I opened my mouth to protest, but Ramirez cut me off, laying one hand over mine.

"I've already fished one woman's body out of a swimming pool. I don't want to make it two. Please. Go home."

I froze. Not so much from the warning, but the heat of Ramirez's hand over mine. I gulped, trying to tell myself I wasn't thirteen and this was not some hunky football player.

"I can't just forget about all this." I didn't add, because I may be carrying his child.

Ramirez put on his Bad Cop face again, the softie side of him swallowed up just as quickly as it appeared. He shook his head at me and muttered something in Spanish before leaving to the tune of a little Asian woman in clogs singing the *Macarena*.

Then he was gone.

I stared at my empty glass. It was good advice. Go home. He was right, I didn't know what I was doing. Maybe Greenway was on a plane to the Caribbean. But then again, maybe he wasn't. Maybe he was tracking Richard down right now, closing in on him, gun drawn, waiting to pounce. The heroic part of me that grew up wearing Wonder Woman Underoos wanted to grab my golden lasso and save Richard from possibly ending up face down in a crystal clear swimming pool.

But the chicken-hearted part of me that had run like hell from room two-twelve knew Ramirez was right. If I kept stumbling along, I might end up stumbling into the barrel of a gun. Was Richard even worth all this?

Last week it would have been a resounding, yes. Today, I was having serious doubts. While I couldn't ignore the Cinderella factor, I couldn't totally write Richard off without hearing his side of the story either. I mean, we'd been together for four months. Most of them really, really good. Okay, so we hadn't had that deep we're-spending-the-rest-of-our-lives-gazing-into-each-others'-eyes talk yet, but I did spend at least three nights a week at his place and we had an understood Friday date-night exclusive.

So, the question was, what to do now? I jiggled the ice cubes in the bottom of my glass. I had no leads, no gun, no CSI guys of my own. I didn't even have a pocket sized pepper spray.

But I did have one thing. A pregnancy test. And with my whole boyfriend status about as hazy as July in the Valley, the thought of facing a murderer was a whole lot less scary than the thought of facing a pink line.

So, I did the only thing I could. I threw a ten on the bar, grabbed my purse, and ran for my red Jeep before Ramirez got too far ahead of me.

* * *

I was the first to admit that the last time I'd tailed Ramirez hadn't exactly been a great success. I really didn't want to encounter any more dead bodies. So, I promised myself I'd stay in the car. But contrary to Ramirez's sexist ideas, I wasn't just going to wait around for things to get worse. And I had a bad feeling things were going to get worse before they got better. Sure it would be great if CSI Guy found a trail leading straight to Greenway, but I didn't think Greenway was that stupid. Or that I was that lucky.

So instead of sitting at home, watching the perky news reporters tell me the cops had no current leads, I was taking my fate into my own hands. I was being proactive. Yes, proactive. That sounded so much better than "interfering in an investigation." Besides, if I just stayed in the car I wasn't really interfering at all. Just spying.

That and I had to admit I was still a little miffed about the girly comment. And what the hell was a *fregadita*?

I pulled back onto Van Nuys and caught up to Ramirez's black SUV at the next light. I stayed two cars behind in the next lane over, willing my Jeep to look small and unnoticeable. As expected, he took a right on Vanowen, heading in the direction of the motel. I let him pull ahead a few more car lengths, feeling reasonably confident I knew where he was going. I lost him as we drove under the 170, but as I slowly cruised past the Moonlight, I saw his SUV parked under that same scraggy palm my Jeep had been only an hour earlier.

I circled the motel and parked down the street under a streetlamp that was blinking its last dying bit of light. Even though it was still a balmy seventy-nine degrees out, I kept the windows rolled up and the doors locked. If the Moonlight had seemed creepy before it was downright horror movie-ish now. I had visions of that scene from *Urban Legend* where the unsuspecting woman sits in her car while an ax murderer springs up from the backseat and slashes until the car fills with red dyed Karo syrup. I shivered. I wanted to keep all my syrup right where it was, thank you very much.

I squinted through the darkness as Ramirez got out of his SUV. There were two black and whites in the lot now, one officer talking into his car radio while the other swept a flashlight along the license plates of the other cars in the lot. Ramirez walked up to the cop with the flashlight, conversing for a moment with the uniform who kept gesturing up to room two-twelve.

I followed Ramirez's gaze up the stairs. The door to the room was open now and I could see the light on. Forms outlined against the ratty curtains, presumably CSI Guy and his many little black bags. The half dressed neighbors on either side of room two-twelve had come out of their rooms, milling around the doorway like moths to a flame.

Ramirez left the uniform and took the stairs two at a time, making long, purposeful strides to Greenway's room. He disappeared inside for a minute, then quickly reemerged. He went back down the stairs and crossed the cracked blacktop to the office. I allowed myself a little smirk at the thought of Metallica cowering under Ramirez's evil eye.

Five minutes later Ramirez emerged from the office and got back in his SUV. The lights turned on and he backed out of the lot, pointing his car down Lankershim in the direction of the freeway. I made myself count to three Mississippi before chasing after him.

More than likely he was just going back to the police station. But, on the off chance Metallica had shared intimate knowledge of Greenway's next destination, I figured it wouldn't hurt to take a little joyride. Besides, though I hated to admit it, my studio was suddenly sounding kind of empty. After the chilling experience tonight, coupled with the knowledge Greenway was still out there somewhere, the thought of being alone wasn't all that appealing. And I didn't even have anyone I could call for a chickenhearted sleepover. Dana was off in hot tub land, and of course Richard was AWOL. I guess I could have called my mom, but then I would have had to spend the evening hearing about her upcoming bachelorette party at Beefcakes and just how many twenties she was taking with her. Which was almost as creepy.

I know it was crazy, but as long as I had Ramirez in my sights, I felt safe. Funny how the taillights of an SUV could be so comforting.

So, I continued to follow Ramirez down Lankershim to the 134. He got on going east, toward Pasadena, but turned off at the 5 south. He drove fast, like he was late for something, weaving in and out of traffic down the 5, chasing it all the way to the 60 east toward Pomona. I struggled to catch up while simultaneously trying to keep at least one semi truck between us. I was determined to be in stealth mode tonight.

My dash clock read seven thirty before Ramirez finally pulled his SUV off the freeway and exited at Azusa and into the residential neighborhood of Hacienda Heights. The houses here were modest, single-family homes that looked like they'd seen generations of children come and go. Originally cookie-cutter tracts in the fifties, the street was now dotted with garage conversions, siding from Sears, and the occasional second story addition. The landscaping was mature, the lawns neatly clipped and littered with big wheels and soccer balls.

Ramirez led me past a house with a baby swing tied up to a tree in the yard and a crisp picket fence outlining the lawn, and I had a moment of suburban panic as my possible future flashed before my eyes. Was this what a pink line meant?

Okay, so I'm not so neurotic as to have a mental breakdown at the mere thought of settling down in soccer mama land. But the thought of giving up my studio (dinky as it may be), of, gulp, cohabiting with Richard, (yes, I was ignoring the Cinderella factor) and becoming Florence Henderson made my hands sweat. With one broken condom was I really ready to give up my whole life for suburbanitehood?

And I hated to admit a teeny tiny (very teeny tiny, mind you) part of me kind of wanted to. I blamed my Cabbage Patch kids for the sudden maternal wistfulness. I'd been programmed since I bought Barbie her dream house, complete with the perfect accessory, her Ken doll, to want all this. And yet as it stared me in the face, I broke out in a cold sweat.

So complete was my fear that I realized I'd lost Ramirez. Crap.

I circled the block, turning at the corner to retrace my steps. On the second go round, I finally spotted his SUV parked on the opposite side of the street under a leafy oak.

I parked at the corner, well away from the dim glare of streetlamps, and slid low in my seat. I could see from here that Ramirez's SUV was empty. He'd already gotten out and presumably gone into one of the houses while I'd circled the block. Crap.

I quickly scanned the two houses on either side of his car. One was completely dark. The other was a squat ranch style with yellow shutters and the blue light of a television set flickering through the front window. The yard was dotted with yucca trees and hula-hoops. Rose bushes lined the walkway, mingling with baseball mitts, Tonka trucks, and an abandoned Raggedy Ann. All of which didn't strike me as the type of hideout Greenway would choose. I silently wondered what Ramirez was doing here.

Then he yanked my psychic thread again.

"Looking for me?" Ramirez's face appeared in my window.

I yelped like a terrier, jumping back in my seat.

"Geeze, you scared the crap out of me."

His eyes crinkled in a half smile, as if he'd meant to. "You're beginning to be a real pain, you know it?"

"We girly girls are like that."

"Don't suppose I could persuade you to go home now, huh?"

I put on my best tough chick face. "No, you can't. I don't know what makes you think you can just order me around like this. It's because I'm a woman, isn't it?"

His half smile widened. "Actually, it's because I carry a badge."

Right. Well, I guess he did have a point there.

I decided to change the subject. "So, where are we?" I asked, gesturing to the sleepy neighborhood.

He glanced at the hula-hoop house. "Nowhere important."

Uh-huh. Like I believed that for a second. "Who's in there?" I asked, craning in my seat to see past the yellow shutters.

Ramirez shook his head. "Trust me, you don't want to know."

"There you go again. Telling me what I want and don't want. Do women really go for this sexist pig thing you've got going on?" But even as I said it I had no doubt that they did.

Ramirez got that I'm-gonna-arrest-you-and-I'm-gonna-like-it twinkle in his eyes again. "Okay. You really want to know?"

I was wavering. But, I hadn't come this far just to be intimidated by some man who thought he could boss me around just because he was sexier than Brad Pitt in a toga. I squared my shoulders. "Yes."

"All right. Let's go in."

This was too easy. There had to be a catch. But, after the stink I'd made, I could hardly chicken out now. (And I had to admit, going to Destination Unknown with Ramirez still sounded better than sitting in my studio alone, waiting for Greenway to jump out and spill my Karo syrup.) So, I grabbed my purse and locked my Jeep, following as Ramirez led the way across the street and up the rose lined path.

The front door was painted a vibrant red with an orange stained-glass window. Ramirez gave a familiar shave-and-a-hair-cut knock and opened the door without waiting for an answer, pushing me in ahead of him.

The air was warmer than outside and smelled like tamales, Pine Sol, and sugar cookies. Music played from somewhere deep in the house, and a chorus of children's voices all vied for attention just beyond my vision. Ramirez walked me into a cozy living room that looked about to burst at the seams with chotchkes of every variety. Colored glass vases, a collection of Anaheim Angels bobble head dolls, homemade afghans in bright greens and assaulting pinks, and glass candle holders painted with pictures of the Virgin Mary filled every conceivable surface. A man in a worn work shirt and jeans dozed in a burnt orange La-Z-Boy in the corner, a black cowboy hat resting on the coffee table beside him. The television I saw from the street was muted, playing a John Wayne western.

Just beyond the living room I could see a kitchen done in baby blue Formica, bustling with round women chattering in rapid Spanish.

I had serious second thoughts about coming in with Ramirez. I'd envisioned questioning a suspect under blaring lamps, breaking into a suburban crack den, even squeezing information out of Greenway's second cousin's neighbor. But I had a sinking feeling I'd walked into something much scarier.

"Hello?" Ramirez called.

The Spanish ceased and five little faces popped out of the kitchen. All were a warm, tan color, topped by waves of thick black hair. One woman seemed about my age, while the other four wore soft wrinkles and streaks of gray through their locks.

The shortest one (and none of them seemed over five feet) clapped her hands in front of her as she spied Ramirez. "*Mijo*, you came!"

"Of course I came." Ramirez walked over to the woman, planting a quick kiss on her cheek. "You didn't think I'd miss your birthday, Mama?"

Mama? Uh oh. Sinking feeling realized.

I tugged at the hem of my dress, wondering if I could make it grow about three inches if I just wished it hard enough. I wasn't fond of meeting anyone's mother dressed like this, let alone one who baked sugar cookies. Maybe if I backed up real slowly I could just disappear out the front door with some shred of my dignity left.

As if he could read my mind, Ramirez said, "Mama, this is Maddie."

I froze as five pairs of deep brown eyes turned on me. So much for backing out the door.

Mama looked me up and down. She raised one thick eyebrow at Ramirez. The other women simply stared at me, their eyes as big and round as their soft faces. All except the younger one. Her eyes narrowed into a tight line and she pursed her lips together.

"Maddie, this my sister BillieJo, and The Aunts— Swoozie, Cookie, and Kiki."

The Aunts stared. BillieJo glared.

"Hi," I said. I did a little one finger wave. No one waved back.

I felt the word "hooker" flashing on my forehead like a neon sign. "I, uh, don't usually dress like this," I said quickly, my cheeks burning brighter than Rudolph's shiny nose.

Mama gave me a slow once over. Her gaze lingered on my hemline. Self-consciously, I gave it another tug south.

"Nice legs," she said.

"Uh…" I looked to Ramirez for an appropriate response. No help there. He crossed his arms over his chest and rocked back on his heels, a smirk pasted on his face that clearly said this was payback for following him around town.

"Thanks," I finally managed.

"I used to have legs like that," Mama went on. "Before I had babies. Babies ruin your legs. Varicose veins, cellulite. It's not pretty. You have any babies?"

"No. No babies." Yet.

"Good for you. Keep those legs as long as you can. I had my first baby when I was seventeen. How old are you?"

"Um. Twenty-nine," I answered. Only it sounded more like a question, as if I was hoping I'd gotten the right answer on the pop quiz

"Oh." Mama leaned in and pseudo whispered. "Are you barren?"

I think I heard Ramirez snort.

"No! No, I'm not barren. I'm just…I have a job."

"Oh. Well, then. Good for you. A career girl. I always wanted to be a career girl. I thought I'd make a really good firefighter."

I tried not to laugh as I pictured Mama's portly frame hauling someone from a burning building.

"So, what do you do?" she asked.

"I design shoes."

Mama looked down at my acrylic chunky heels.

"Not these," I added quickly. "I design children's shoes."

Mama perked up. "See, she does like children. This one's good. I like her." Mama gave Ramirez a pat on the cheek.

"Glad you approve," he said. He really was enjoying this too much.

Mama gave me a pat on the cheek too, for good measure. Then she gestured to Ramirez. "Make him use condoms. You gotta keep those legs as long as you can."

I think I swallowed my tongue. I looked to Ramirez to dispel his mother's idea that we needed condoms. But he was trying too hard not to laugh.

"Well," Mama said to the room at large, "tamales are ready, let's eat."

I blinked hard, watching Mama's stout frame waddle back into the kitchen. The Aunts followed as one, BillieJo bringing up the rear with one last glare at me over her shoulder.

I was still contemplating whether it was too late to bolt for the door when I felt Ramirez's breath on my neck.

"I told you, you didn't want to come in here," he murmured. He shot me a grin to rival the Cheshire cat's as he grabbed my hand and led me into the kitchen.

I was so going to get him for this.

CHAPTER TEN

———

Ramirez led me outside to a spacious backyard that made my paltry window box of geraniums look downright pathetic. Three picnic style tables were set up on the lawn, covered in brightly color tablecloths. Mismatched chairs and benches surrounded them, while piles of fragrant tamales, chilies, and empanadas sat atop. Strings of lights had been hung between the tall oak trees and a battered piñata swung from one of the lower branches. A handful of dark haired children sat beneath it, lollipop sticks protruding from their mouths.

"Uncle Jack," one of them yelled, flying at Ramirez. Two more little girls followed suit and soon Ramirez had candy fingered rug rats permanently affixed to both his legs.

My turn to smirk a little. "Uncle Jack" was about the last role I'd have picture Ramirez in. But, to his credit, he didn't even grimace as one of his nieces made a chocolate covered handprint on his white shirt.

Mama came out carrying another tray of tamales and sat down on one of the benches. This seemed to be the signal as suddenly a swarm of people appeared from nowhere. BillieJo and three other young women came out the sliding glass doors, followed by the man I'd seen dozing in the La-Z-Boy. Two men came around the side of the house, both with an unmistakable resemblance to Ramirez, though one was a little pudgier and the other wore his dark hair in a ponytail at the nape of his neck.

Mama shoved a plate into my hands, with a commanding, "Eat, eat," and under her watchful eye I piled one of everything on my plate, for fear of offending her. (I figured my outfit was offensive enough for one evening.)

As we sat down to eat, two more men emerged from the house, guitars slung over their shoulders as they converged on the food, laughing, talking, and generally adding to the roar of voices that seemed to surround me.

Now, my grandmother is, as I may have mentioned, Irish Catholic. Before my grandfather bought his one-way ticket to St. Peter's, we used to spend every Christmas Eve at their house. All seven of my aunts and uncles, all nineteen of my cousins, and all forty gazillion of their little darlings running around the house in plaid Christmas dresses and tiny red bow ties. So, I'm no stranger to big families. But I had never in my life encountered people who could talk so loudly and yet eat so much, all at the same time. I was in awe.

And if I'd hoped to fade into the background, I was sorely disappointed. Mama pulled me down on the bench beside her and proceeded to introduce me to each and every family remember in attendance. I met Ramirez's brothers, Bart, Dillon, Marshal, and Clint. Along with BillieJo there was Clint's wife, Amelia, Bart's wife, Maria, and cousins, Mary Jane and José. In addition to the ten or so nieces and nephews whose names I knew I wouldn't remember past dessert.

While their volume began to rival that of Mulligan's amateur hour, somehow, instead of feeling lost in the crowd, their noise was actually kind of comforting. Like a big warm blanket filtering out the rest of the world and all its problems. I swear for a half a second I forgot everything else that had gone on today and actually began to relax as Mama shoveled a second helping onto my plate.

"I like to see a girl eat," Mama said with approval as I dug in. "So many of these young girls are too skinny. Not like you. You got some meat on you."

I paused, forkful of empanada halfway to my mouth. Maybe I should have quit at two. "Thanks," I answered uncertainly.

"Of course, my Jackie, he likes a woman with some curves."

Jackie? Too cute. I looked across the table at Ramirez, eating mole enchiladas with one hand while jiggling a toddler in bright pink ruffles on his knee.

"Can I ask you a question, Mrs. Ramirez?"

"Call me Mama. Everyone calls me Mama."

"Okay…" I hesitated. "Mama." I felt funny calling someone else's mother "Mama." Especially if that someone's mother was under the false impression I was dating her son. But I couldn't very well tell her I was tailing him around now that I'd eaten her homemade empanadas. Ramirez had me over a barrel and by the way he kept glancing across the table and flashing that dimple at me, I think he knew it too.

"What do you want to know, dear?"

"What does *fregadita* mean?" I asked.

Mama looked thoughtful for a moment. "It means little pain in the back side. Why?"

I resisted the urge to toss an empanada at Ramirez while he was holding a child. "No reason," I said instead.

"It's such a nice night. I'm glad Jackie could make it. You know, the weatherman, he say it was going to rain."

"It never rains in L.A."

"That's what I said. But that newscaster, he say rain. I knew he was wrong. Mama knows." She nodded sagely at me and I couldn't help but start to like her.

After we'd been fully stuffed with Mexican sweet breads, cinnamon rolls, and sugar cookies with little green sprinkles on top, the guitar slingers tuned up their instruments and began playing a slow, soft rhythm. It was soothing and, along with the two servings of spicy food settling in my belly, left me feeling full and content. Dare I say, almost peaceful?

A state which ended with a jolt as I felt a warm hand land on the small of my back.

Ramirez leaned down and whispered, "Let's dance."

I thought about protesting as he grabbed my hand and led me to the lawn where Clint and his wife were already swaying to the music. But then again, he was a cop and it didn't seem wise to tick him off. (It had nothing to do with the way his deep voice so close to my ear produced animal sex visions again. I swear!)

Ramirez slung one arm casually around my waist, taking my right hand in his as we moved in slow time with the music. He was surprisingly graceful on his feet, moving almost like I'd imagine that long, sleek panther on his arm would. Dancing with him suddenly made me feel like Ginger Rogers. It was nice.

A little too nice. And, I noticed as that familiar heat began to pool somewhere south of my belly button, a little too intimate. A little too easy to get used to.

I cleared my throat, trying to come up with some mundane conversation to cool the heat wave flooding my body.

"So, uh, your sister has an unusual name. Why BillieJo?"

Ramirez smiled. "What, you think all Hispanic people should be named José or Maria?"

At the risk of being lumped in with grand dragons in white sheets, I resisted the urge to point out that there were, in fact, a José and Maria in attendance. "No, no, I didn't mean that at all. It's, just, well, BillieJo isn't a name you hear everyday in L.A. Maybe in the south. Or Texas. Or someplace, um, more cowboy-ish." Then I remembered the dozing man in the cowboy hat. "Not that there aren't Hispanic cowboys. I mean, I'm sure there are some Hispanic cowboys. It's just, they aren't named BillieJo. Well, except your sister. Who is clearly not a cowboy." I was dying here.

"Relax," he said, pulling me just a smidgen closer to him. "I'm just yanking your chain."

"Oh." I pretended I didn't notice the hormone signals my stupid body started flashing me as his hips touched mine. Didn't my body know this was a totally inappropriate time to be thinking of jumping some guy's bones?

Ramirez seemed unaware. Or maybe just a little too used to dancing with girls in hookerwear.

"BillieJo," he continued, "is a character on *Petticoat Junction*. Bart's from *Maverick*. Marshall, well every TV western has a Marshal. See a trend? When Mom and Dad moved here from Mexico in the sixties, Mom learned to speak English by watching those western shows on TV. She became a little attached to them."

"How'd you escape it?"

He flashed his white teeth at me. "Jackson Wyoming Ramirez."

"Ouch."

"Tell me about it."

"So, what was it like growing up with so many siblings?"

"Crowded." He smiled. "I think I was fifteen before my mom finally stopped dressing me in hand-me-downs."

"You poor thing," I answered, appropriately horrified.

He laughed. One of those real person laughs, not the smirky cop ones I'd gotten to know so well. Again I had a little talk with my body about those hormone signals.

"No pity, please, Miss Fashion Designer. Having older brothers had some advantages too. There was always a stack of *Playboy*'s under the mattress."

"I should have known you were one of *those* boys."

"*Those* boys?"

"I bet you looked up girls' skirts in class too."

The wicked twinkle in his eyes answered that question clearly enough.

"What about you? Something tells me you were no angel, Miss Girly Girl."

"I can't imagine what you mean."

"You strike me as the kind of girl who took her own peek in the boy's locker room now and then."

"It's the clothes. The spandex gives the wrong impression."

"Uh-huh." He didn't believe that anymore than he believed I'd go home and knit after this.

"So," I said, clearly changing the subject. "I think BillieJo doesn't like me much." I glanced across the lawn to find her still glaring, her arms crossed over her ample chest.

"She's just a little overprotective."

"Older sister syndrome?"

"Younger. By two years. She's the baby of the family, always following me and my friends around when we were young."

"Hmm. I bet she was a real *fregadita*." I let the word roll slowly off my tongue.

Ramirez's eyes crinkled at the corners. "You've been talking to Mama?"

"Uh-huh. Pain in the ass, huh?"

"Relax. You're a cute little pain in the ass." He winked at me and I was rendered momentarily speechless.

"What about you," he asked. "Any annoying little sisters?"

Clearing my throat, I willed myself to get a grasp on the hormone thing. "No I'm an only child. It's just been my mom and me growing up. Though she's getting married soon, so I guess our family's growing a little. Nothing like this, though." I gestured to the lawn, now full of adults and children alike. The cowboy was dozing again, this time leaning his folding chair against the sliding glass doors, his hat pulled low over his eyes. Mama was swaying her round body in time with the music, a contented smile on her face as she watched her children dance.

"Well, anytime you want to borrow a family for awhile, you're welcome to mine. Though, you might want to leave the hooker clothes at home next time." He winked, that smirk returning.

"Thanks for the tip, wise guy."

But the comment pulled me out of my empanada and guitar music stupor just enough to remember why I was dressed like a Pretty Woman. To remember the unreal events of my evening thus far, and the five million loose ends of my life.

"You think they've found anything at the motel yet?" I asked.

"They'll call me if they do. In the meantime, just relax a little."

Relax. Right. The problem was I was getting *too* relaxed. With the abundant food, the warm company, the crowded, festive atmosphere of the backyard, I'd almost completely forgotten about Richard, Greenway and the whole mess. So, what did that say about me? Did I really care so little about the man whose child I was quite possibly carrying that a plate full of empanadas and a cop with a sexy grin could make me forget him in the span of one evening?

But even as I was attacked with serious guilt (the likes of which I hadn't felt since I'd confessed to my grandmother I hadn't been to mass since Easter) I didn't let go of Ramirez's hand. I didn't step away, and I didn't protest when his arm curled around my waist, his hand resting on the small of my back. I was so going to hell, wasn't I?

Luckily my eternal soul was saved as Ramirez's cell phone chirped to life on his belt. He picked it up, glancing briefly at the number before answering it without so much as a look of apology in my direction.

"Ramirez," he said, stepping off to semi-privacy at the far side of the yard.

I wandered back over to the picnic tables, sitting on a bench as I watched Ramirez talk. It was hard to tell in the dark, but I thought I saw his Bad Cop face return, the lines of his jaw tense, his eyes that impenetrable dark cloud again. I wondered if the call had anything to do with Greenway. Maybe CSI Guy had found something useful after all. Then I wondered if Ramirez would share it or just tear out of here with a "go home," again. It was hard to tell. He'd almost seemed like a real person a minute ago, but back into cop mode, I wasn't sure.

"He works too much." Mama came up behind me, offering a glass of water. I took it gratefully, not admitting even to myself how heated dancing with Ramirez had made me.

"Always that phone going off. Always the beeper. Clint works at the teddy bear factory in Industry. Now that's a good job. Go to work in the morning. Make the bears. Come home at night and see his wife and kids. Good steady job."

"Jack's good at his job." What irrational idea made me suddenly defend Ramirez, I have no clue. But I did. "He's a good cop."

"You better make sure those condoms don't break. You marry this one, you'll never see him."

Unfortunately, it was a little late for the broken condom talk.

"Mama," Ramirez said, coming up behind me. "I'm sorry, but we've got to go." He flipped his phone shut, the hard look still in his eyes.

"Oh, so soon?" Mama's face fell. Then she shot me an I-told-you-so look.

"Sorry, Mama." Ramirez leaned down to kiss on her on the cheek. "I'll call you this weekend."

Ramirez grabbed my arm and steered me back toward the house. I barely got out an, "It was nice to meet you," before I was propelled back through the chotchke-laden house to the front door.

I didn't like the urgency in Ramirez's movements any more than I did the hard line of his jaw. My stomach was rapidly sinking like quicksand.

"What?" I asked as soon as we were out of earshot of Mama. "What's happened? Is it Richard?"

His eyes narrowed at the mention of Richard as he shoved me out the front door and practically ran to his SUV.

"What? What is it?" My voice was rising into the range of hysterics now and I had terrible visions of attending Richard's funeral beside Cinderella. "Please tell me what's going on?"

He stopped. "It's Greenway."

"They found him? When? Where?"

"Just a few minutes ago. In a Dumpster behind the motel." He paused. "With a gunshot wound to the head."

CHAPTER ELEVEN

———

I blinked hard, digesting this information.

"But he was just alive," I protested. "He shot at me."

"Well, he's not shooting anyone now. Get in your car and I'll follow you to the motel."

I wasn't sure I'd heard him right. "You want me to go with you?"

Ramirez turned around and fixed me with a stare. "You're going to follow me anyway, aren't you?"

I hated being this predictable. "Yes."

"At least this way I can keep an eye on you." He turned and strode to his car.

I tried to get over my shock and clattered to my Jeep, quickly roaring it to life as Ramirez made a u-turn and waited for me to pull out. I did, retracing our drive back to the freeway with Ramirez's headlights as a constant companion.

The drive back to the 5 and west to North Hollywood took over half an hour. Long enough for the implications of this latest development to sink in. If Greenway had been shot, that meant someone had to have killed him. All this time I was assuming that Greenway was the one who'd killed his wife. But if that was true, who'd killed Greenway? Three people knew where Greenway hid the twenty million. Two were dead. I clenched my teeth together to keep them from chattering as I did the math. That meant only one was left.

Richard.

I focused on the task of driving through the late night traffic to keep my mind from rolling this fact over and over like a snowball out of control. There were two possibilities now staring me in the face, neither one particularly pleasant. Either Richard was in a Dumpster of his own somewhere or…

Richard was pulling the trigger.

That thought sent a chill straight through me, prompting me to flip on the heater despite the seventy-plus temperature outside.

The Richard I knew folded his socks into perfect pairs in his drawer, drank non-fat milk, and had asked permission to even kiss me the first time. The Richard I knew did not shoot people.

Then again, the Richard I knew didn't have a wife either.

As Ramirez tailed me onto the 134 another horrible thought occurred to me. Dana and I had heard shots earlier. At the time we'd assumed Greenway was shooting at us. But what if it was the other way around. What if someone had been shooting Greenway? Oh my God. That made Dana and me earwitnesses to a murder. I had a sudden vision of me in the witness protection program, wearing some really horrible *Married to the Mob* stretch pants like Michelle Pfeiffer. I shivered again.

I pulled into the parking lot of the Moonlight Inn, Ramirez close behind me. Again, residents were out on the balconies, men in stained robes and women dressed uncomfortably like myself. Metallica stood outside his office talking with a uniformed officer who was making notes in a small black book. I parked my Jeep and got out as Ramirez pulled into the spot beside me.

Metallica spotted me, his eyes round and pupils suspiciously dilated. "That's her!" he shouted. "That's one of those crazy ho's I told you about. They killed that dude!"

The officer looked up, one hand instinctively hovering over the gun holstered at his hip.

"I got it." Ramirez appeared at my side, waving to the uniform that he had the "crazy ho" under control. He leaned in close to my ear, his voice low. "Lucy, you got some splainin' to do."

I bit my lip. No kidding.

Ramirez steered me past Metallica and into the cockroach infested _ront O__ice. He sat me down on a hard plastic chair as he leaned against the Formica counter, arms crossed over his chest. "Looks like paperwork's inevitable at this point. You better tell me what went on here tonight."

I tried to read Ramirez's expression in the flickering glare of the Moonlight's neon sign. No luck. I couldn't tell if I was currently being questioned as a suspect, witness, or just a cute little pain in the ass.

I'd watched enough TV dramas to know that when the cops put on their we've-got-to-talk face, the first thing you do is call your lawyer. But considering my lawyer was currently nowhere to be found, I cracked under Ramirez's steady gaze and told him everything, right down to the look in Dana's eyes as she'd grabbed a handful of Metallica's shirt.

Ramirez's gaze didn't waver. He didn't crack a smile or blink an eye. Nothing. Not even call me girly. I bit my lip again, hoping I'd done the right thing in talking.

"So, what now?" I asked.

"What now is you go home and let me handle this. I don't want to see any more hookers, red Jeeps, or designer shoes until this whole mess is straightened out. Got it?"

I nodded meekly.

"And if, for any reason, Richard gets in touch with you, you are to call me right away. Not go for a manicure first. Right away."

I nodded again, though I felt the manicure comment was uncalled for.

CSI Guy emerged from room two-twelve, a handful of black bags in tow as he clomped down the metal stairs.

"Wait here," Ramirez commanded, stalking out the glass doors and intercepting CSI Guy at the bottom of the stairs.

For once, I did as told, wrapping my arms around myself as I strained to hear what CSI Guy and Ramirez were talking about through the open doors. Unfortunately, all I got was a "…hair fibers," "…ridge detail," and a "…back to the lab for processing." Which put together could mean just about anything.

Ramirez finished with CSI Guy and walked over to a group of men standing around a black van with the word "coroner" on it. I shuddered.

Okay, so I had no great love for Greenway. But just yesterday I'd been on the phone with the man. It was unnerving to think of someone being here, and then suddenly not being here. Like at any moment *I* could not be here. Again I had that creepy feeling of being the dimwitted blonde in the horror movie who the entire audience knows will end up getting chased across the lawn in her underwear by the ax murderer at the end of act two. Only I didn't have a face for my ax murderer now.

Obviously Greenway hadn't shot himself. It's a little hard to dispose of one's own body in a Dumpster. But I really couldn't put Richard's face there either. Richard wasn't a killer. He was an attorney. Yes, I know, not the highest of life forms, but not a murderer either. There had to be another explanation.

Only I wasn't entirely sure Ramirez was going to look for it. It didn't take a rocket scientist to figure out that Richard was no longer a "person of interest." In fact, I had a sinking feeling as CSI Guy joined Ramirez and the ME, that Richard's status had just been upgraded to full-fledged suspect.

Ramirez broke away from the group and crossed the cracked macadam to the office again. He paused in front of me, his eyes calculating as he stared down.

"You sure you didn't go into Greenway's room?"

A wave of dread rolled through my stomach.

"Yes. Why?"

He didn't answer, just crossed his arms over his chest. "Look, I know you've been less than honest with me in the past, but now's the time to come clean."

"I never went in Greenway's room. I told you, we knocked, then we heard shots and ran. Why? What did he tell you?" I tried to look past him to CSI Guy, honestly a little hurt that my evidence collector would turn on me like this after my intimate encounter with his lint roller.

"We found blonde hairs in Greenway's room and impressions in the carpet that CSI thinks came from a stiletto heel."

I looked down at my shoes. "For your information these are not stilettos. They are platform heels."

His eyes narrowed, the Bad Cop face not budging.

"You don't seriously think I had anything to do with this? That I actually killed him?"

"Look, I don't know what to think. Your boyfriend, whom you seem to know *nothing* about, disappears along with twenty mil and this guy," he gestured to Metallica, "this guy here says he saw you and your friend go up to Greenway's room tonight. And apparently a woman with blonde hair and a thing for high heels was in his room recently enough that the shoe impressions are still in the carpet."

"Ask CSI Guy," I sputtered. "He has a bunch of my hair. He'll tell you it's not mine. You've got to believe me. I had nothing to do with this."

Ramirez sighed. "I want to believe you, but you're not making it real easy. What the hell am I supposed to tell my superiors? Let alone the press?"

"Tell them whatever you want. I did not shoot Greenway."

Ramirez sighed again, then began rubbing his temple. "Will you go home now?"

"Gladly." I was on the verge of tears but I'm proud to say I kept them at bay. The last thing I wanted to do was bawl like a baby in front of Bad Cop.

"Good. And don't take this the wrong way, but stay away from me, okay?"

"No problem." I spit the words out a little more harshly than I meant to, banking on my anger to keep the tears from flowing down my cheeks.

I turned and stalked across the parking lot with as much dignity as a hooker in four-inch heels can muster. And wouldn't you know it, the second I began fumbling in my little purse for my keys, I felt a big fat drop hit the back of my neck. I looked down to see more drops hitting the blacktop with an acrid smell of wet motor oil. It was raining. Great. One more thing I can say I was wrong about tonight.

I was wrong to let Dana talk me into dressing like a hooker, wrong to think I could find a murderer on my own, wrong to ever trust Ramirez. And last but not least, I was apparently wrong about the weather too. I cursed the weather gods right along with Ramirez's superior attitude as I found my key and got in my Jeep. I made it all the way out of the driveway and down the street before I finally let the tears run loose.

I think I'd been a pretty tough chick up until now. I'd managed to keep my cool even when under threat of gunfire, arrest, and pregnancy. But suddenly it all came rushing at me and once the tears started I couldn't make them stop. Maybe it was because I'd heard a man get shot, or because my cheating ex-boyfriend was now the prime suspect in a murder investigation, or because for half a second Ramirez actually thought I had something to do with this even when his mother thought we were making like rabbits. Or maybe it was just all of it. The whole ridiculous, awful evening. Everything was spiraling out of control and I was powerless to stop it. I felt very alone, very vulnerable, and, I hated to admit, oh-so-very girly as I cried my guts out down the 405.

I was crying so hard it took me a minute to realize what the flashing lights in my rearview mirror were. I blinked, wiping away the tears and saw a CHP glued to my back bumper. Oh crap. I looked down at the speedometer. Seventy-five. Oh really crappy crap.

I tried to pull myself together as I slowed and pulled off to the side of the road. I flipped down my mirrored visor, wiping at the mascara streaks running down my face. Eeek. I looked like Tammy Faye's evil twin. I was still doing hiccup sobs as the officer came around to the passenger side and motioned for me to roll down the window.

"Good evening, ma'am," he said, leaning his elbows on my driver side door. He was clean shaven and looked about twenty, with clear blue eyes and pudgy cheeks that warned he may never lose his baby fat. A radio was clipped to his shirt beside a CHP badge that looked like he polished it nightly.

I took one look at the badge and couldn't help it. I burst into tears again. Yes, I know, I was so not cutting it as a Bond Girl right now. But this was just the thing to top off my horrible night. A speeding ticket. I was in serious feeling-sorry-for-myself mode and no amount of streaked mascara was going to stop the flood of tears.

The poor officer looked about as uncomfortable as I felt and, had I not been in the throws of my own hysteria, I might have felt sorry for him.

"I'm sorry ma'am, but I'm going to need to see your license and registration."

I retrieved my license from my purse and the registration from the glove box, still sobbing uncontrollably as I handed them over.

"I'm sorry, ma'am," the officer said uncomfortably, "But I'm going to have to write you a ticket."

I tried to be brave. "No, (sniff, sniff) it's okay. How fast was I going?"

"Seventy-five."

"I'm so, so, so, sorry." I started sniveling again. "It's just...I'm dressed like a hooker. And I really, really hate spandex. And Ramirez's mother saw me in this. And she's right. I've always liked my legs. But if I'm having Richard's baby they're going to be all shot to hell. And then it started raining. Rain is very bad for purples."

The officer just stared at me. "Have you been drinking tonight ma'am?"

"No. No, I have not been drinking. I only had a Diet Coke at the bar. But then Ramirez showed up and I really wanted a martini. But I couldn't have one because of the Muppet. And, oh my aura is just ruined now. Can you believe it, it never rains in L.A.?"

"I'm going to need to give you a breathalyzer test, ma'am."

"Oh God. I can't go to jail. Look at me. I'm a hooker!"

"Ma'am, please step out of the car." All sympathy had gone out of CHP Guy's eyes, his hands hovering near the cuffs on his utility belt. Nothing highway patrol loves less than a drunk driver. Except maybe a drunk hooker driver.

"Please, I'm not drunk. I'm just...I'm just..." I searched for words to describe the night I'd had. I came up with nil. "I'm...I'm Detective Ramirez's girlfriend!"

Oh God. Why did I say that?

CHP Guy looked dubious, but his hand was off his cuffs. "Detective Ramirez?"

I decided to go with it. "Yes, he works in homicide. You can look him up."

"Do you have his badge number?"

Crap. Badge number. Then I remembered the business card still tucked in my purse. "Uh, just a minute." I grabbed my purse and dumped the contents onto the passenger seat, spilling my cell phone, a tampon, tube of lipstick, a breath mint, a handful of change, and Ramirez's business card. I read off the numbers.

"2374." I handed the card to the officer.

He took it, going back to his squad car. I watched in the rearview mirror, praying he didn't call Ramirez to ask he if was dating a hysterical hooker. Luckily, I only saw him punch a few keys on his keyboard before returning, apparently satisfied.

"All right," he said, handing back the business card along with my registration and license. "I'm going to give you a warning this time. But please slow down. And, uh, don't worry," he said awkwardly. "It's going to be okay."

I swallowed. "Thanks," I sniffed out. Though I didn't really believe him. Things were so far from okay, it would take a layover in Cincinnati to get there.

I watched the cop pull back onto the freeway, trying to get a hold of myself well enough to drive back home. I took deep breaths and finally got the hiccupping under control before pulling back onto the freeway.

I slowly navigated the oil slick roads, watching the unexpected rain gather in the gutters, creating mini floods along the drainage impaired L.A. streets. By the time I pulled up to my studio, it was an all out downpour. I covered my hair with an old copy of *Vogue* I found in the back seat and clacked up the stairs, letting myself into my silent apartment.

At that point I was too tired to feel scared, alone, or any other emotion that had assaulted me during the evening. All I wanted was my warm cozy bed and the familiar, uncomplicated Letterman to lull me to sleep. I stripped out of the wet spandex and wrapped myself in a Lakers T-shirt before snuggling under my quilted blankets. I didn't even get to Dave's first guest before I fell asleep.

* * *

I was sitting at the edge of a tiled swimming pool watching a man swim laps. I couldn't tear my gaze away. His long, sleek form cut through the water, the muscles in his back flexing as he swam for the far side of the pool. It was like a Cool Water commercial, his movements in slow motion so every muscle tensed, every move was exaggerated. As he hit the end of the pool and began swimming back toward me, I felt water falling on me. It was raining. Fat, clear drops hit the glassy surface of the water making rhythmic sounds like nature's orchestra.

The man swam closer and I leaned over the edge of the pool to get a closer look. But suddenly I was wearing Strawberry Shortcake high tops that were three sizes too small and I tripped on the sparkly laces. I began to fall toward the water. It seemed like I was falling forever, as the rain orchestra picked up tempo, plinking out a frantic William Tell Overture. I screamed, and the man stopped swimming. He reached up to catch me. And that's when I noticed the black panther tattooed on his right bicep.

* * *

I opened my eyes, jerking to a sitting position. My gaze whipped wildly around me as if expecting the swimming man to appear. All I saw were the tangled sheets on my bed, harsh sunlight slanting through my windows and a pile of rain soaked spandex on my floor. The only thing that remained of my dream was the strain of William Tell coming from the region of my purse. I rubbed my eyes, fumbling with sleep clumsy hands for my cell phone.

"Hello?" I mumbled, still trying to shake the image of Ramirez's tattooed muscles.

"It's gone." Mom's voice assaulted my ears with a high-pitched screech.

"Mom?" I rolled over to look at the clock on my kitchen wall. Six-thirty. I groaned.

"Maddie, the cliff is gone. The whole thing is just gone."

I blinked the cobwebs out of my eyes, trying to figure out what she was talking about. "What's gone? What cliff?"

"The cliff in Malibu," she shrieked. "Where I'm supposed to get married *tomorrow*! It's gone. The rain caused a landslide and the whole cliff side fell into the ocean last night. It's just a big rocky, muddy mess. Maddie, what am I going to do?"

Oh. That cliff.

"Mom, don't panic. We'll think of something. Did you call the Malibu office?"

"Yes, yes. I talked to them first thing this morning. They said they'd refund the deposit for the site, but Maddie where on earth am I going to have the wedding now? Oh God. This is your grandmother's fault. She said we should get married in a church. She said God would never forgive me if I didn't get married in the Catholic Church. Now look, I've pissed off God so badly he's destroying Malibu."

My head was pounding, screaming for a double mocha espresso. "Where are you, Mom?"

"I'm at Fernando's."

"Okay, give me twenty minutes, I'll meet you there, and we'll think of something."

"This is it Maddie. I've heard about these sorts of Catholic curses. I'm doomed. This marriage is doomed. Oh God. I've doomed Ralph too."

"I'm hanging up now, Mom."

I pressed the end button and flopped back onto my bed. I closed my eyes, hoping that maybe *this* was the dream and I was *really* going to wake up soon. I lay there for a good five minutes before I cracked one eye open. Nope. No dream. Damn.

Somehow I dragged my exhausted body to the bathroom and managed to shower, dry my hair, and throw on a little makeup without gasping in horror at the sight of my puffy eyes. After the good, long cry I'd had last night I resembled a bug-eyed cartoon character. That's it, no more feeling sorry for myself. My eyes couldn't take it. I quickly slipped on a pale blue sundress and a pair of low-heeled, silver mules before deciding I was fit for human eyes again.

After checking my voice mail, just in case Ramirez left a message saying he had Richard in custody, I grabbed my keys and headed for my Jeep.

Fifteen minutes later I pulled up to Fernando's. I parked on the near empty street (Beverly Hills doesn't rise before ten unless it's Oscar night.) and pushed through the glass doors.

"Dahling, thank God you're here!" Marco greeted me. He had his hair spiked up in crisp little points today, his eyeliner even thicker than usual. He leaned in and pseudo whispered. "I put your mom in the back. She's pulling a Whitney Houston freak-out on us."

"Where's Ralph?"

"*Fernando*," Marco emphasized, "is with a client. He's almost done." He motioned to the sole chair being used at this unearthly hour. Faux Dad was doing a color rinse on a small Hispanic woman.

"Mrs. Lopez. Jen's Mom." He nodded solemnly. "She always comes in early to avoid the tabloids."

"Ah. I see."

"Come on. That psychic lady is with your mom, but I don't think she's actually helping things. She said she had a vision of a tornado."

I rolled my eyes, praying Mrs. Rosenblatt would at least refrain from comment on my aura today. Of course, the fact I hadn't been to confessional in about five years is probably why God didn't have time to get to my prayer by the time Marco and I crossed to the back room.

"Your aura looks awful. Were you out in the rain last night?" Mrs. Rosenblatt narrowed her eyes at me.

"A little."

She opened her mouth to warn me of the universal dangers of aura soaking, but I quickly cut her off. "I know, I know. Rain isn't good for purples."

She looked me up and down the way one might a leper. "Oh *bubbee*, you're way beyond purple now."

Trying not to get self conscious about the state of my aura, I leaned down and kissed Mom's cheek. "I'm so sorry about the cliff."

Mom looked like she'd been crying harder than I had. Her nose and cheeks were red and splotchy like she'd spent the weekend at the Venice boardwalk without sunscreen. She was still wearing her nightgown underneath a gray trench coat with blue tube socks and a pair of Nike's. The effect was sadly comic

"Malibu was so beautiful," Mom sniffed.

"But it was such a long drive," I said, trying to put a positive spin on this. "Maybe we can find somewhere closer?"

"Maybe," Mom squeaked out. She pulled a handful of tissues from her pocket and blew her nose.

"At this late date? Oh honey, you are dreaming," Marco said. I shot him a look that could wither a cactus.

"Come on, there's got to be something?" I glanced down at Mom. She had that Old Faithful look about her. Like any minute tears would come gushing with landmark intensity.

"Albert said there's nothing in L.A. County," Mrs. Rosenblatt argued.

"Who's Albert?"

"My spirit guide."

Great. Just what we needed. A pessimistic spirit guide.

Just in case Albert hadn't done his homework, I asked Marco to pull out the L.A. County phone book. I won't tell you what kind of I-told-you-so look Mrs. Rosenblatt gave me when half an hour later I'd gone through every conceivable site with no luck. None could accommodate a wedding of this size on such short notice.

"Albert is never wrong." Mrs. Rosenblatt informed me. "He was a fact checker for the *New York Times* in his earthly existence."

I ignored her with no small effort. "Okay, well, maybe there's something in Orange County? Or Ventura?"

Again Marco went to retrieve more phone books. Marco took Riverside County, Mrs. Rosenblatt took Orange, and I took Ventura, while Mom sat in the corner and took a Xanax.

Just as Faux Dad joined us, saying Mrs. Lopez's roots had never looked better, Marco hit pay dirt. It wasn't much, but a small hotel in Riverside had a back garden they sometimes rented out for weddings. They'd had a last minute cancellation when the bride-to-be found a pair of someone else's Victoria's Secrets in the groom-to-be's pick-up truck, and the garden was free for tomorrow afternoon. They said they even had the chairs and tables rented for the previously cancelled wedding, so we'd be all set. As long as it didn't rain. Mom made the sign of the cross at that, but Mrs. Rosenblatt assured her that Albert said it wasn't scheduled to rain again until November. I promised I'd check the weather channel, just in case.

Wedding crisis averted, I went home. My answering machine was blinking furiously when I stepped in the door. The first message was from Tot Trots, asking why they hadn't gotten the Strawberry Shortcake designs yet. I glanced guiltily at my drawing table as I deleted the message.

The next was from Ramirez. I bit my lip trying not to picture the image from my dream as his voice filled my studio.

"This is your *boyfriend* calling. Don't drive so fast next time, okay?" End of message. I couldn't tell if he was amused or annoyed by my antics with the CHP last night. I told myself it didn't matter. As long as the word "warrant" didn't enter into the picture, it didn't matter what Ramirez thought of me.

But instead of deleting it, I saved the message, skipping on to the next one.

It was from Dana, asking if a) she was a bad person for sleeping with Liao on the first date, and b) if I'd seen anything on the news about Greenway's arrest.

It felt like I'd lived a lifetime since I'd left Dana at Mulligans and I wasn't at all sure I could relay the events of the previous evening to her with any amount of coherency. At least not before coffee.

Too tired to hoof it to Starbucks, I flipped on my Mr. Coffee, dumping in two generous scoops of French Roast as I turned on the television, hoping to get the latest Greenway update on the noon news. Two carjackings in Compton, a mudslide warning in the Hollywood Hills, and one minor celebrity arrested for drunk driving. No news of Greenway or Richard. Which I guess should have been comforting. No news meant at least my boyfriend wasn't behind bars. But instead of relieved, the non-news made me feel antsy.

I'll be the first to admit, I don't have a really great history of patience. I was one of those kids who always peeked in Mom's closet for a preview of my Christmas and birthday presents. After a first date, I can never wait for the guy to call (even though I read *The Rules* twice and managed to wait three whole hours once) and even though I really, really meant to wait until we'd been seeing each other for a couple weeks first, I slept with Richard on our second date. So just sitting by the phone, waiting for Richard to turn up in handcuffs, was producing a bite-your-fingernails, crawl-up-a-wall feeling that was so not working for me.

I even debated calling Cinderella to see if she'd heard anything from him. Which should tell you just how desperate I was because calling Cinderella meant acknowledging that she actually existed, and that ranked below sucking up to Jasmine on the list of things I wanted to do this lifetime.

My internal whining was cut short as the familiar blonde news reporter piped up from the TV.

"Last night the body of missing business mogul, Devon Greenway, was found by authorities at a North Hollywood motel."

I grabbed the remote and turned it up, watching images of the Moonlight Inn flicker across the screen. It was daylight now but the parking lot was still littered with police cars and yellow crime scene tape. I grimaced as Metallica's greasy face filled the screen.

"There were two of them. These chicks. And they were like really buff, like pro wrestlers or something. I tried to fight them off, but they were like totally strong. I think they were on steroids."

I rolled my eyes.

The cameraman cut away to an image of a green Dumpster. The coffee churned in my empty stomach as I listened to the reporter remind the viewing public this was the same Greenway whose wife was found dead earlier this week.

Then Ramirez's face filled the screen. My stomach rolled for a whole different reason. He seemed tired, like he hadn't slept, but I hated how sexy the five o-clock shadow dusting his jaw looked.

A reporter from another station shoved a microphone at Ramirez, yelling questions from the mob of press. "Do you have a murder weapon?"

Ramirez answered with a standard, "We're still in the process of recovering a weapon."

"Do you have any suspects?" another reporter demanded.

The mob went quiet as Ramirez answered. "We do."

"Detective Ramirez," the first reporter shouted, "Are you prepared to name them at this time?"

Ramirez looked squarely at the camera and I could swear he was talking directly to me. "Based on our current evidence, we've issued a warrant for the arrest of Mr. Greenway's attorney. Richard Howe."

CHAPTER TWELVE

‒‒‒‒‒

I stared at the television, my brain half listening and half screaming that this was some mistake. Richard wanted for murder? This couldn't be happening.

A picture of Richard from the office Christmas party flashed across the screen. I'd bet anything Jasmine had furnished it to the press. They were probably descending on Dewy, Cheatum & Howe like vultures right about now. I had a mental image of Jasmine's Elvis smirk preening for the cameras on the six o'clock news. I think I was going to be sick. I sat down hard on my futon as the reporter made appropriately concerned faces, then cut to a Doritos commercial.

Ramirez was going to arrest Richard. I knew Ramirez well enough to know that there wasn't a whole lot I could do to stop that. Sure I could put on my Bond Girl outfit again and search Richard's office for the umpteenth time, but what good would it really do? I had no idea what I was doing. I was the worst Nancy Drew ever. Every time I tried to help, another dead body showed up. I'd like to think it was coincidence but I made a mental note to go to mass on Sunday with my grandmother just in case.

On the other hand, the search to find Richard was an all out manhunt now. Every cop in the city would be looking for him. And not for whoever *really* killed Greenway. Because I was still relatively confident that Richard wasn't capable of killing anyone.

Which is why even though I knew I should take Ramirez's advice and leave this to the professionals, I grabbed a lined notepad and began scribbling.

I wrote the word "Suspects" at the top of the page in big bold letters. My pen hovered in the air, poised to write Richard's name down on the list. But even though I was pretty pissed off at the cheating bastard, I couldn't bring myself to do it. So, instead I made a compromise. I amended the "Suspects" with an "other than Richard." There, that was a better starting place.

Only my mind was a blank when I tried to list them. I didn't have any suspects. All I had to go on was a blonde hair and a stiletto impression. Which I was pretty sure Ramirez still thought were mine. I wrote "blonde in heels" on the list. Gee. That narrowed the field to 95% of L.A.'s population.

Obviously I needed more to go on. And it was equally as obvious that following Ramirez around town wasn't a good idea anymore. Besides the fact that he'd be on the lookout for a red Jeep now, I had a feeling he'd been *this* close to hauling me downtown last night. And I didn't want to tempt the man. Especially if he hadn't slept. Lord only knew how grouchy Bad Cop got with no sleep.

So that meant Sherlock Fashion was on her own. I stared down at the notepad again. It was a pretty pathetic list. If I was going to convince Ramirez that Mystery Blonde was a suspect at all I needed more. Which meant going back to the Moonlight.

I picked up my cell and dialed Dana's number, hoping she was up for playing Cagney to my Lacey again. (Never mind that the reality was more like an Ethel to my Lucy.) Unfortunately, No Neck Guy answered the phone at the Actor's Duplex and informed me (through a series of cave-man worthy grunts) Dana hadn't come home yet. Still out hot-tubbing with Liao no doubt. I said to have her call me when she got in and hung up.

As much as I dreaded going back into the bowels of the Valley alone, it was either that or draw kiddie shoes. And I was so not in a kiddie shoes place right now.

I grabbed my keys and purse and headed out to my Jeep, braving the afternoon traffic into North Hollywood.

There was an overturned big rig on the 405 and a police chase on the 101, so by the time I reached Vanowen again the Moonlight Inn was clear of reporters and CSI teams. In fact, save for the bright yellow crime tape still gracing the door of room two-twelve, it looked like business as usual. Radios blared, spandex clad women bade good-bye to their "gentleman callers," and the parking lot pharmaceutical trade had resumed in full force. North Hollywood was quick to bounce back from one little shooting.

I parked the Jeep and avoided glancing in the direction of the green Dumpsters as I made my way to the _ront O__ice.

I pulled open the smudged, glass doors and saw Metallica was on duty again. He'd changed into an AC/DC shirt, but his greasy hair betrayed that he hadn't taken time to shower before coming back to work. He stared for a moment before recognition kicked in.

"Oh hell. It's you!" He ducked down below the counter. "Please don't shoot."

I rolled my eyes. "Do I look like I'm carrying a gun?"

Metallica peeked his head up over the Formica. He did an up and down thing with his eyes, his gaze resting on my breasts. A grin broke out on his face. "Nope. You look niiiiice." He nodded, drawing out the word.

Hmmm…maybe I should start carrying a gun.

"Get a grip. They're just mammary glands."

"Dude, I think the cops are looking for you. You chicks like totally messed that guy up."

"We didn't kill him."

He narrowed his eyes at me. "You sure?"

"Yes!"

"'Cause I wouldn't tell no one. I mean, when you think of it, it's actually kind of hot. Chicks with guns. Like a Laura Croft thing. Laura Croft is hot."

I had a feeling any woman with a pulse was hot in Metallica's world.

"Sorry to interrupt your wet dream, but we didn't kill him. In fact, the police think my boyfriend killed him."

"Dude!"

"I know!"

Metallica leaned in. I tried not to grimace at the scent of stale weed and breakfast burrito. "Did your boyfriend kill him 'cause he was your john?"

"No! God, no. I'm not really a hooker."

Metallica looked me up and down again. "You sure?"

"Yes, I'm sure."

He grinned, showing off a mouth in serious need of some Crest White Strips. "You *could* be one. You'd make a really hot hooker."

I felt my left eye begin to twitch. This was getting nowhere.

"Did you see anyone else go up to room two-twelve last night?"

"Nope. Just you, your friend, and that dude they found in the Dumpster."

Damn. But, on the bright side, at least he didn't say he saw a lawyer in tailored slacks.

"Could anyone have gone up when you weren't looking? Like maybe you went 'out back?'" I put my thumb and index finger up to my mouth in a smoking motion.

He giggled. "Hey, anything's possible, babe."

"How about the parking lot. See anyone suspicious hanging around?"

Metallica grinned. Right. Stupid question.

"Anyone who didn't look like they belonged here? Anyone…with money?" Or the vaguest notion of hygiene.

Metallica chewed on his chapped lips, squinting off into space. "Nope."

I was beginning to feel like I'd wasted a trip to the Valley for nothing. I tried one last angle. "How about this. Did you see any blondes last night? Wearing high heels?"

"Dude, that would have been hot."

Great. He was like Beavis and Butthead all rolled into one. Well, what did I expect? The man's brain probably looked like Swiss cheese.

Then a thought struck me. Dana and I had had to weasel Greenway's room number out of Metallica. If Metallica hadn't seen the blonde, that meant she already knew where Greenway was staying. Either she followed him, which I didn't think was likely considering Greenway would be pretty careful about who he led to his hideout, or else Greenway trusted her enough to give her the room number. I mentally added another item to the Suspects list. Blonde in heels, Greenway's trusted confidant.

Maybe a mistress? I wouldn't put it past him. During our short phone conversation, Greenway hadn't seemed like the type to balk at extra-marital affairs.

So, I was looking for a blonde mistress in heels. All right, it wasn't a Colombo moment, but at least it was something.

"Thanks a ton," I said to Metallica.

"Thanks for what?"

"For not seeing anything."

"Dude, I not see stuff all the time."

I didn't doubt it.

* * *

My cell started ringing as I got back in my Jeep. I flipped it open as I pulled back onto Vanowen.

"Hello?"

"Mads, it's Ralph."

"Hi Ralph. How's Mom doing?"

"Better. She's still trying to get a Catholic priest to go bless the hotel gardens before the ceremony, but at least she's stopped eyeing her rosary."

That was a start.

"Anyway," he continued, "I was just calling to remind you about the bachelorette party tonight. Not that I thought you'd forget, but, well, I just thought I'd remind you."

"I wasn't going to forget."

"Right. Of course not." Faux Dad cleared his throat. "I knew you'd be there. I just…wanted to make sure."

Okay, I had forgotten. What was it with this wedding that I seemed to be blocking it out of my memory?

"Don't worry, Ralph. I'll be there. Cross my heart."

I hung up with Faux Dad, ignoring the icky feeling that washed over me at the combination of Mom and male strippers, and dialed in my number to check my messages again. Only Dana, saying she was back from hot-tubbing. Nothing from Ramirez. Nothing from Richard.

I called Dana back as I swung into an In-N-Out Burger, and filled her in on the latest developments over a double-double and fries. I also made her promise to go with me to Beefcakes tomorrow. I didn't think I could stomach it alone.

As I hung up with Dana and dabbed at a spot of mustard on my skirt with a paper napkin (the burger was messy, but oh-so-worth it) I pulled out my Suspects list again. So, who was this blonde? The problem was I didn't know anything about Greenway, aside from the cliff notes version Ramirez had given me. What I needed was more dirt on Greenway's personal life. Like nosey neighbor or *National Enquirer* type dirt. Since I didn't see Greenway's neighbors gossiping with prime suspect number two (a.k.a. me! Ugh!) I figured a trip to the library was my best bet at ferreting out the gory details of Greenway's social exploits. If there was dirt to be gotten, I felt confident that back issues of the *L.A. Informer* were the place to find it.

I hopped back on the 405, making a quick stop back at home to change out of my mustard spotted clothes and into my version of library wear—tweed skirt, white silk blouse, and low heeled loafers—before heading to the Santa Monica library. I was on a mission to view every bit of microfilm they had on Devon Greenway.

Which turned out to be a lot. Apparently Greenway was not only a frequent story in the gossip columns, but also in the business section, due to the new micro chip innovations of his company, Newtone Technologies. I scanned through page after blurry page of microfilm, the constant hum of the machine my only companion. This was the side of detective work they didn't show on HBO. The no-frills-and-even-less-glamour side. It made the kiddie shoes look tempting again.

If I'd hoped for a headline that read "Greenway Spotted with Blonde, Homicidal Mistress at Charity Gala" I was sorely disappointed. What I found instead was page after page of ribbon cuttings, IPO filings, and company prospects analysis.

Two hours later my eyes were permanently stuck in squint mode and my nose was itchy with dust, but I knew every detail of Greenway's life, business or social. And unfortunately, a lack of blondes hadn't been one of Greenway's problems. In fact, through the course of the press's two year infatuation with all things Greenway, it was speculated he'd had no less than three mistresses. Andi Jameson, Carol Carter, and, get this, Bunny

Hoffenmeyer. All blonde. (My money was on Bunny. Who could grow up with a name like that and *not* be homicidal?)

I wrote all three names down on my suspects list, ignoring the fact that they didn't get me a whole lot closer to earning Richard that get-out-of-jail-free card. Sure I had the names of Greenway's *known* mistresses, but who knew how many had slipped by the press? Greenway struck me as the slick type.

But, just to be thorough, I looked up all three blondies in the library's yellow pages before heading home. Andi Jameson was easy enough to find, listed in a condo in Encino. Otherwise known as Silicone Valley. I called her number, but she wasn't home. So I left a message saying I was a friend of Greenway's and wanted to ask her a few questions.

There were about fifty Carol Carters, so I reluctantly wrote her address down as "unknown."

Bunny Hoffenmeyer, as it turned out, was an adult film star, number unlisted. I did, however, find the production company she worked for. Big Boy Films in Sherman Oaks. Great. Back to the Valley.

It was late afternoon and hitting that day's high of 96 degrees according to the bank on the corner of Westwood and National. I cranked my air conditioner as far as it would go as I hopped on the 405 and reluctantly made the trip back over the hills. A thick layer of smog held tight to the curves of the mountains, covering the Valley with a sickly gray color that made me wonder why anyone would live here by choice. On the other hand, it did strengthen Bunny's motive. Twenty million dollars would go a long way toward buying her way into the Beverly set.

Another ten minutes of fighting freeway traffic and I was cruising down Sepulveda, a street lined with warehouses that passed themselves off as production studios for rent. Large, gray, and rusty, they didn't resemble Universal Studios in the least. And, I ventured to guess, neither did their films. Most were straight to video or foreign market pictures. Or, in the case of Big Boy Productions, tailored for a more mature audience. (Read: kinky.) Big Boy was located in a gunmetal gray building covered in corrugated metal siding. I parked in the lot beside a lunch wagon and stared at the building.

K—here's the thing. I'm not really a porn kind of girl. I mean, I've *seen* porn. Once. When my college boyfriend tried to convince me it was hot to see close-ups of strangers' privates while we made love. (Needless to say I broke up with Voyeur Boy soon after.) But honestly the closest I'd ever come to knowing the insides of the adult film industry was Marky Mark's performances as Dirk Diggler in *Boogie Nights*. And that was as close as I wanted to come.

Damn Richard. This was all his fault.

I took a deep breath and forced myself out of the car and across the two yards of parking lot to the unmarked door of Big Boy Productions. I almost covered my eyes as I walked in.

If I'd been expecting a lava lamp induced orgy, I was disappointed. The room I stepped into looked like just about every office reception area I'd ever been in. In fact, with the exception of a bright red light bulb flashing over the door, it bore an unnerving resemblance to Dewy, Cheatum & Howe's front office. Only instead of one Jasmine, there were three. Three women behind expensive looking desks, all blonde Anna Nicole Smith look-alikes, all Double D's barely concealed by itty, bitty pink crop tops with the words "Big Boy" stretched across their implants, and all three staring up at me.

I gulped, suddenly feeling like Granny Prude in my library attire.

"Uh, hi," I said to the Double D closest to the door. "I'm looking for Bunny Hoffenmeyer."

The Double D shifted in her seat and I resisted the urge to look away in case an implant escaped her crop top's precarious hold. "And you are?" she asked in a breathy, Marilyn Monroe sort of voice.

"Um. Maddie."

She looked at my prim tweed skirt and frowned. "Are you doing a scene together?"

"No!" I said a little more loudly than I'd intended.

"Right." She looked me up and down again. "I didn't think so."

I wasn't sure whether I was relieved or insulted.

"I actually wanted to talk to her about a mutual acquaintance of ours. Devon Greenway."

Double D's face softened. "Oh. Right. That guy she was dating. I heard about him on the news. Really sad."

"Very sad," I agreed, nodding and mimicking Perky Reporter Woman's appropriately concerned faces. "Did he ever come in here with Bunny?"

Double D smiled, showing off a row of slightly crooked teeth. "Actually, her name's Myrtle. Bunny's just a stage thing."

Myrtle Hoffenmeyer? I think I liked Bunny better.

"And, sure, he was here a few times. He was really cute. And rich." Blondie sighed. "Myrtle was real lucky to meet him."

Lucky. Right. Lucky she wasn't swimming face down right about now. Which brought me back to her current whereabouts…

"So, is Bu—uh, Myrtle here today?"

"Oh, sure. She's just finishing a scene in studio two." Blondie indicated a pair of doors to her right.

I cut a look to the doors. I had an unnerving feeling *that* was where the orgies took place.

"Um, do you mind if I wait here until she's done with her, um…scene?" I asked.

"Sure, no prob." Double D grinned and indicated a pair of padded chairs along the wall. I sat down, glad that the front office seemed to be soundproofed.

Ten minutes later the red light above the door shut off and a sound like a fire alarm blared through the building. I must have jumped as Double D reassured me, "That means they're done shooting. It should be safe to go back there now if you'd like."

"Thanks." I stood up and pushed through the double doors, hoping Bunny had robed.

The studios of Big Boy weren't pretending to be anything other than a Valley warehouse. Walls were covered in rusted metal (and not the chic rust of Fernando's, but the real kind caused by years of corrosion), large pipes ran along the ceiling, and the floor was a cracked concrete. The only break in the industrial look were the three-walled rooms made of painted plywood that were supposed to resembled bedrooms. At least that was my guess by the enormous beds scattered through the warehouse.

A group of people were huddled around one. Luckily, they seemed to be dispersing, men winding up lengths of cable and women wearing silky looking bathrobes, with slightly mussed bedroom hair. I felt my cheeks growing hot as I averted my eyes.

I recognized Bunny right away from her photographs with Greenway in the *L.A. Informer*. She was sitting on a stool by a plywood bedroom, cigarette between her acrylic nails as she watched the grips check the camera. She was my height, but about five pounds slimmer and filled with enough silicone that she might topple over at any second. I had a hard time picturing her hauling Greenway's body all the way downstairs and out to the Moonlight's Dumpsters. Still, no stone unturned.

"Bunny Hoffenmeyer?" I asked.

She looked at me with a disinterested stare. "Yeah?"

"Hi. I'm Maddie, uh…Ramirez." Okay, why I gave her that name, I didn't know. But for some reason I didn't want her to know who I was really was. At least not until I knew if she owned a gun.

"Hi," Bunny said, blowing smoke up toward the ceiling.

"Hi. I, uh, I was wondering if I could ask you some questions about Devon Greenway?"

Her eyes clouded. "Why?"

Why. Very good question. "Well, I uh, I'm from the *L.A. Informer* and, uh, we're doing a story on Greenway's death. We wanted to include some interviews from those close to him."

Bunny still looked dubious, so I tried to sweeten the pot. "We'd love to include some pictures, too. It would be great exposure for you." No pun intended.

Bunny straightened in her chair at the mention of pictures. "What do you want to know?"

Did you kill him? But I figured blunt wasn't the way to go. They always finessed the suspects a little first on *Law & Order*. I put on my best finessing voice. "I heard you and Greenway were close."

She smirked. "You could say that."

I had a feeling I was going to regret this next question. "How close?"

Bunny raised an eyebrow. "I screwed him occasionally, if that's what you're asking."

At least she didn't mince words.

"Right. So, when was the last time you, uh…saw Greenway?"

She took a long drag from the cigarette. "Last Thursday."

I perked up. Thursday had been the night Richard canceled dinner with me to meet Greenway. I wondered if Bunny had been there.

"What did you do?"

"We had dinner at Le Petite's. This totally expensive French place on Ventura. Then he had to meet his lawyer. Some Ken Doll in a suit."

Hey! That was my Ken Doll she was talking about. But, I had to admit, now that she mentioned it, Richard did resemble Ken a little. Perfect plastic façade—hollow on the inside. Ugh.

"Do you know what the meeting was about?"

She tilted her head and scrutinized me. "I dunno. Some business stuff. What did I care?"

I felt my bubble of hope deflating. Even if Porn Star Barbie had been present at Richard and Greenway's meeting, I doubted any of it would penetrate her silicone filled head.

"So, you haven't seen him since Thursday?"

She blew out a slow stream of smoke at the ceiling. "No. I broke it off with him."

"Really? Why?" Honestly Greenway and Bunny seemed like a perfect fit.

"Cause I found some chick's thong in his pocket."

"His wife's?"

Bunny smirked again. "Honey, wives don't wear stuff like this. This was a leopard print, mesh thong. He was screwing someone else."

I'm pretty sure my eyes strayed to the bed where Bunny had just finished her scene. I had a hard time believing she was a stickler for monogamy.

"Hey, this is just work," she defended. "I fake it at work. What Devon and I had was the real deal. And if he was sticking his real deal to some other chick, I didn't want any part of it."

Fair enough.

"Any idea who the thong belonged to?"

Bunny smirked again. "Some slut. I think he was meeting her for nooners, 'cause he never answered his phone around lunchtime."

"So, just for the record, where were you last night?" Even though Bunny was slipping down my list of suspects I figured it didn't hurt to be thorough.

"Here. Shooting a scene for *Babes in Boyland*."

Ugh. A porn pun. "Okay. Well, I, uh, don't want to take up any more of your time." I reached out to shake her hand, then thought better of it, not knowing where that hand had been. Instead I waved a little good-bye as I turned and headed for the reception area.

"Hey wait a minute!"

I spun around. "Yeah?"

"What about the pictures?"

Right, pictures. "The photographer will be out tomorrow," I lied. Gee, I was getting better at this. "Thanks again."

Back in my Jeep, I pulled out my Suspects list again. I wasn't entirely convinced Porn Star Barbie wasn't my blondie, but I was having a hard time picturing her hacking into Greenway's accounts and transferring twenty million to unknown whereabouts. She hadn't struck me as the sharpest crayon in the box. I added, "leopard thong, nooners" under "blonde in heels." Hmmm…Bunny was right. She did sound like a slut.

I was just merging back onto the 405, watching the sun sink into a hazy, glowing orb below the hills, when my cell phone rang. I glanced down at the number. Faux Dad. Oh crap, what did I forget now?

"Hello?"

"Where are you?"

"On the 405. Why?"

"Good. Cause your mom's at Beefcakes already and she's starting to worry about you."

D'oh! I slapped my forehead with my palm. Beefcakes. "Right. I was just on my way there."

Faux Dad heaved a sigh of relief into the receiver. "Good. 'Cause for a minute there, I thought maybe you'd forgotten again."

"Who me? Never."

Faux Dad paused. "Mads, you seem a little distracted lately. Is there something on your mind?"

I resisted the urge to break out in manic laughter.

"I'm fine." Ha! "Sorry, Ralph, I gotta go. I'm going through the canyon."

I hung up and made a quick maneuver into the right lane, merging onto the 2 East toward Beefcakes.

This was turning out to be quite a week for me. Hookers, and Porn Stars, and Strippers. Oh my!

CHAPTER THIRTEEN

———

Beefcakes was located between La Brea and Highland in an old Hollywood speakeasy that had been turned into a Mecca for bachelorettes, divorcees, and horny housewives. The interior was done in all black with pink velvety sofas lining the walls. Down the middle of the floor was a catwalk, surrounded by purple tables and chairs where hordes of screaming, middle-aged women with dollar bills in their hands acted like teenagers at a Hillary Duff concert. I spied Mom and Mrs. Rosenblatt at one of the tables near the end of the runway. Beside them was a cowgirl in Calamity Jane attire screaming out boisterous *wahoo's* as "Fireman Bob" took to the stage.

"Mads!" Mom yelled above the girlish squeals. All traces of her post-cliff trauma were gone. A cosmopolitan in one hand, she bobbed her head in time with the pulsating music. Mom was dressed in her party chick clothes tonight. A black spandex halter top, minus the much needed bra, a pair of polka dotted capris, and red Converse sneakers. In honor of the special occasion, her blue eye-shadow reached all the way to her eyebrows tonight. Mrs. Rosenblatt sat at a table beside her, dressed in a purple flowered muumuu that perfectly matched the two chairs she took up.

"Having fun?" I asked as I gave Mom a quick hug.

"I'll say. Oh, God, Mads, isn't he a hunk?"

I looked up at Fireman Bob, dressed in boots, suspenders and little else. I was instantly reminded how long it had been since I'd had sex, as my eyes strayed to his little red G-string.

"Check out that package," Mrs. Rosenblatt said, as if she could read my mind. "Reminds me of my fourth husband, Lenny.

Lenny was royal putz, but the Universe blessed him with a package like you wouldn't believe."

"That's nothing. You should see my Ralphie." Mom held her two index fingers ten inches apart, wiggling her eyebrows up and down.

Ew! Mom and sex—two things I never wanted to think about in the same breath. I felt like putting my fingers in my ears and chanting, "I can't hear you."

"Maddie, you made it!" The exuberant cowgirl turned around. I did a mental forehead smack. Dana.

"Nice boots, cowgirl," I said.

"I came straight from a shoot. Charmin commercial."

"As in toilet paper?"

"Cowboy's invoke the image of strength. No one wants weak toilet paper. So," she asked, leaning in close, "how goes the great boyfriend search?"

I quickly filled her in on my mistress theory, punctuated by her occasional *wahoo's* as Fireman Bob dropped his suspenders. I finished off by recounting my visit to Big Boy studios with Porn Star Barbie.

"Did you say Bunny Hoffenmeyer?" Mrs. Rosenblatt asked, coming up behind me with a fresh drink in hand.

"Yes. Why? Do you know her?"

"Actually, my Lenny used to work with her."

I blinked at her. "What do you mean, 'used to work with her?' You were married to a porn star?" I could feel my nose scrunching into an icky face.

"No, no, no. Not that Lenny couldn't have been, mind you. But he was her insurance broker. You gotta have a lot of insurance in that industry. As Big Boy's owner, Bunny brought him a whole lotta business."

"Wait—owner?" I'd pegged Bunny as a dimwitted double D, not a savvy entrepreneur.

"Oh yeah. Bunny was raking it in back when I was married to Lenny. But then she expanded the whole operation into soft core. You know, stuff with storylines and candlelight. Erotica for ladies."

"And that didn't do well?"

"She lost her shirt. No pun intended. Turns out women don't buy as much porn as men."

Go figure.

"Last I heard Bunny was in debt up to her implants," Mrs. Rosenblatt continued. "I heard she's even trying to get some mainstream roles now to pay the bills. Poor thing."

Right. Poor thing. Poor enough to bump Greenway off for the money? After my interview, I'd moved Bunny to the bottom of my suspects list, thinking her IQ rivaled Jasmine's for lowest in L.A. County. But now I had a feeling Bunny was sharper than she let on. If she could fake an orgasm I guess she could fake innocence too.

"Want a drink, Maddie?" Mom asked, signaling a shirtless waiter.

Did I ever. "I'll have a Diet Coke."

"Oh come on, honey. Live a little!" Mrs. Rosenblatt drained her glass and set it on the waiter's tray. "How about a Virgin Mary?" she suggested.

Honestly, I was sick to death of Diet Coke. As long as it was virgin, I decided I could afford to live a little tonight.

"Okay. A virgin Mary."

Mrs. Rosenblatt ordered one for me and one for herself. Cowgirl Dana, staying in character, ordered a shot of Jack Daniels. Mom ordered another cosmo and stuck a ten in the waiter's Speedo. (Ew, ew, ew!) By the time Fireman Bob had collected his suspenders and cleared off the stage, we all had fresh drinks in hand and I had that nauseous, my-mom's-talking-about-sex feeling somewhat under control.

Music started to pulse from the speakers again and the crowd took to their feet, craning to see the next beefcake.

"*Look out ladies*," the MC warned. "*Because here comes Damien. And he's been a bad, bad boy.*"

The sound of a motorcycle engine revved through the speakers as a man in all leather appeared on the stage in front of a cloud of smoke. He strutted down the catwalk, shedding his leather jacket to reveal a six pack Budweiser would be jealous of.

"Oh my God." Mom made the sign of the cross.

"What was that for?" asked Mr. Rosenblatt.

"I just had the unholiest of thoughts."

Ick. Okay, so I *almost* had that mom's-talking-about-sex nausea under control. I took a big gulp of my Virgin Mary in hopes it would settle my stomach. It wasn't half bad, really. Kind of like an extra spicy bloody Mary with a twist of lime. Not a martini, but definitely better than another Diet Coke.

Damien gyrated down the catwalk, shedding leather like a snake until Mom grabbed a cocktail napkin and started fanning herself. "Whew, I think that man just gave me a hot flash."

"That man is hung. You think he'd go for an older woman?" Mrs. Rosenblatt asked, elbowing me in the ribs.

I tried to be kind. "He's probably gay."

Mrs. Rosenblatt scrutinized Damien as he stripped off his leather chaps to reveal a thong with a Harley Davidson logo.

I took a big sip of my Virgin Mary. Wow, he did have a nice package. I took another sip.

"I just love a man in leather," Mrs. Rosenblatt continued. "I saw this documentary about how dominatrixes tame their men with leather whips. Now I don't go in for all that chains stuff, but I could go for a guy in leather."

I drained my glass and signaled the waiter for another.

"Ralphie doesn't like leather," Mom chimed in. "But he's nuts about lace. I bought this adorable lace teddy at the mall today. One look and we'll be spending the whole honeymoon in bed." Mom winked one heavily shadowed eye. "If you know what I mean."

If a person could die of ickiness, I was just about flat-lining. I searched frantically for that waiter with my fresh Virgin Mary. Luckily, he appeared just as Damien gyrated his way in our direction and Mom dug into her purse for more green.

"Take it all off!" Dana commanded, waving her cowgirl hat in the air.

Damien complied, doing away with the Harley thong and going full monty on us.

Mrs. Rosenblatt nudged me in the ribs. "I told you he was hung."

I admit. I stared. It was hard not to. Especially when I now realized how poorly Richard measured up against the Damiens of the world. Yikes. What had I been missing?

And then out of nowhere, I thought of Ramirez. I wondered if he was a Damien or Richard. I took another sip of my drink and tried really hard not to picture Ramirez in a leather thong.

"Over here, bad boy," my mother yelled, waving her five dollar bill in the air. Damien strutted closer and collected the cash with his teeth. Mom giggled like a sixth grader. I tried not to look.

Dana grabbed my arm, her nails digging into me. "Oh my God, Maddie, did you see who that is?"

I looked up at Damien, squinting through the smoke and strobing lights to get a good look at his face. (Which, I had to admit, I'd not yet really seen, being a little distracted by certain other parts of his anatomy.) He did look a little familiar. But as Damien turned our direction, it was the neck that gave it away. Or lack thereof. "Is that your roommate?"

Dana nodded and I swore I saw drool form at the corner of her mouth. "I had no freaking idea he was this built."

No Neck Guy winked at Dana, then gyrated his way to the other side of the stage.

"You know that guy?" Mrs. Rosenblatt asked. "He's got a *tuchis* like granite."

"*Give it up for Biker Damien,*" the MC said as Damien gathered his chaps and headed off stage.

Mom grabbed another cocktail napkin and began fanning herself.

"Um, will you excuse me for a minute?" Dana didn't wait for an answer before disappearing toward the stage.

I drained my second glass and signaled for another. I could easily get addicted to these things. The waiter returned with my drink just as the music started up and "Officer Dan" took the stage, wearing a cop uniform amidst flashing red lights. Mom and Mrs. Rosenblatt were instantly on their feet again, waving dollar bills. Maybe it was the spicy Virgin Mary, but I was starting to get into the swing of things. I even shouted a cowgirl holler of my own when Dan tossed his blue shirt into the crowd—badge and all.

I wondered how Ramirez would look in a cop uniform.

Duh, he'd look sexy! The man looked sexy in just about anything. I wondered how he'd look in *nothing*…

Ugh! What was I thinking? I instantly felt guilty. I was possibly carrying Richard's child and here I was not only ogling half naked men, but fantasizing about Ramirez's package.

But I realized as I took another long sip of my Virgin Mary that it was Richard's fault really. If he hadn't up and left, I never would have gone looking for him, then I never would have met Ramirez and I wouldn't be here comparing the size of his ding-dong with Officer Dan's. See, it was all Richard's fault.

In fact, I realized, all the problems in my life lately were because of him. He'd gotten me into this whole mess, and what's more, he didn't even have the decency to tell me where he was. Even Greenway told his mistress where he was.

And what kind of scum marries Cinderella anyway? What, does he think he's some kind of Prince Charming? Ha! I mentally snorted. More like Prince Anal. He folded his socks for crying out loud. What kind of a man does that?

I bet Ramirez didn't fold his socks. I bet he just threw his socks in with his underwear in one big mess. Socks mixed with with…briefs? Boxers? I wondered what kind of underwear Ramirez wore. I pictured him as a briefs guy. Not those Hanes things from Kmart, but the really sexy Calvin ones. Maybe in gray or slate blue. Slate blue would be a good color on him.

Officer Dan ripped off his break-away pants, revealing a black G-string that read L.A.P.D.

"Woo hoo," I yelled, waving my drink in the air. A little splashed on my wrist, but I didn't care. In fact, I realized, I was feeling pretty good. Better than I had in days. "Show me your gun, officer hottie!"

"You tell 'em, Maddie," Mrs. Rosenblatt commanded, slightly slurring her words. Then leaned in and added, "I think I'm getting just a teeny bit tipsy."

I froze. Glass halfway to my lips. Tipsy? What did she mean, *tipsy*? My gaze whipped from her empty Virgin Mary glass to my own. Sure, I was feeling a little happy, but that was because of the naked men, right?

I grabbed Mrs. Rosenblatt by the arm. "What's in a Virgin Mary?"

"Tomato juice, lime, cayenne."

I heaved a sigh of relief.

"And vodka. Lots of vodka."

I froze. "Vodka? But you said it was virgin!"

Mrs. Rosenblatt laughed. "*Bubbee*, they call it a Virgin Mary, cause you drink too many, and you won't even remember the sex that night. It'll be like immaculate conception."

Oh my God. I was the world's worst mother. And I wasn't even a mother yet! I was awful, terrible, selfish, stupid. I was going straight to hell.

I was going to throw up.

"Don't worry. Nothing a little aspirin in the morning won't cure."

Right. Aspirin. I bit my lip to keep from blurting out what a horrible thing I just did. Potentially did, that is. I guess if I wasn't sure I was pregnant, I couldn't be sure I'd done something really, really awful. Damn Richard. This was all his fault.

Dana walked up, a clothed Damien a.k.a. No Neck Guy in tow. The grin on her face said she'd have no trouble remembering the sex tonight. "Hey, we're gonna head back home. Thanks for inviting me Mrs. Springer. We'll see you tomorrow for the big day."

Mom and Mrs. Rosenblatt gave Dana hugs, Mrs. Rosenblatt all the while eyeing No Neck Guy's crotch like a dog might a big beefy Milk Bone.

The icky warred with morning sickness, which warred with guilt, which warred with the mass amount of vodka I'd apparently consumed that night. I willed my stomach to stay put as the room swayed.

"Can you drop me off at home first?" I begged.

"Sure, Maddie."

Dana, No Neck and I all piled in to her Saturn. I sat in the back, trying to avert my eyes as Dana and No Neck held hands and made kissy faces. Instead I slouched down in my seat and closed my eyes so I didn't have to watch the scenery wizz past the window in a noxious blur.

Luckily, the drive was short and a few minutes later Dana was walking me to the door of my studio. Any other time I could have walked myself in, but have you ever tried to walk in three-inch heels under the influence of vodka?

"Are you drunk?" Dana asked.

Duh. "I think so."

"I thought you weren't drinking because of..." She trailed off, looking at my belly.

"I'm not. I mean, I wasn't. It was an accident."

"An accident?"

"I thought the virgins were virgin."

Dana gave me a funny look. But considering she had a hot stripper in the car, she didn't interrogate further. "Get some sleep," she commanded. "You want me to come drive you to the wedding in the morning?"

"No. It's fine. I'll get a cab."

"Okay, well, call me. But, uh," she glanced back at No Neck. "Just not too early, k?"

I nodded. Not a good idea. I put a hand to my head to make the scenery stop spinning. I watched Dana pull away, then walked inside. That is, after fumbling with the key for a good five minutes first. I hated being drunk.

But most of all, I realized as I collapsed onto my futon and stared at the ceiling, I hated Richard. Maybe it was the vodka, or maybe the full monty, or maybe the fact I'd been inside a porn studio today, but no matter what explanations he might try to conjure up, I realized I hated Richard. There was no excuse for doing this to me. Look at me! I was a mess. I was a bundle of nerves, anxiety, and I'd just *possibly* poisoned my *maybe* child. Oh God. I was an awful, awful person. Nothing in the world could make this day worse.

And then my doorbell rang.

I lay there, deciding if I even remembered how to move my limbs. After the third ring, I finally managed a vertical position and staggered to the door. I looked through the peephole and think I actually gasped out loud.

"I know you're in there, I can see your light under the door. Open up."

I bit my lip. I could let him in. But, see, here's the thing: I've been known to be a little over friendly when I've been drinking. Which is why I don't often indulge. In fact, I have a pitcher of margaritas to blame for my second date sleepover with Richard. Knowing I was past my common sense limit, coupled with, as Mom would say, the unholy thoughts I'd been having earlier at Beefcakes, I wasn't sure it was really a good idea to let him in.

He pounded on the door again. "I can hear you breathing. Open the door."

Then again, it's never a good idea to disobey a cop.

I unhooked the latch, turned the deadbolt, and opened the door to find myself face to face with Ramirez. Sexy day-old stubble and all.

CHAPTER FOURTEEN

——————

I blinked. God he looked good. He still didn't look like he'd slept much, but the five o'clock shadow had grown into this sexy George Clooney thing that made his jaw look like it belonged in a Schick commercial. He was dressed in his usual uniform of butt hugging jeans and a black T-shirt. His eyes were hooded and dark, his hair just a little mussed. This was exactly how I imagined he'd look after a really long night of really excellent sex.

Down girl. See what I mean about alcohol and me?

"Where have you been?" he asked. "Didn't you get my messages?"

I turned around. Sure enough the light on my machine was blinking like mad.

"No, I didn't. I just got in. Why?"

"Can I come in?"

I bit my lip, hesitating. The rational voice in my head said, tell him to leave. Close the door. Do not talk to sexy cops when you're drunk. Only the Beefcakes patron in me said, yes, please, come in. Take your clothes off. Hop into my bed.

And considering the amount of vodka Beefcakes Girl had consumed, she was getting really loud. So loud she was overpowering the rational voice.

"Sure." I stood back to allow him entry.

He stepped into the room. And I swear my eyes went straight to his leather thong region. Boxers or briefs? I just couldn't tell.

"So," I said, clearing my throat loudly. "What did you want?"

"I just wanted to let you know we ran an analysis on the hairs found in the motel room. They weren't yours."

"I told you so." Ugh. I sounded five. "I mean, I'm glad you checked. I'm glad we cleared that up."

Ramirez looked at me kind of funny, but didn't comment. "Yeah, well I just wanted to let you know you're officially not a suspect."

"Well, duh," I smacked my head with the palm of my hand. "I don't even own a leopard thong."

Ramirez raised one eyebrow. "Leopard thong?"

"And I so don't do nooners. Well, not unless it's a really special occasion. Or the guy's really hot. But I always leave with my panties on."

Ramirez's eyes creased at the corners, twinkling with that Big Bad Wolf look again. "Good to know."

I took a deep breath. Yes, I was aware I sounded frighteningly like Bunny Hoffenmeyer and I wasn't making a whole lot of sense. But somehow the connection between my brain and my mouth seemed to have shorted out. I grabbed onto the kitchen counter for support, as the room was starting to look like a Tilt-A-Whirl again.

"What I mean to say is, I'm glad I didn't kill him. I mean, I'm glad you know I didn't kill him. I know I didn't kill him. But now you know that I know I didn't kill him. Even though he's dead."

The corner of Ramirez's mouth quivered. "Uh-huh."

"I know that you know that I know that I didn't kill him." I paused. Hmmm…that didn't sound quite right. Let me try again. "I mean, I wasn't there. No, I was there, but not *there* there, as in not in his room, there." There. That sounded better. Kind of.

The quiver turned into a full fledged grin. "Are you drunk?"

"No!" I rolled my eyes and did my best as-if face. "I'm so *not* drunk. I'm the opposite of drunk. I'm…" I paused trying to come up with the word. "…the other thing."

"Sober?" Ramirez supplied, still grinning.

"Right. That's me. Sober Maddie." It might have been more convincing if my hand hadn't slipped off the counter just then, throwing me so off balance I tripped on one of my heels and nearly fell.

Nearly, because Ramirez reached out with quick cop-like reflexes and caught me in his arms. Strong arms. I put my hands up to balance and came up against a chest like a brick wall. I felt his heart beating beneath his six-day-a-week-at-the-gym muscles. I think I sighed.

"You okay?" His face was inches from mine. His eyes still twinkling with amusement.

"Uh-huh," I managed. Even though my limbs felt like Jell-O and I could swear visions of Damien's package were swimming through my head. I suddenly had a burning desire to know for sure whether Ramirez was a boxers or briefs guy.

"Love the outfit," he said, still holding me around the waist. His eyes dipped down to my Librarian wear.

"You're mocking me again aren't you?"

"Just a little."

"It went over big at the porn studio too."

Ramirez's eyebrow shot up again. "Porn Studio?" His grin widened, showing off a row of white teeth. *The better to eat you right up with my dear.*

"See, I knew there was a little bad girl in you." His voice was low and deep in a way that made me warm in all the right places.

I was still pressed against his chest and his hooded eyes looked wide awake now, intent on me. Making me think serious bad girl thoughts. Thoughts of bad cops in boxers.

Or better yet, nothing at all.

Try as I might to rein in Beefcakes Girl, her eyes strayed downward. Past his brick wall chest, beyond six-pack territory, until they zeroed in on that denim covered package.

"Are you staring at my crotch?"

At least I had the decency to blush. At least, I think it was a blush. Or maybe just one of Mom's hot flashes at the totally X-rated thoughts racing through my mind.

"I was just wondering if you're a boxers or briefs guy." Did I say that out loud? Oh lord, I must be really drunk.

Before I had time to take back my Sluts-R-Us statement, Ramirez tightened his grip on my waist, pulling my body flush with his.

I think I had an on-the-spot orgasm.

His head dipped down, his lips grazing my ear. "Briefs," he whispered.

And then he kissed me.

And not one of those nippy, soft, kissy things. This was a *kiss*. A serious lust-inspiring, picturing-you-naked-all-day, you're-so-going-to-remember-the-sex-no-matter-how-many-Virgin-Marys-you-accidentally-drank kind of kiss. One that left no question in my mind whether Ramirez was a Damien or a Richard beneath all those clothes. I knew for a fact that Richards didn't kiss like this. He was a Damien through and through.

His hands slid up my shirt and I did a quick mental inventory. Legs shaved? No granny panties? Just in case condom still in my purse? Check, check, and check. Beefcakes Girl did a mental *woohoo!* as I kissed him back.

His tongue touched mine and I suddenly felt like Ramirez was wearing way too many clothes. I slid my hands down his chest, fumbling like a nervous teenager at his belt buckle until his T-shirt came untucked. He didn't protest in the least as I slid the fabric up and over his head. Though he did groan a little as I trailed my hands down his abdomen. Good lord, this guy was built. I bet he worked out more than Dana.

Ramirez picked me up like I weighed less than nothing and sat me on the kitchen counter. My skirt hiked up as his hands slid up my thighs, past my knees, past the oh-that-tickles spot, and on into where's-that-freaking-condom territory.

I went back to fumbling with his belt buckle again. We were suddenly in a race. Who could get their clothes off fastest and the winner received the orgasm of their life. Ramirez's shoes went flying across the room. My silk blouse was ripped off so fast one of the buttons popped off, pinging against my microwave. My bra was down around my waist and I heard the unmistakable sound of Ramirez's zipper sliding open.

And then he froze. Okay, through my vodka-hormone cocktail it took me a second to realize he wasn't kissing me back anymore. But when I did, I saw he was staring at a spot behind me.

"What?" I asked. "What's wrong?"

"What is *that*?"

I turned around to see what he was staring at. My heart sank.

The EPT.

"Uh, it's nothing. Just, um, a little pregnancy test."

It was as if I'd said, "Just a little nuclear bomb." Ramirez instantly put two feet between us, still staring at the bomb like it might go off any second. "Why do you have a pregnancy test on your kitchen counter? Are you pregnant?" He stared at my belly. Thankfully, I was still flat as a board. But I could see him mentally putting a basketball there.

"No! I mean, I don't know. I don't think so. Well…maybe."

His gaze whipped wildly from the test to me. Then he muttered a, "Jesus," and sat down on my futon, scrubbing a hand over his face.

I slid off the counter, shrugging back into my bra as I sat down beside him.

"Richard's?" he asked.

I nodded.

"Jesus," he said again. "Why didn't you tell me?"

"I didn't know if there was anything to tell. And, well, I don't know, you're a cop and you thought I was in Greenway's room. And then you came here and you looked so nice and you kissed me, and that was *really* nice, and well, I just kind of forgot to mention it."

"You forgot?" He stared at me.

"Uh-huh." In my defense, Ramirez shirtless was enough to make a woman forget her own name.

"Hell, this is…this was…" He waved his arms from me to the EPT, seemingly searching for the right words.

My heart bottomed out when he found them.

"A mistake," he finally said. "This was a huge mistake coming here."

A mistake. My bottom lip quivered. Okay, so maybe it was a mistake. In fact, I'm sure had we actually had sex, I would have been thinking the same thing as soon as the Virgin Marys wore off. But did he have to say it like that?

I wrapped my arms around my middle, suddenly very conscious of the fact my shirt was on the other side of the room.

"Maybe you should just go then," I said. Then bit my lower lip to stop that damn quivering.

"You're right. I should go." Ramirez got up and retrieved his shirt from the floor.

"Fine," I spat back. I'm not sure why I was so mad at him, but it beat being mad at myself. "Go then."

"Hey, look, I didn't mean for this to happen. I didn't come here for this," he said, gesturing the counter where we'd been *this* close to being the stars of our very own porno flick.

"Oh, so you're saying this is my fault? That I threw myself at you? That I'm some kind of drunken hussy?" The closer the words hit to home the louder I said them. Damn. I had thrown myself a little hadn't I? But he'd been more than willing to catch me.

"I didn't say that. You're not a drunken—" He paused. "Wait, you're pregnant and you went out and got drunk?" He stared at me as if I'd just confessed to shooting my grandmother.

That did it. The quivering lip shook out of control and big fat tears rolled out of my eyes. Did I mention I also tend to get a little emotional when I'm drunk?

"I-I-I'm a horrible p-p-person," I wailed.

"Oh, Jesus."

"I'll be a horrible m-m-mother."

Ramirez sat down beside me. "No, you won't. I'm sure you'll be a fine mother."

"I didn't mean to get drunk. I was tricked. I would n-n-never hurt a baby." My words were coming out in big slobbery sobs and I was pretty sure my nose was running too. This was about as unsexy as you could get.

"Hey, it's okay. I'm sure the baby is okay."

"If there is a baby," I reminded him between sniffles.

"Right. If there is one." He put his arm around me.

"I'm sorry." I sniffed again. "I'm a mess."

Ramirez looked at me. He pushed one stray strand of hair behind my ear. Oddly enough it was an even more intimate gesture than having his hands up my shirt. More…touching. Wow. Who knew Bad Cop had a soft side?

"You're not a mess. You'll make a beautiful mother."

Okay, so I knew he was lying. I was so far from beautiful right now. My mascara must be in streaks, my nose was running and red, and I'm sure my eyes were once again puffier than the Michelin man. But it was a nice lie. And he was a nice guy to say it.

"I'm sorry," I said again. "I'm sure you have stuff to do. Important Bad Cop stuff."

He smiled. Not that smirky smile and not the sexy, wolfish grin either. Just a smile, like maybe deep down he really didn't think I was such a mess after all. "Nope," he said. "I've got nowhere to go."

He pulled me close to him and I laid my head down on his chest. I could hear his heart beating. It was a comforting sound. He smelled like fresh laundry and mellow aftershave. I took a deep breath, inhaling his scent.

I closed my eyes. I wasn't sure if it was the vodka, the good cry, or Ramirez's steady heartbeat beneath my cheek, but for the first time in days I felt peaceful. Calm, peaceful and so very relaxed. I closed my eyes and let my thoughts drift, feeling utterly comfortable in Ramirez's arms.

* * *

I heard a phone ringing, echoing through my head like a car with too much bass. Slowly I flexed one limb, then the other. My neck was stiff, like I'd fallen asleep sitting up and my mouth felt like sandpaper. I managed to open one eye a crack.

And saw Ramirez.

Yikes!

I blinked hard against the assault of sunlight coming through my windows. What the hell was Ramirez doing in my apartment? His head was lolled back on the futon cushions, his mouth slightly open as he slept, making deep breathing sounds. Slowly it came back to me as I watched him. The Virgin Mary's, the EPT. Ramirez's hands up my shirt.

Uhn. I groaned. Oh God, I'd practically thrown myself at him. And then bawled all over him. I'd made a drunken fool of myself. I shook my head. Ouch. And I had the headache to prove it. And where the hell was that ringing coming from?

I dove for my purse on the floor, every movement jarring my head until it pounded like a marching band. Oh my God, someone stop the ringing!

"Hello?" I croaked as I found my cell phone.

"Maddie! Where the hell are you?"

I held the phone away from my ear, Dana's shrill shriek assaulting me in so many ways I couldn't keep track.

"Shhhhh. Hangover."

"Oh my God, Mads. You're hung over? I knew I should have picked you up this morning."

Picked me up?

And then through my hung over haze I had a moment of clarity. Oh crap. The wedding!

I spun around, producing a new round of pain in my temples, and looked at the clock on my kitchen wall. Oh crap. 10:00!

"Maddie? Are you still there? The ceremony starts in half an hour. Your mom is starting to freak."

"I'll be right there. Don't start without me"

I hung up, throwing the phone down on the carpet.

"Crap!"

Ramirez opened one sleepy eye. "What time is it?"

"Ten. I'm late. I gotta go. Crap!" I ran to my closet and pulled the Purple People Eater out of its garment bag. I didn't even take the time to grimace as I stripped off the rest of my librarian outfit and threw it over my head.

Had I more time I might have waited until Ramirez was gone to strip down. As it was, I think the sight of me half naked and running around like a crazy woman woke him up quickly enough.

"Late for what?"

"Wedding. Mom's wedding. Riverside. Crap!" I panted, trying to get the Purple People Eater closed in the back.

Ramirez stood up and helped me with the zipper.

"Thanks."

"How late are you?" he asked, still rubbing his eyes.

"Late. Riverside in half an hour late. I am so freaking late!" I looked wildly around for my dyed purple shoes. I found one under my drawing table and hopped around looking for the other as I scooped my cell phone back into my purse.

"Okay, I'll drive."

I stopped hopping and stared.

Okay—my first thought when Mom told me she was getting married (after the initial shock that Ralph was, in fact, straight) was of the awesome act of God it would take to get Richard to come to the wedding with me. We'd only been dating four months and the Wedding Date is really more of a six months-and-up kind of event. Rating just after meet-the-parents, and just before buying a puppy together. After weeks of procrastinating, and weeks more of begging, pleading, and playing the we're-not-having-sex-until-you-relent game, I'd finally convinced Richard to go on the promise he could leave early if they started doing the chicken dance.

And, after one drunken night of Maddie the Horny Tear Factory, Ramirez wanted to go to the wedding with me?

I must have looked as shocked as I felt, because Ramirez grinned as he explained.

"My car has a siren. We'll be able to get through traffic."

Right. Siren. Duh.

I shook off the tiny prickle of disappointment that he wanted a quick route and not an evening of close dancing with me as I found my other shoe and made a mad dash for Ramirez's SUV.

Usually the drive from Santa Monica to Riverside is a good hour and a half—Santa Monica bordering the ocean and Riverside bordering the last known outpost of civilization before heading into the desert of doublewides between L.A. and Las Vegas. However, with Ramirez's police siren blaring down the 10, we made it in twenty-five. It was a good thing too because as we pulled up in front of the Garden Grande Motel, Mom and Mrs. Rosenblatt were pacing up and down like two vintage kitschy Energizer bunnies.

"Where the hell have you been?" Mom shrieked at me as I catapulted myself from the car.

"Sorry, I overslept."

Mrs. Rosenblatt looked Ramirez up and down. Her gaze settled in his package region. "I can see why."

My cheeks turned into two flaming pools of lava.

Ramirez just grinned.

"You, come with me," Mrs. Rosenblatt instructed him. "I've got the perfect seat for you." Before I could protest she grabbed Ramirez by the arm and steered him toward the back garden.

"No he's just dropping me off, and…" I trailed off. What was the point? Mrs. Rosenblatt would probably just lecture me on the importance of sex for a healthy aura.

Ramirez just shrugged and grinned at me over his shoulder as Mrs. Rosenblatt led him away. If I hadn't known better, I'd have thought he was enjoying this.

"Where is Richard?" Mom looked from me to Ramirez's retreating form with narrowed eyes.

"Uh, well, Richard is kind of, um…"

Mom waved her hands in the air. "Never mind. It doesn't matter. You're here. I'm getting married. That's all that matters."

Mom's hands stopped waving. Her eyes got round. She visibly paled under her thick layer of foundation and startling blue eyeliner. "Oh God. I'm getting married."

And then my mother began to hyperventilate. Right there on the sidewalk in front of the Garden Grande Motel in an empire waisted wedding dress with a two foot long train Mom had the breakdown to end all breakdowns.

"Oh God. I don't think I can do this, Maddie. I mean, I want this," she went on, "But oh my God, I'm getting *married*, and I swore I would never do this again, and maybe we should wait, maybe we should do it in the church after all, what if God really does want me to be Catholic, and what if he puts a curse upon our marriage, Maddie, you know I can't take another failed marriage, I *need* God to be on my side, Mads."

My head pounded, the marching band bringing out the big cymbals. "Take a breath. Pause for a period."

Mom took another deep breath, still looking like she needed a paper bag. "What am I going to do if I blow this marriage too? I don't know if I can do this."

"Mom, if you don't want to do this, now's the time."

Am I a bad person that I almost hoped she'd change her mind and I could go home and commune with my Mr. Coffee instead of parading down the aisle in Barney on Crack for all to see?

She bit her lip, creating little red lipstick flecks on her teeth.

"I do Mads. But, it's just been the two of us for so long. And, well, Ralph's great, but everything's about to change. And I don't know if I can take it. The change. Maybe I'm just too old for change."

And I realized as I stared at my mother's '80's blue eye shadow and lipstick stained teeth, so was I. Maybe that was why I'd blocked out all things wedding for the past three months. I was afraid things were going to change. That I'd lose my Keds-with-floral-Muumuus Mom to Fernando's ultra chic world.

And just as quickly I realized how ridiculous that was. There wasn't a designer in Beverly Hills strong enough to pry my mom out of her 1983 ways, and to be honest, I didn't think Ralph even wanted to try. Any man who would love Mom, blue eye-shadow and all, passed muster with me.

I wasn't losing a mom. I was gaining a dad. A Faux Dad.

"Mom, do you love Ralph?"

Mom nodded without hesitation. "I do."

I gave her arm a quick squeeze. "Then let's go get married."

Mom's eyes teared up, and she caught me in a hug that crushed my ribs even harder than the Purple People Eater. I held onto her hand as we took our places behind a boxwood hedge just as the strains of the wedding march began to play.

CHAPTER FIFTEEN

"Everybody on the dance floor for the chicken dance!"

Ramirez leaned in close. "Just so you know, this more than makes up for dinner at my mom's."

No kidding.

Actually Ramirez had been a pretty good sport about this whole thing, sitting all the way through the ceremony, even when my Irish Catholic Grandmother started saying her rosary halfway through the I-do's, and even when every one of my cousins, aunts, uncles, and members of my mother's Internet chat groups insisted on meeting Maddie's New Guy. All things considered, Bad Cop was turning out to be an okay date.

We were seated at one of the ten round tables in the Garden Grande's "great hall" (Think Elk's lodge décor—peeling wood-toned vinyl walls and grade school cafeteria linoleum). Molly the Breeder sat across from me with her husband, Stan. Dana and an exhausted looking No Neck Guy were flapping their wings on the dance floor, and Ramirez was sitting on my left. Beside him sat my Irish Catholic Grandmother, back straight, lips pinched into a tight line, eyes narrow and shrewd, flicking between Ramirez's tell-tale stubble and my naked left finger.

"Maddison, are you going to mass tomorrow morning?" she asked, her steely blue eyes squinting up at me. (Despite my petite status, my grandmother makes me look like a giant, topping out at just under 4'11".)

"Of course, Grandmother." I figured this didn't really count as a lie because it was for a good cause. If my grandmother thought I didn't go to mass, she might have a heart attack and die here on the spot. So, really, I was saving her life with this lie. Very noble, when you look at it that way.

"How about the new guy?" She gestured to Ramirez as if he weren't there. "Does he go to mass?"

"Uh..." I was stumped.

"My family goes to St. John Vianney," Ramirez cut in.

He was Catholic? Ohmigod. I think my grandmother might just die a happy woman. Maddie had actually brought home a good Catholic boy. Well, a Catholic boy at any rate. The jury was still out on the good part.

My grandmother's eyes narrowed like a cat's. "St. John Vianney? Do you know Father Michael?" She was testing him.

"I do. In fact I worked with him last year to establish an after school program to keep teens away from crime. I'll tell him you've been asking after him."

Grandmother's wrinkles parted in a small smile, nodding, and I had a sneaking suspicion mentally booking the St. Mark's chapel for the Springer-Ramirez wedding.

Ramirez leaned in close. "I think granny likes me." Then he winked at me and I felt his hand rest on my knee.

I jumped. I wasn't entirely sure if Ramirez was here as my ride, my date, or to keep me under surveillance in case Richard tried to contact me. Granted, I'd just spent the night drooling on his chest. And he *was* here with me at my mother's wedding, charming the dentures off Grandmother. And, as I'd sampled last night, he'd take home the gold in the kissing Olympics.

But with the vodka slowly seeping out of my system, reality was rearing her ugly head again. And in reality, Ramirez was on a case, Richard was on the lam, and I was somehow stuck in the middle, not sure whose side to be on.

I was pretty sure I now hated Richard. It was hard not to hate a man who married a Disney character. But somehow I wasn't ready to totally write him off either. At least, not without hearing his side of the story. Even without taking into account my late factor, Richard and I had a history together. And I wasn't quite ready to throw that all away. The whole situation still left me with a squishy sensation in my stomach, like that time in second grade when I'd eaten a bad burrito and done one too many flips around the monkey bars.

But I didn't move Ramirez's hand.

"Wasn't it a lovely ceremony?" Molly piped in.

Grandmother snorted. "No priest. Civilized people get married in a church with a priest, not on some lawn." She turned to Ramirez. "Molly got married at St. Mark's. *All* our girls get married at St. Mark's," she emphasized.

Ramirez gave me the raised eyebrow. I pretended to find an interesting piece of lint on the Purple People Eater.

"Our wedding was so beautiful," Molly went on. "We had the traditional white roses everywhere, and my gown was this white, lace creation that had this long, lovely train tha— Stan, get your son, he's climbing on the podium again. Anyway, the train went on for miles. I had to have a train bearer, can you believe it? I felt just like a princess and—Stan, get him, he's going to pull the whole thing over! What was I saying? Oh, yes, St. Mark's. Well, it was just a lovely ceremony. You have to get Father Jacobs to do your wedding, he's just the most—Stan, I swear if you feed that boy any more cake I'm going to castrate you! Get him down from there, now! Anyway, where was I?"

I stared, my jaw hanging open like a cartoon. I think I was having a terrible glimpse into my future. Like the ghost of pregnancy hormones yet to come. I grabbed my water glass and took a big gulp, trying to fend off hysteria, and made a mental note to take that test when I got home.

Stan mumbled something that sounded like "four more months of this," before leaving the table to wrangle his cake eating monsters.

"Molly has three children already," Grandmother informed Ramirez. "If you want a big family, you'll have to start soon. Maddie's not getting any younger, you know."

I choked on the water, making coughing sounds as I tried not to spew it across the table.

Ramirez looked like he was trying hard not to laugh. "We'll get right on that." He flashed Grandma a smile that was all teeth and I felt his fingers curl around my knee.

I took another sip of water.

"I'm glad to hear that." In fact, Grandmother looked about as pleased as when Molly had promised she'd *think* about sending her oldest boy in to the priesthood.

Great. My mom's bouquet not even cold yet and already Grandmother was trying to marry me off with a corral full of cake eating, podium toppling monsters of my own. I tried to think of a tactful way of saying Ramirez was just my ride.

My ride who kept squeezing my knee under the table.

Before I could sort that one out, my cell phone rang. Grandmother gave me a stern look that obviously said cell phones were on the *War and Peace* sized list of things she didn't approve of.

"Excuse me," I said, grabbing my phone and stepping away from the table. The readout was an 818 area code I didn't recognize.

"Hello?" I answered, putting a hand over my other ear to block out the strains of the chicken dance.

"Hi. I'm returning a call from Maddie Springer?"

"This is Maddie?"

"This is Andi Jameson."

My ears perked up. Mistress number two.

"Yes, thanks for calling me back. I actually wanted to ask you a of couple questions about Devon Greenway."

Andi was quiet on the other end.

"You did know him, right?"

"Yes," she said hesitantly. "Who did you say you were again?"

I decided to stick with the story I'd told Bunny. "I'm with the *L.A. Informer.* We're doing a piece on Mr. Greenway's tragic passing and I'm speaking to anyone who was close to him."

Andi didn't respond. But, she didn't hang up either, so I plowed ahead. "From what I understand, you used to date Mr. Greenway?"

"Listen, I don't know if I feel comfortable talking about this to the press."

Crap. I bit my lip, trying to think fast. Think like a used car salesman.

"Okay, here's the deal. I'm not really with the press. I, uh, I dated Greenway too, and I was just trying to find out how many other women he screwed over by failing to mention he was married." Okay, a lie. But the anger about having a boyfriend forgetting to mention his marriage was real.

And it seemed to hit home.

"God, you too?" Andi sighed into the phone. "Would you believe I didn't even find out about it until I saw his wife's body on the news. What a cheating scum."

"No kidding." Now we were getting somewhere. I wondered just how angry Andi had been when she saw the news. Angry enough to kill someone?

"How long did you date Devon?" I asked.

"Six months. He said he was going to marry me. He said he was going to buy me a big house in the hills and we'd get married. What a load of bullcrap."

"Yep, men are scum." I was getting into this. "All men should be required to have their marital status tattooed on their foreheads."

"Better yet, tattoo it on their dicks."

Ouch. "So, when was the last time you saw Devon?"

"A couple weeks ago. He said he was going out of town for a while. Bastard. Probably just shacking up with some whore. No offense."

"None taken." Wow, she was really pissed. I wondered if I could goad her into telling me if she owned a gun. "Man, when I found out about his wife, I was so angry, I could have killed him. I guess someone beat me to it." I laughed nervously.

Andi was quiet.

I prodded a little further. "I sure would like to shake the woman's hand who did it. She did us both a huge favor, huh?"

Silence again. Damn. Maybe I'd laid it on too thick.

Then she spoke in a slow, calm voice. "You want to know what I did?"

The hairs on the back of my neck stood up. Was I about to hear a murder confession? I was almost afraid to ask. "What?"

"I drove to his house, and I snuck into the garage and carved the words 'pencil dick' into the hood of his precious Mercedes." Andi burst out laughing.

Damn. Not the confession I'd been looking for. However, I filed the pencil dick thing away for future reference. Richard did think a little too highly of his beamer...

"Mind if I ask where you were two nights ago?" I asked as Andi finally got her laughter under control.

"Yoga Class. I'm trying to find some inner peace."

Good plan.

"Oh, hey, one more thing. Um, you don't happen to own a leopard print thong, do you?" I asked.

"No. Why?"

"Oh, no reason. Thanks again."

I hung up, not feeling like I'd really learned anything. Expect that Andi Jameson had anger management issues. Not that I blamed her. Keying a fifty thousand dollar car did sound sort of therapeutic. I mentally added her name to the list of contenders for When Mistresses Attack.

I flipped my phone shut and turned around to find Ramirez standing behind me.

I let out a little, "Eek!"

"Who was that?" he asked.

"No one. Nobody. Just a friend."

He narrowed his eyes at me and I felt my cheeks growing hot. "This friend wouldn't happen to be wanted for murder would he?"

I put my hands on my hips. "Just what are you implying?"

"Nothing. But you would tell me if Richard called you, right?"

"Of course I would." Only it came out sounding so weak I don't think either of us was convinced. Which of course made me even more defensive. "Are you saying you don't trust me?"

"I didn't say that."

"But you implied it? Just like you implied you were going to give my grandmother a handful of Catholic babies. I'll have you know I'm not a baby factory. I have good legs! I'm not throwing that away. And I can most certainly have friends who call me who aren't Richard. And I can talk to them any time I want without answering to you."

"Oh Jesus." Ramirez rolled his eyes.

"What? What is that? That eye-rolly thing?"

"You're getting hormonal on me now aren't you?"

Okay, if there's one thing you don't *ever* say to a woman on the edge it's that she's hormonal.

"I'm *what*? Look, you're the one that came to my apartment last night, Mr. I-can't-keep-my-pants-on. So don't *you* lecture *me* about hormones."

Ramirez grinned, that infuriatingly sexy dimple flashing in his cheek. "I didn't hear you complain last night."

"Yeah, well, I was drunk."

He took a step closer. "Are you drunk now?"

"What? No, I'm not drunk now, I'm—"

But I didn't get to finish my rant as Ramirez's mouth was suddenly covering mine. I was poised to push him away with enough force to knock that sexy grin off his face, but the second his lips touched mine, the only thing I felt was a serious case of lust. Starting in my chest and settling somewhere between my legs. I grabbed onto his neck, more for support than anything, my body melting like a Hershey's kiss on a sunny day. That's it. No denying it. I had a case of the I-want-Ramirezes, and I had it bad.

Just as the back seat of Ramirez's SUV was starting to sound pretty good, he stepped back.

"What was that?" I asked between short breaths. I think I was panting.

He grinned. "That was me proving a point. Any complaints?"

It was official. I hated him.

My head hurt and I think my hangover was back. Only I felt tired, grouchy and squishy stomached all at the same time.

Ramirez was first and foremost a cop. And despite the fact my grandmother might think he was a good catholic boy, he was not happily-ever-after material. Or even boyfriend material for that matter. Besides, I already had a boyfriend. Sort of.

"Look, I, uh, I need to use the ladies room."

What I needed was a cold shower. And then a shrink. Ramirez the Hormone Machine had me so confused I didn't know what I felt anymore. One minute I'm designing Strawberry Shortcake high tops and wondering when those cute suede boots would go on sale, and the next I'm tracking down murderers, dressing as a hooker and visiting porn studios. Not to mention making out with sexy detectives at my mother's wedding. It was all too much.

I left Ramirez in the great hall and rounded the corner into the motel lobby, not even sure where I was going. I walked up to the front desk.

"Excuse me, where's your ladies' room?"

The clerk indicated a narrow hallway. "Down the hall, to the left."

"Thanks." I followed the hallway, ignoring the peeling paisley wallpaper and shag carpeting beneath my feet. In fact, I was so self-absorbed with the *Law & Order* meets *I Love Lucy* farce my life had become that I didn't even see him until I plowed smack into the man coming out of the men's room.

"Oh, sorry, I—"

I paused. My eyes growing wide, my jaw dropping and my heart doing one big thump in my chest. I looked up and stared right into the perfect blue eyes of Mr. Cinderella himself.

Richard.

CHAPTER SIXTEEN

———

"Maddie?" Richard looked wildly from side to side as if expecting I'd brought the entire mounted Calvary with me. Which, I guess I almost had, if you counted the wedding guests. "What the hell are you doing here?"

I tried to answer but I think I'd swallowed my tongue. It was like seeing a ghost. He was dressed in the same pressed slacks I'd come to expect, his button down shirt opened at the collar, covered by a tasteful sport coat. He looked like he'd just come from the office, or a client meeting, instead of being on the run for the last week. I almost wanted to reach out and touch him just to make sure I wasn't hallucinating this whole thing.

Either that or smack him across his perfectly shaved cheeks.

"Me?" I finally gasped out, in sort of a strangled cry. "What the hell are *you* doing here?"

"Nothing." Richard shifted from foot to foot, still looking over my shoulder at the empty lobby. "I mean, I, uh, I've been staying here for a few days. I just needed to get away for a while."

I snorted. "Away from Greenway or away from the cops? Oh, I know, maybe away from your wife."

He froze. His eyes meeting mine. "You know about her."

"Richard, I know everything." Which was a slight exaggeration.

"Look, maybe we should just go up to my room and talk." He looked over my shoulder again.

I bit my lip. I was dying to ask Richard about a million different questions, starting with what the hell is up with Cinderella? But, while I mostly believed Richard had nothing to do with the hole in Greenway's head, I was still a little reluctant to go off alone with him.

He must have sensed it because he grabbed my hand in both of his and looked at me with those sad little boy eyes that always melted me. "Please, pumpkin?"

I took a deep breath. "Fine, we'll go up to your room." I told myself it was because I didn't want Molly the Breeder to stumble into the lobby and witness me ripping the designer slacks wearing crap weasel a new one. Not because hearing him call me pumpkin suddenly filled me with a longing for a simpler time when deciding if I should be leaving my toothbrush in Richard's medicine cabinet was my biggest worry. "But just for a minute," I added. "I have to get back to the reception."

"Reception?" He glanced down at my gown as if just noticing the purple monstrosity for the first time.

"Yes, reception. My mom just got married. The wedding was going to be in Malibu, but weather issues forced us…" I glanced around at the Elk's Lodge chic interior. "…here. You were supposed to go with me, you know."

"Right. Sorry, pumpkin."

Only he didn't look sorry at all. He looked nervous. And he kept glancing back at the lobby like any second he expected someone to come bursting through the doors with guns drawn. Maybe Ramirez.

I shuddered at that thought, suddenly as eager to get Richard out of sight as he was.

I followed him down the hall to the elevators and up to the second floor. He paused outside room two-fourteen and unlocked the door. The room wasn't much to speak of. A double bed covered with a desert motif spread, two watery prints on the wall and a TV stand and small writing desk in one corner. All standard roadside motel issue. Richard immediately went to the windows and peeked out between the rust colored curtains.

"Richard, maybe you should tell me what's going on here."

"Nothing's going on. I told you, I just needed to get away."

"Right. And this is really Club Med. Time to quit shoveling the bullcrap, Richard."

He crossed the room and sat down on the bed. He still looked jumpy, his body humming with nervous energy. "All right, look, Maddie. I'll tell you. But I don't want you to get mad at me."

Fat chance of that. But I nodded anyway.

Richard sighed. "I didn't mean for things to get this out of hand. And I'm sorry I just left like that, but I couldn't take the chance of anyone following me. I had to get out of there."

"Because of Greenway?"

"Yeah."

I sat down beside him. He looked so pathetic I almost felt sorry for him. "Maybe you'd better start at the beginning."

Richard sighed again. Then he proceeded to tell much the same story Ramirez had. Richard had been in debt. So, when his client, Devon Greenway, wanted to shuffle some money around, Richard had agreed to help set up the dummy corporations in Mrs. Greenway's name in exchange for a small cut of the profits. Two million dollars small. (He so owed me a pair of really expensive Blahniks when this was all over.) The plan had been to funnel everything into Swiss bank accounts and no one would be the wiser. Only an over zealous accounting clerk at Securities and Exchange had found a minor accounting error. That's when everything started to go wrong.

To make matters worse, somewhere in all the paper shuffling, the twenty mil had disappeared. Greenway had suspected Richard of taking it, and Richard had suspected Greenway was holding out on him. Neither was willing to leave town without it, but with Newtone suddenly under investigation, they'd both gone into hiding.

"How do you just lose twenty million dollars?" I asked when he finished the narrative.

"I don't know. We had the money travel through a series of different accounts to lose the paper trail. And it's not in any of them."

"Well, who had access to those accounts?"

"Just Greenway, his wife, and I." Richard paused. He must have read the facts settling on my face because he quickly protested, his voice going high and whiney. "Look, I know this looks bad, but you've got to believe me. I had nothing to do with killing anyone. I've been here the whole time. Pumpkin, I swear I wouldn't do that."

As much as this new whiney side of Richard was starting to annoy me, I was inclined to believe him. I didn't think Richard had the stomach to shoot a man. Never mind drive into the Valley.

An alternative brewed in the back of my mind as Richard got up and checked the windows again. Bunny had admitted that she'd been present at one of Greenway and Richard's meetings. What if Greenway had been as careless with his other lady friends? What if one of the Bimbo Parade was smarter than she appeared? Unfortunately the list of Greenway's bedtime playmates was about as long as my mother's vintage wedding train.

I was about to ask Richard what he knew about Greenway's extra curricular activities when a knock sounded at the door. My stomach jumped into my throat.

Ramirez.

Richard leapt away from the window, his gaze whipping wildly from me to the door.

"Who is that?"

I bit my lip. "Well, I, uh, kind of got a replacement date to the wedding."

"Replacement date?"

"More like a ride, really." With the added perks of knee grabbing and French kissing.

Richard waved his hands in the air. "Look, just get rid of him."

"Open up, police," I heard Ramirez yell from the other side of the door.

"Police?!" Richard's voice rose two octaves, and he looked like he had ants in his pants, jumping from one foot to the other. "You're dating the police?"

Okay, I wasn't sure how suddenly Mr. Did-I-forget-to-mention-I'm-Married was making me feel guilty, but I kind of did. "Sort of. It's that detective that came to see you. Ramirez."

"Detective Ramirez!? You brought him here?"

"I didn't bring him. He kind of brought himself." Which was the truth.

"Well, make him go away."

Ramirez banged on the door again.

"Richard, you can't run forever," I reasoned. "You have to turn yourself in."

I moved toward the door.

But Richard stopped me, laying a hand on my arm. "Don't do this to me. Please, pumpkin."

Ugh. I was beginning to hate this pumpkin thing.

As it turned out I didn't have a choice. Before I could even jerk free of Richard's grip, Ramirez burst through the door, gun drawn. I was pretty impressed. It was very Bruce Willis.

"Oh God!" Richard retreated to the far side of the room, hands up in a surrender motion. "Don't shoot—I'm unarmed. I know the law. You can't shoot an unarmed man."

Ramirez looked from me to Richard. He raised his eyebrows, silently asking if I was really serious about this clown. At the moment, I was having my doubts.

"Are you okay?" Ramirez asked me.

"I'm fine." I paused. "He didn't do it." I know, it was a feeble attempt, but I had to make it. And, I realized, I honestly believed it. It was painfully obvious now that Richard didn't have the guts to shoot anyone.

But it made any trace of Ramirez's concern for my safety disappear. His face settled into those hard Schick commercial lines and just like that he was the unreadable Bad Cop again. He crossed the room in one quick stride and before I could say Miranda Rights, Richard's hands were cuffed behind his back and Ramirez was doing the right to remain silent speech.

A lump knotted in my throat and I balled my fists at my sides. Only right at the moment I wasn't sure who to be more angry at. Richard for getting involved in such a stupid scheme to begin with, or Ramirez for arresting the father of my possible child. Or, to be honest, myself, for leading Ramirez right to him. I suddenly wondered if this had been Ramirez's plan all along. Why he'd sat through my mother's kitschy wedding and made nice with Grandmother.

"You can't do this," I protested. "He's innocent. He didn't kill anyone."

Ramirez wasn't moved. He didn't even look at me, dialing a number into his cell phone instead, and requesting backup.

"He was here the whole time. Please, don't do this." God, I was pleading as pathetically as Richard had been just a minute ago.

Only Ramirez wasn't half as receptive as I'd been.

"I have a warrant," he responded in a flat monotone. "He's wanted for murder. I have to take him in."

"But, but…you kissed me!"

Both Ramirez and Richard turned to look at me. Then at each other. Uh oh. I could feel the testosterone level rising in the air.

"It was just a little kiss," I squeaked out.

Had Richard not been in handcuffs, I'd like to think he would have decked Ramirez. In reality, Ramirez would have had him flat on the floor before he even threw a punch. Either way, they let the animosity lie between them untouched as there was little Richard could do besides glare.

Ramirez held Richard by the shoulder and escorted him to the door. He paused as their little parade passed me. "I assume you can find another ride home."

And then he left.

Crap. I picked up the lamp on the writing desk and threw it on the floor with all my might. Just my luck it was plastic and kind of bounced on the shag carpet instead of making a satisfying crash. Tears welled behind my eyes, but I was damned if I was going to cry again. I'd done enough of that in the last few days to last me a lifetime. And especially not over two idiots like Richard and Ramirez.

I hated them both. Richard could rot in jail for all I cared and Ramirez…Well Ramirez could kiss my granny panties. He'd had his tongue down my throat not fifteen minutes ago and now wouldn't even listen to me. Just like a man. That was it. I was through with all of them. The whole male species. Maybe I'd make my grandmother proud and go join a convent after all.

Speaking of Grandmother…

I was pretty sure if I sat here feeling sorry for myself much longer, someone from the reception would come looking for me. And I so didn't want to have to explain this to my relatives. How many Hail Marys did one get for sleeping with criminals?

Because it hit me, that's just what Richard was. Even if he hadn't had anything to do with the murders, he'd flat out confessed to the embezzlement. White collar or no, that was a crime. I was carrying a criminal's baby. Maybe.

That squishy burrito turned into a lead weight in my stomach.

I left the room, closing Richard's door behind me and took the elevator back down to the lobby. I was sure in a matter of minutes Ramirez's backup would have CSI teams combing the room for any speck of incriminating evidence. And I wasn't in the mood for a lint roll right now.

I hightailed it back into the main hall just in time to see Mom throwing her bouquet. Both Mrs. Rosenblatt and Dana made a mad dash for it. A few beads popped off Mrs. Rosenblatt's muumuu, but Dana caught the flowers in the end. Then gazed starry eyed at No Neck. Poor guy, he didn't know what he'd gotten himself into.

I think I put on a passably convincing façade of everything was hunky dory in Maddie's life for the rest of the reception. I avoided Grandmother's not-so-subtle hinting over my biological clock versus Ramirez's suitable Catholic husband status, and even managed not to scratch my own eyeballs out through the removal of the garter belt, which I now knew should never be attempted by any bride over the age of forty. Yick.

By the time we were all blowing bubbles out of tiny bell shaped wands as Mom and Faux Dad jumped into their 1974 Mercedes with the words "just married" in shaving cream on the back window, I felt like I'd run a marathon. If I had to keep the plastic smile wedged on my face any longer I had a feeling I'd permanently end up looking like Perky Reporter Woman.

And as I watched them drive away I had a sudden and profound feeling of loneliness. Richard was on his way to prison, Ramirez—whatever that was between us—was over, Dana and No Neck had left hand in hand for another night of great sex at the Actor's Duplex, and even Mom and Faux Dad were in their own little honeymoon world for two weeks in Hawaii. It was just me and the Purple People Eater. Deep sigh.

Mrs. Rosenblatt agreed to give me a ride back to Beefcakes, where my little red Jeep had spent the night. It was dark by the time I finally drove up to my studio and I was beyond tired. I was in that state of feeling sorry for myself that comes just before the walking dead phase of exhaustion. I trudged up the stairs and unlocked the door, not even bothering to turn on the lights before I collapsed onto my futon.

I gave myself five minutes to cry. Just five. Then, I was going to be done, finished. Over that creep for good. Never mind I wasn't quite sure which creep I was talking about.

Richard, right? I mean, Richard was the one I should be getting over. He was the one I'd been dating for the past five months, all the while blind to the fact he'd been married to Cinderella on the side. Richard's betrayal was what should be eating me up inside.

Only, as I closed my eyes all I could think about was the way Ramirez's lips had tasted on mine. Like canapés and champagne.

God I was pathetic.

I rolled over and buried my head in a pillow, my only comfort knowing that tomorrow couldn't possibly be worse than today had been.

* * *

I felt sunlight hit my face the next morning, but was almost afraid to open my eyes for fear of what new disaster might await me. Tornado? Hurricane? Plague? It wouldn't surprise me. With the way my life was going my aura must be a pukey puce by now.

I summoned up all my courage and cracked one eye open.

No detectives sleeping beside me. No cell phone ringing. No screeching brides or best friends. So far so good.

Gingerly I got up and flipped on my Mr. Coffee. After two strong cups I turned on the news to see if Richard had made the morning report.

Perky Reporter Woman did a ten second snippet on the arrest of Devon Greenway's lawyer, but the whole story was losing steam and had been sandwiched between a segment on a school closure in Watts and a dog that sniffed out heroin at the airport. The press had moved on.

And, honestly, I should too. Richard probably had a whole team of lawyers surrounding him by now, pulling every rabbit out of their legal hats to get him safely back to his leather and chrome condo. What could I possibly do to help that they couldn't? More importantly, why did I even want to?

I sighed. My gaze straying to the EPT on the counter.

That's why.

I stared at the little pink box. It stared back, and I could swear it was silently mocking me. (bok, bok, bok)

"Fine, I'll take the damn test!" I yelled to the universe at large. I picked up the stupid little box and marched into the bathroom. After reading the instructions only three times (My hands were shaking just a little.), I ascertained that I was supposed to pee for five full seconds on the little cottony strip. Five seconds? This was going to take some preparation.

I went back to the kitchen and grabbed a liter of Diet Coke from the fridge. I downed half of it, only getting slightly fizzy nosed from the bubbles. I waited ten minutes, then took the Coke back into the bathroom with me. It was now or never.

I clipped my hair back, took a deep breath, and did the whole peeing thing. Which ended up being way more complicated than it sounded. When I finished, I set the test down on my bathroom counter to wait. One line negative. Two lines…I'd be asking my mother to pick up another basinet full of booties and binkies. I took a fortifying swig of Diet Coke as I watched the hands on my watch crawl by. Three minutes.

Okay, I could do this. I was a tough chick. Whatever those pink lines threw at me, I could handle this, right? Okay, so maybe I'd have to take little Ritchie Junior to visit his father behind bars, and maybe I'd never again fit into that cute Dolce crop top again, but I could do this. Of course, I'd have to get a second job. Tot Trots barely kept me in Top Ramen and pumps, there was no way I could raise a baby on that salary. I looked around my dinky studio. And I'd probably have to move back in with Mom and Faux Dad. And the Jeep would have to go. No way was a convertible Jeep safe for a baby to ride in. Oh God, would I have to get a mini van? I had a vision of myself in Mom clothes from Target, driving a beige Odyssey and living in the room above my parents' garage.

Not surprisingly, I started to hyperventilate again. I sat down hard on the tiled floor and put my head between my knees. Unfortunately, as I flipped my head down, my hair clip came undone, flying across the tiny room and knocking into the bottle of Diet Coke. Which swayed precariously on its plastic bottom, then, as I watched in slow motion horror, fell over and spilled bubbly liquid all over the EPT.

"Crap!" I jumped up and grabbed a bath towel, dabbing at the test. I looked down. It was soaked, the cottony swap at the end quickly swelling up like a sponge as the little windows turned a murky caramel color. I squinted, trying to make out any faint lines. Preferably just one of them.

Nothing.

"Crap, crap, crap!"

I sank back down to the floor. Great. Now what?

I stared at the ruined EPT. The way I saw it, I had two options. One, go back to the drug store, pick up a new test, and go through his whole thing again. Or, two, hop back on the denial train (Because it was probably just stress anyway. I mean, sometimes stress messed up your hormones, right? And I *had* been under a tad bit of stress lately.), and go back to ticking off blonde murder suspects to earn my boyfriend that get-out-of-jail-free card.

Which was scarier, murderers or a pregnancy test? After my mini van vision, that was a no-brainer.

I tossed the Coke-stained test in the trash and threw on a pair of butt hugging jeans with my favorite red mules, mentally picking up my suspects list again. The only one I had left was Carol Carter. And the only thing the *L.A. Informer* had mentioned about her was that she was an aspiring actress. If she was anything like Dana, she probably spent her Sundays at the gym, toning and shaping for the coming week of auditions. It was a long shot, but I hopped in my Jeep and pointed it in the direction of the Sunset Gym.

Twenty minutes later I was showing my membership card to the steroid gatekeeper and trying hard not to inhale the stale eau d' perspiration as I scanned the crowded workout room for Dana's perky blonde ponytail. The place was packed with film execs trying to sweat off their weekly diet of doughnuts and wanna-be starlets shaking every silicone body part imaginable in hopes of being discovered as the next *Baywatch* babe. I finally spotted Dana coaching a dark-haired man covered in veiny muscles on the leg lift machine in the corner.

Feeling conspicuously out of place in my heels, I picked my way over the medicine balls and stretch mats to the leg lifter.

"Thirteen, fourteen, fifteen…and rest. Okay, check your pulse, Sasha. You shouldn't let it get over one-sixty."

Sasha nodded, sweat trickling off his forehead as he applied two fingers to his neck.

"Dana?" I made a little one finger, come-here sign.

She saw me and waved. "Hey, what's up?" Dana looked down at my heels and frowned. "You can't work out in those."

I rolled my eyes. "Can I talk to you for a sec?"

"Shoot."

I glanced at Sasha.

"Oh, sorry," Dana said. "Maddie, this is Sasha. I told you about him, he's the pyramid bottom for the Cirqué Fantastique. Sasha, my best friend, Maddie."

"I have been pleased to met you," Sasha said in a heavy accent.

"Me too. Uh, Dana, can I talk to you?"

"Sure. Sasha, do two more sets and we'll move on to something else."

Sasha nodded and went back to his leg lifts as Dana followed me out of earshot.

"What's with the Russian?" I asked.

"Isn't he hot?"

I glanced over at him, veins popping out on his neck as he lifted a stack of metal weights. "I guess, in a steroid-happy kind of way. But what about your roommate?"

"Who, Mr. Asshole the Stripper?"

Uh oh. Trouble in the Actor's Duplex.

"What happened? You two were all over each other last night."

Dana snorted. "That's what I thought too. Only when we got back home I put the bridal bouquet in the freezer and he freaked out. He said he couldn't understand why I'd want to keep it. And I said, 'Well duh, I caught the bouquet.' And he said, 'Well, what's so special about that?' And I said, 'Well duh! It means I'm the next to get married.' And he totally freaked out. I mean, I didn't say I wanted to get married *to him, right now.* But he flipped. He said that he was suffocating. That he wasn't ready for a ball and chain. Do I look like a ball and chain?"

"Typical man." I really was beginning to hate the whole gender.

"No kidding. Anyway, I was like totally crying and Sasha called and he took me out for a cocktail, and, well, we ended up back at his place."

Dana has got to be the only woman I know who can start a story out getting dumped by one guy and end it in some other guy's bed.

"Anyway, what's up with you?" she asked. "How goes the Charlie's Angels search?"

Apparently Dana hadn't seen the news yet, her attention being consumed by a limber Russian all night. I quickly filled her in on last night's disaster as she gestured Sasha through two more rounds of Cybex torture. It took longer than I thought because the sight of Sasha's muscles straining proved to be a little distracting for Dana, but as we moved on to the rowing machine, I produced the printout from the library, showing her Carol Carter's picture.

"Do you recognize her?" I asked. "She's an actress and I thought maybe she worked out here."

Dana and Sasha both leaned in to look.

Sasha let out a low whistle. "She is having the boob that are big like cantaloupe."

"They're fake," I pointed out.

Dana squinted at the photo. "What did you say her name was?"

"Carol Carter."

"I never see boob like this. Boob back home, flat. Like pancake food. Like biting of bug." Sasha looked up at me. "Like you."

Yep. I hated all men.

"The name sounds familiar," Dana said, still staring at the photo. "Oh! You know what? We were both up for the role of Bikini Girl in that teen movie last month."

"You be very good Bikini Girl." Sasha looked Dana up and down. "Very good."

"Thank you! I thought so too. But I never got a call back."

"Those director blind. You are very good body. You have the curvy boob."

"Oh, you're so sweet!" Dana leaned down and kissed Sasha. I looked away before I got a glimpse of Russian tongue.

"Back to Carol Carter," I interrupted. "You don't happen to have her number, do you?" I asked.

"No, sorry. But I do know who her agent is. Charlie Platt. He's in that big building on the corner of Le Brea and Hollywood."

"Dana, you're a goddess." I could have hugged her if she wasn't covered in gym sweat.

"You sure boob is fake?" Sasha was still staring at the photo of Carol Carter. "Is very bouncy looking."

"Trust me, nature does not come in those sizes," I said.

He nodded. "Yes. Maybe true. Not so curvy, like Dana."

Dana giggled and kissed Sasha again. This time I definitely saw tongue. Ew.

"Well, I'll, uh, leave you two to your workout..." I trailed off as I backed away, but I was pretty sure no one was listening to me anymore.

I ran back to my Jeep and called information for the number of the Platt Agency. Unfortunately I got a recording saying they would be closed until four. I glanced down at my dash clock. Noon. I decided McDonald's was as good a place as any to wait it out and put my Jeep into gear, hitting the drive through. Fifteen minutes later I was making my way through a Big Mac, large fries, and a strawberry milkshake. Which unfortunately reminded me of Strawberry Shortcake. And my ever more tenuous employment with Tot Trots. I still hadn't called them back and I had a feeling if I didn't get those high top designs done soon, unemployment would be edging its way closer to the top of my list of problems.

With a sigh, I finished off my fries and pointed my Jeep toward home. If I put in a good hour of drawing before going to find Carol Carter, at least I could call Tot Trots back with a clear conscience. I even made myself stop by Rite Aid on the way home and bought a new pregnancy test. This time I got the deluxe digital version, which the pharmacists assured me was virtually indestructible.

Only as I pulled up to my studio, there stood the one thing in the world I wanted to see even less right now than two baby pink lines. Ramirez.

CHAPTER SEVENTEEN

———

His arms were crossed over his chest and his hair was wet, like he'd just showered, as he lounged against my front door. I had a bad feeling that if I got too close I'd smell that fresh Ivory and aftershave mix that had me sniffing my futon cushions like a bloodhound last night.

I told myself not to breathe any of it in as I got out of my Jeep. I'd pretend that he had no effect on me. He didn't. So what if he'd seduced me, met my family, and then used me to get to Richard. I was not going to lose it. I was not an emotional girly girl. I was tough. I was Demi Moore in *G.I. Jane.* I was Uma Thurman in *Kill Bill.* I was cool. Calm. In control.

"Hi," he said.

"Hi? Hi!? Don't you dare 'hi' me. You arrested my boyfriend! After feeling me up. And you have the nerve to make my grandmother like you. You know how long I'm going to have to hear her ask about that nice Catholic boy now? So don't you dare 'hi' me, you…you…pig!" Cool, in control Maddie. Yep, that's me. Ugh.

"I had a warrant." His voice was infuriatingly calm. Which of course made mine rise that much more.

"You used me!"

"Me? Maddie I'm not the one who got you pregnant then ditched you for a flea trap in Riverside."

"Look, I know you think Richard did this, but I've been looking into Greenway's past—"

Ramirez rolled his eyes. "Jesus, didn't I tell you to leave this alone?"

I gritted my teeth and ignored him. "Do you want to know what I found out or not?"

"Fine. Can we go inside first?"

I gave him the evil eye, but had to agree that Richard's status as a felon was not high on the list of things I wanted to share with my neighbors. I unlocked the door to my apartment, marching in ahead of him and laying my new EPT on the kitchen counter. Ramirez didn't wait for an invitation before following me in. He leaned against the door frame counter, arms still crossed over his chest, one eyebrow raised in anticipation.

"So? Let's hear it," he said with a this-oughta-be-good expression on his face.

I ignored the look, instead sharing my brilliant mistress theory and filling him in on my chats with Greenway's string of big breasted girlfriends. "And all three are blonde and might own stilettos," I finished. "I'm not sure. I haven't gotten access to their closets yet."

Ramirez rolled his eyes again. "Wonderful. The great shoe detective."

"Hey, you were the one who told me about the shoe clue." Okay, put like that it did sound like it belonged in a Scooby-Doo episode. But I stood my ground, putting my hands on my hips and doing my best don't-mess-with-me face.

"So, you want me to believe there's some mysterious thong wearing woman going around killing people?"

"Not people, just Greenway. And maybe his wife."

Ramirez shook his head. "This is ridiculous. The investigation is closed."

"How can it be closed? You don't even have a murder weapon yet."

Ramirez went silent.

I felt that lead weight settle in my belly again. "Do you have a murder weapon?"

"The report came back from ballistics. Greenway was shot with a .22, the same caliber weapon Richard bought for his wife last year. She says he asked to borrow it before he left town and now it's missing."

I bit my lip. "That doesn't mean Richard pulled the trigger."

Ramirez threw his hands up. "I don't understand how you can possibly think this guy's innocent."

"What makes you so sure he's not?" I countered, my voice starting to rise again.

"Because he's an asshole! He lied to you, Maddie. He lied to the police, he lied to his wife. He's a criminal."

"But he's not a murderer."

"What, because some porn star found a thong?"

"Hey, if you'd get your head out of your macho man ass for two seconds, you'd see that there were other people with plenty of motive to want Greenway dead. You were the one who said there was a stiletto impression and blonde hairs in the room."

"For God's sakes, Greenway probably had a hooker in his room."

"Metallica said we were the only hookers he saw."

"Great, so your witnesses are a porn star and a stoner. Gee, you're really building a case, Nancy Drew."

"Hey, I don't appreciate your tone of voice."

"I don't appreciate you sticking your nose into my investigation."

"I thought you said your investigation was closed."

"It is!"

"Fine!"

"Fine!"

We paused for a breath, both our nostrils flaring, glaring like two prize fighters about to start round three.

Then Ramirez glanced down at the kitchen counter. "Taken that test yet?"

"Get out!" I pointed a straight arm at the front door. "Get out, get out, get out!" Okay, so I'd become a scene out of *Women on the Verge of a Nervous Breakdown*. But he was hitting below the belt now.

"Fine," he yelled one more time before Bad Cop turned and slammed the door behind him.

I picked up the new EPT and threw it across the room at the closed front door. It bounced on the floor with a little plop. Which wasn't nearly satisfying enough. So, I picked it up and jumped up and down on it a few times. My heel hit the little plastic window with a satisfying crunch. Apparently "virtually indestructible" didn't take into consideration a pissed off woman with spiky heels.

I stared at the ruined pile of plastic. Damn. What was wrong with me that I couldn't take a simple pregnancy test without becoming Calamity Jane? Did everything I touched have to fall to pieces? That's it. I seriously needed therapy.

Ice cream therapy.

I got back in my Jeep, drove straight to the nearest Ben & Jerry's shop and ordered a pint of Chunky Monkey. I sat in the parking lot and ate the entire thing.

Unfortunately, as I licked bananas and chocolate from my plastic spoon, I realized part of what Ramirez had said was true. Richard *was* a liar. He'd kept his marriage secret from me. And that was a hell of an omission. But part of me still hoped he had a reasonable explanation. Granted it was a very small part. Smaller even than my bite-of-bug boobs. But it was still there, itching at the back of my mind. Urging me to polish off the last of my ice cream therapy and point my Jeep in the direction of Richard's office. I wasn't sure where Ramirez's cop friends were keeping Richard, but I knew someone at Dewy, Cheatum & Howe would. And it was time to have a little chat with my boyfriend.

I took the 10 into downtown, parking across the street from the law offices as I wasn't in any sort of mood to walk the two blocks from the garage. Especially since I could feel the afternoon heat creeping into the high nineties again. Instead, I anteed up the change for the meter and gratefully rode the air conditioned elevator up to the fourth floor.

As usual, Jasmine was standing sentinel at her desk. She looked up and quickly closed whatever screen she'd been working on. I suspected another highly productive solitaire game.

"You again," she said. "You're not getting past me this time." She wagged an acrylic nail at me in scolding.

"Relax, Receptionist Barbie. I'm here to see about Richard."

She gave me a big, toothy smile, which I could swear actually said kiss-off-bitch. "Richard is indisposed, as you may have heard."

"I know. I want to speak to whoever is handling his case."

"Do you have an appointment?"

I gritted my teeth. I counted to ten. I promised myself another pint of B&J's if I made it out of here without strangling her. "No. I don't have an appointment."

She smirked. I think she lived for people who didn't have appointments. "Please have a seat and I'll let Mr. Chesterton know you're here. But," she added with obvious glee in her eyes, "it could be awhile. Mr. Chesterton's *very* busy right now."

I matched her kiss-off-bitch smile with one of my own. "I'll wait."

I sat down in a leather chair near the door as Miss PP dialed Mr. Chesterton's extension. She spoke to him for a few minutes, then hung up. "He'll be with you in a moment," she said. Which of course by the satisfied gleam in her eyes translated to: Get comfy. It could be awhile.

I held my tongue, instead watching as she opened her computer screen again, her eyes intent on what I guessed was a very difficult card game for a woman whose head was filled with silicone. Her evil Barbie sense must have felt my eyes on her as she turned around and caught me staring.

"What?" she asked, one hand on her hip.

"Nothing. I'm just amazed at how much you get done around here."

She narrowed her eyes. "Sarcasm isn't a very attractive trait."

"Neither is bitchiness."

Jasmine scowled at me. At least, she tried to scowl. Her eyebrows just kind of just twitched.

"Your eyebrows are twitching."

Jasmine's hands immediately went to her forehead, and I had a moment of glee myself as she self-consciously pulled out a compact.

"For your information I'm frowning at you. It's the Botox. Dr. Bradley says I can't frown for another three days."

Ugh. Mental forehead slap.

"Well, you look very placid."

Jasmine snapped her compact shut again. "Thank you."

I refrained from pointing out that it wasn't a compliment.

I was spared further conversation about Jasmine's cosmetic procedure number five thousand and one as the frosted doors opened and Mr. Chesterton ambled up to me.

"Miss Springer, we're so sorry to hear about Richard's legal troubles," he said, taking one of my hands in both of his. Mr. Chesterton reminded me of an over sized teddy bear, tall with fuzzy cheeks and large hairy hands. He had a loud, deep voice that sounded like Raymond Burr, which, I'm told, he used to full advantage in front of a jury. I felt a little better knowing he was in charge of Richard's defense.

Right behind him was Althea, looking especially dowdy today in a checked cardigan, corduroy A-line that reached mid calf, and low heeled loafers. Her eyes never strayed higher than knee level as she stood meekly beside her employer.

"I can't tell you how eager we all are to get this whole unpleasantness cleared up," Chesterton continued. "We're sparing no expense on Richard's account."

Althea nodded beside him like a bobble head.

"Thank you," I said. "I feel better knowing someone's on Richard's side. I was kind of worried that the police aren't looking at any other suspects now."

Mr. Chesterton tilted his head. "Other suspects?"

"Well, if Richard didn't do it, someone else had to," I reasoned.

Mr. Chesterton gave me a blank look. Like the thought of Richard's innocence hadn't even occurred to him. Or, perhaps closer to the mark, just didn't interest him. Dewy, Cheatum & Howe, like most attorneys outside of a television sound stage, had no time for such trivial matters as guilt and innocence. It was all about probable cause, technicalities, loopholes, and very large retainers.

Trying my best to appeal to Mr. Chesterton's human side, (Some lawyers have those, right?) I quickly outlined my mistress theory. I admit, after the less than appreciative reception it had just gotten with Ramirez, I was a little reluctant, especially with Jasmine hanging on my every word, but at this point, I didn't have much to lose. I was *so* not doing visitations at San Quentin.

Only when I finished, Mr. Chesterton's blank face gave way to the kind of patient smile one wore with whiney children or small, disobedient dogs. "That's all very...interesting. But I'll tell you what, why don't you just let me worry about how to get Richard out of this jam."

It was that leave-it-to-the-big-boys speech again. I was really beginning to get tired of all these *big boys* screwing with *my* life.

"I want to help," I insisted.

Mr. Chesterton put on a placating smile. "Well, honey, you know what you could do that would really help Richard the most?" he asked.

I bit my lip. "What?" So help me God, if he said go home and knit I was going to lose it.

"Be Richard's moral support in all this. He needs someone in his corner. A cheerleader, if you will."

I'm proud to say I didn't laugh out loud. Not even a little snicker.

"Should I go buy pompoms, too?"

Luckily my sarcasm was lost on Chesterton. "You just leave everything to me. We'll get Richard home soon."

I gave up. It was clear Mr. Chesterton cared even less than Ramirez about the growing list of women with a grudge against Greenway. And I'd had enough arguing with pigheaded men for one day. Instead I listened in silence while Chesterton informed me that Richard was being arraigned this morning and asking for bail. Unfortunately, since Richard had already run, it was more likely he'd remain in the custody of the State until trial.

He all but patted me on the head as he sent me on my way and disappeared into the back offices again. I resisted the urge to flip him the bird as he walked away. Men!

Althea lingered behind, biting her lip as she edged a little closer to me. "You really think maybe one of Greenway's girlfriends killed him?" she asked, her voice hushed as if just talking about murder might endanger her.

I sighed, watching Jasmine type away out of the corner of my eye. Despite her attempts at looking uninterested, I'd bet my favorite Gucci boots she'd been careful to overhear every word. "I don't know. Maybe. I know Greenway was careless where women were concerned."

"Have you gone to the police with this yet?"

I cringed, remembering Ramirez's mocking tone. "As far as they're concerned the investigation is closed."

"Poor Mr. Howe." Althea's eyes dropped to the maroon carpeting and I swear they looked misty behind her coke bottle lenses. I had a feeling Althea might be the only other person on the planet who didn't think Richard was capable of shooting someone. I made a mental note to take her for a cut and color at Fernando's when this was all over.

"Don't worry," I said, surprising even myself. "I know he didn't do this. And one way or another, we'll prove it." I gave Althea a reassuring smile.

She sniffed, nodding. "Right. Well, I'll make sure Mr. Chesterton sets up a visitation with Richard for you. It will probably be sometime tomorrow. Is that okay?"

I nodded, thanking Althea even as visions of Richard in prison garb threatened morning sickness again. As I rode the elevator back down to my Jeep, I tried to feel reassured that Chesterton was doing all he could to free Richard. But all I felt was an overwhelming sense of pressure. If I didn't find Greenway's killer soon, Richard would stand trial for murder. I really hoped Carol Carter owned a .22. Because I was running out of options.

*   *   *

At exactly four-o-two I was circling the block between Fairfax and LaBrea on Hollywood Boulevard for a parking place that wasn't too blister-producingly far from the Platt Agency. I got lucky on my third try and parked between the Happy Time Go cleaners and Phat Chan's Hollywood souvenir shop. After reluctantly feeding the meter I clubbed my steering wheel and walked around the corner to the small, white building that housed the Platt Agency. Blissful air conditioning greeted me as I swung through the front doors and took in the décor. The reception room was done in a vintage theme a la Doris Day meets Rock Hudson. Big plastic flowers on the wall, retro square sofa and chairs, and olive green area rugs in geometric patterns on the polished floors. The nostalgia theme was reinforced by the occupants of the room. No less than half a dozen Marilyn Monroe look-alikes. I blinked, taking in the range from Seven Year Itch Marilyn to Happy Birthday Mr. President Marilyn. Yikes. That was a lot of peroxide.

Two folding tables were set up along one wall, stacks of headshots on one and coffee, Styrofoam cups, and untouched doughnuts on the other. In the center of the room was a kidney-shaped reception desk. Behind it sat a dark haired woman in tortoise shell glasses and the bored expression of someone who didn't appreciate having to work on a Sunday.

"Excuse me?" I said, wading through the sea of blonde bombshells.

She looked up, giving me the once over. "Are you here for the audition?" she asked in a voice with a New York edge to it.

"Me? No. Actually, I'm here to see Carol Carter. I understand she's a client of yours?"

"She is," the receptionist said. "But she's not here."

"Maybe you could give me her number?"

"Uh, hold on a sec," the receptionist gave the one finger universal wait sign as a Marilyn in a pink sweater and pumps pushed her way to the desk.

"I'm here for the—" the breathy blonde started.

Bored Receptionist cut her off. "I know, I know. The Lifetime movie. Sign in on the table, the sides are next to the sign in sheet. Leave your headshot on the pile." She shook her head as Marilyn tottered off on two-inch heels. Then mumbled something that sounded like, "I need a raise."

She turned back to me. "I'm sorry, who did you say you were?"

I took a deep breath, pulling out the speech I'd prepared in the car on the way over here. "I'm with Springer Productions. We saw Carol Carter's headshot and think she's perfect for our latest film. Do you think I could get her number from you?"

"I'm sorry," the receptionist informed me. "Miss Carter is on location in Toronto. She's there shooting a pilot for FOX."

"Canada? How long has she been in Canada?"

"Since last Wednesday."

I tried not to let my disappointment show. If Carol Carter had been out of the country all week she couldn't very well have put the hole in Greenway's head. I was beginning to feel like I was on a wild goose chase.

"Would you like me to set something up for next week?" the receptionist asked, looking past me as another Marilyn came through the door.

"Uh, no, that's okay. We'll check back then."

"Excuse me," the new Marilyn said, brushing up beside me in saddle shoes, a pencil skirt, and a pink polka dotted blouse that was two sizes too small. "I'm here for the *Goodbye Norma Jean* audition, and I..." Newbie Marilyn trailed off as she trained her eyes on me.

It took me a second to realize why, but as I stared at those big blue eyes, then lower to those big round implants, recognition hit me like a smack in the head. Bunny.

"You!" she breathed, pointing at me. "What are you doing here?"

"Uh—" Again with the stumped thing. Irrationally I looked to the receptionist, who seemed to have perked up. Apparently her day was becoming more interesting.

Bunny planted her hands on her hips. "I hung around the studio all day yesterday and your photographer never showed up."

"Huh. Go figure." I tried to edge toward the door, but Bunny and her double D's were suddenly blocking my way.

"You know what I think?" she said.

I shook my head, glancing around the sea of blond bombshells for an escape route.

"I think you're not even a real reporter."

"Reporter?" Slightly Less Bored Receptionist narrowed her eyes at me behind her frames. "I thought you said you were with Springer Productions?"

"Uh..." I looked from Marilyn to the receptionist. Wondering why my cell phone never rang at times like this. Now would be an excellent time for Mom to call with a wedding emergency or for Dana to need break–up therapy. I looked down at my purse. Silent. Damn.

"Look, here's the truth," I said, breaking under the pressure of two pairs of glaring eyes, "I'm looking into the murder of Devon Greenway. And, from what I understand, both you," I gestured to Bunny, "and Carol Carter dated Greenway."

"So?" Bunny challenged. "Devon dated lots of women."

"Which makes for lots of people with reasons to want him dead."

Bunny narrowed her eyes at me. "You think I killed Devon?"

I shrugged.

"This is better than *Desperate Housewives!*" Our receptionist was practically beaming out of her seat now. Two more Marilyns walked in, but she just waved them toward the coffee table, her eyes brighter than the Hollywood sign.

"Look, Devon may have been an ass," Bunny conceded. "But there's no way you're pinning his murder on me. Besides, didn't they arrest his lawyer?"

I cringed. "Sort of. But the police are still investigating."

Bunny put her hands on her hips, her implants jutting towards me, the buttons on her blouse straining against the pressure. "Are you the police?"

I bit my lip. "No."

"Then I don't have to answer anything."

"She's right," the receptionist said. "I saw it on *Law & Order*. She doesn't have to answer you."

"In fact," Bunny went on, advancing on me, "I think maybe it's time *you* answered some questions. Who are you, anyway?"

"Me? I'm, uh…" I'm cornered.

Thinking fast, I reached into my purse and flipped my Motorola open. "Sorry I have to take this." I pretended to push the "on" button and held it to my ear. "Hello?" I said into the silence.

"I didn't hear it ring," Helpful Receptionist said.

Bunny crossed her arms over her chest. "Me neither."

"Vibrate," I mouthed to them as I nodded and made appropriate listening noises. "Uh-huh…sure…right…"

I'd like to think my acting skills would have been pretty convincing if my phone hadn't picked that moment to start ringing the William Tell overture.

Bunny smirked. "I think your phone is ringing."

Damn. Note to self: I sucked at undercover work. "Uh, I gotta go." I made a break for it, through the front doors and down the street. All the while being serenaded by the William Tell Overture still trilling from the cell in my hand. I rounded the corner and made it to my Jeep, quickly locking the doors against any killer Marilyn Monroes before I picked up my call.

"Hello?" I breathed into the phone, the unexpected sprint causing me to pant like a golden retriever.

"Hey, it's me," Dana's voice came through. "Listen, I just remembered something else about Carol Carter."

"What?"

"She's on location in Canada right now."

Does my friend have timing or what? "Yeah, I just found that out."

"Oh. Sorry. Well, listen, I got a call for an audition tomorrow and I was wondering if I could come over in the morning and borrow something to wear. It's a campy sixties thing, kinda modern *Mod Squad* and none of my clothes are right for the part."

"Sure. Mi closet es su closet."

"Thank, hon. Oh, Sasha's calling me, gotta go." And Dana hung up.

I flipped my phone shut and took a moment to get my breathing under control again before hopping back on the 10 toward Santa Monica. Unfortunately, my day had been a bust and I was no closer to knowing who killed Greenway than Ramirez was. All I'd accomplished was alienate a pissy porn star and discover that Richard's lawyer was an old-school chauvinist. I wasn't even fully prepared to cross Carol Carter off my list of evil girlfriends. Sure she had an alibi, but what if she'd hired someone to bump Greenway off? I know, I was grasping now, but I was desperate.

I stopped at Von's on the way home to pick up a frozen pizza and another liter of Diet Coke. Then somehow a dozen Krispy Kremes jumped into my cart, along with another pint of

Chunky Monkey. I didn't fight it. I figured my dismal encounter at the Platt Agency called for major calorie comfort.

It was dark before I pulled up to my studio. I wasn't sure if I was relieved or disappointed not to see Ramirez's SUV gracing my driveway again. As much as I hated the fact we fought over everything I did, at least it beat the silence I knew was waiting for me inside.

I opened my door and flipped on the lights. Then tripped over something on the floor.

"What the—?" I looked down. It was the crushed EPT.

God I hated that thing. That thing had started this whole mess. I had a married ex(ish)-boyfriend sitting in jail, a sexy cop showing up at my apartment at all hours, a killer Barbie running around shooting people, and *I* had to deal with a freaking pregnancy test!

And the worst part was, I still didn't even know how I felt about it. A baby. I mean, I guess I wanted a baby someday. Who didn't like babies, right? Babies were cute, soft, cuddly. I mean, I'd be a monster not to want a baby, right?

The awful thing was, I kind of did want a baby. I got this warm Florence Henderson feeling when I thought about it that scared the crap out of me. But Florence had had a loving husband, a house in the suburbs, and Alice. I didn't have any of those things. I wasn't sure I could do family right now. At least, not alone.

For some odd reason, the image of Ramirez's family popped into my head. The big backyard filled with laughing children. Mama's soft, smiling face. The battered piñata hanging from a tree limb. Ramirez, holding his little niece on his lap, his pants sticky with lollipop fingerprints. The air thick with the scent of empanadas and sugar cookies. Then music. And dancing. And the feel of Ramirez's body against mine as we close danced…

I groaned. I picked up the EPT and threw it in the trash can under my sink. There. One less thing to think about.

I was just contemplating whether or not I should take the can out to the Dumpster in the back of the building, when the phone rang.

"Hello?" I answered.

There was a pause on the other end, but I heard breathing.

"Hello?" I tried again, envisioning Richard trying to make a call while rapists and murderers breathed down his neck.

Only the voice I heard wasn't Richard's. It was a woman's.

"Greenway deserved what he got. Leave it alone. Or the next bullet's for you."

CHAPTER EIGHTEEN

―――――

I froze, the receiver still glued to my ear as the line went dead. Ohmigod. Had it been Bunny? Andi? Thong woman? I couldn't tell. The voice had been kind of muffled. It was a woman. That much I knew. And she was pissed.

I shivered and quickly replaced the receiver as if she could reach through the phone and shoot me as easily as she'd done Greenway. If ever I needed confirmation that Richard was innocent, that was it.

How had she gotten my number? How did she even know who I was? Did she know where I lived too?

I ran to the front door and checked the lock. Still in place. I unlocked and relocked it again just in case. Then I checked all the windows and shut the blinds. I had the irrational urge to hide under my futon. Instead, remembering my own stint crouching in Richard's closet, I quickly scanned mine. I was relieved to find no one hiding in my seasonal sweaters.

After checking the lock on the front door one more time I sat down on my futon and turned the television on really loud. Trying to fill the now menacing silence with *Seinfeld* reruns. Only I wasn't paying attention to Jerry. I was listening for sounds outside. Like the sounds of a crazed thong wearing, stiletto walking, blonde, homicidal maniac. I turned *Seinfeld* down so I could hear better.

I was truly getting freaked out.

What I needed was a weapon. Something in case Homicidal Barbie tried to break in during the night. Like a sharp knife or a heavy wrench. Unfortunately, since I didn't cook or do carburetors, I didn't have either. My eyes scanned the room for anything heavy enough to conk a Barbie on the head. I grabbed my dusty Thighmaster from the closet and jumped back onto my futon.

Nope. Still didn't feel safe.

Reluctantly, I pulled Ramirez's number out of my purse. I stared at it. The right thing to do was call the cops, right? I mean, I'd just received a death threat. This was the sort of thing cops did. Respond to calls like this.

Only, after the way we'd verbally sparred this morning, I didn't really want to be the one to make first contact. I mean, I didn't want Ramirez to think this was just some excuse to call him. If I called him first, that made me the loser right?

I bit my lip, deciding which was worse, being a loser or being Barbie prey. I grabbed my cordless and dialed the number. It rang once. And then I chickened out and hung up. Crap. I was a loser.

The phone rang in my hand and I jumped about three feet in the air. My hands shook as I pressed the on button.

"Hello?" Oh God, please let it be a telemarketer.

"Maddie?"

No such luck. It was Ramirez.

"Oh, hi."

"Did you just call me? Your number came up on my caller ID."

I cursed modern invention.

"Oh, uh, yeah. Sort of."

"Sort of?"

"Fine. I called and hung up. Happy?"

There was a pause on the other end. I expected laughter but instead his voice held a note of concern. "What's going on? Are you okay?"

Damn. I hated that I was acting like a teenager and he was being all concerned and touching. Maddie, you are seriously screwed up girl.

"Yes. I'm okay. I just got a disturbing phone call."

A pause again. "Tell me about it."

So I did. It didn't take very long. It was a short call, but the chill in the caller's voice was leaving a long impact. When I finished there was a silence on the other end again.

"Do you want me to come over?" he asked.

Boy, did I. And I wasn't even thinking about sex. Much. Just the thought of Bad Cop with his big bad gun guarding my door made me feel a lot less like hiding under my futon. On the other hand, calling and hanging up had been pretty girly of me. And asking him to come spend the night just because some woman was crank calling me would be *really* girly. So, despite the fact that my insides were screaming, "Yes, come over, bring your gun, and let's get naked," I managed to muster up some pride.

"No, thanks. I've got my Thighmaster. I'm fine. Really."

I could hear him sighing on the other end. I don't think he believed that any more than I did.

Finally he said, "You have my number, right?"

"Yes."

"Put it on speed dial." Then he hung up.

I turned off the ringer and complied, adding Ramirez's number to my speed dial. Then I clutched my Thighmaster in one hand as my pride and I hunkered down for a long night. Punctuated by dreams of killer Mattel dolls and naked Ramirez. Was my subconscious screwed up or what?

* * *

The next morning I woke up early and checked to make sure all the doors and windows were still locked. They were. Which should have made me feel better, but only served to heighten my paranoia. I skipped the shower—visions of Janet Leigh's psycho scene playing through my head—and downed two cups of coffee instead as I quickly got dressed.

I checked my messages and found one from Althea saying that visiting hours at the prison were from two to four, and she'd put me on the list to see Richard. I said a silent thank you that at least someone was on my side.

The second message was from Dana. She'd changed her mind about borrowing an outfit, but now she needed a new pair of boots. So, did I want to shoe shop with her?

On the one hand, it seemed kind of frivolous to be shopping while my boyfriend was in jail and my life was quickly crumbling around me. On the other, a new pair of shoes always helped me think more clearly…

I quickly called Dana back and told her I'd meet her at Neiman's in half an hour.

* * *

Neiman Marcus was located in Beverly Hills just three blocks from Wilshire's famous Miracle Mile, teeming with museums, restaurants, and most importantly, store after designer store filled with fashion temptation for the visa challenged such as myself. I rounded the block, parking in the garage, and found Dana sitting in Neiman's shoe department, a pile of boots on the seat beside her.

"You're late," she said.

What was with people continually pointing this out?

"Sorry. I had a long night."

"Ooo…with your detective?"

"No!" Thanks to my stupid pride. "And he's not *my* detective. He's just *a* detective." Who kept showing up in my dreams naked. Ugh.

"Too bad. So…" Dana got that wicked twinkle in her eyes. The one that through many years of friendship I'd come to associate with short-term men. "Ask me about my night with Sasha." She wiggled her eyebrows up and down.

"Would you hate me if I said I'd rather not?"

"It was fabulous! Maddie, the man is a machine." She held up four fingers. "Four times. Four separate orgasms in one night. Can you imagine?"

I was ashamed to say, I almost couldn't.

"I'm telling you, he's like the Energizer Bunny. He just goes, and goes, and goes…"

"I get the point."

"And the best part is…" She leaned in close, pseudo whispering. "…he has a friend. Micha." She winked at me. "Wanna double date tonight?"

I admit, the Energizer Bunny aspect was tempting. "Dana, I have a boyfriend." Sort of.

She cocked her head at me. "I thought you said he was married? And, like, in jail?"

I hated that she had a point. "Can we not talk about this right now?"

She shrugged. "Okay, whatever. Just, think about it, okay?" She held up four fingers again.

I rolled my eyes and quickly changed the subject. "Are those Prada?"

"Uh-huh. You likey?" Dana wiggled her toes in a pair of camel colored calfskin boots.

"Likey? Honey, I'm in lovey. Can you afford Prada?" I asked.

"I wish. But I can afford to try them on."

As if on cue a salesman emerged from the back room, carrying three more boot boxes that he deposited on the seat beside Dana.

"Thank you, David," she said reading his name tag. "You're an absolute doll." Then she flashed him her biggest, flirtiest smile. "And would you mind checking if you have these," she pointed to a pair of spike heeled Gucci's, "in black?"

"No problem." He then looked expectantly at me.

"Oh, I, uh…" I looked from the calfskin Prada to the salesman. What the hell. "And those in a seven and a half."

Twenty minute later I was warring with my Visa over whether or not there was any chance in hell I could afford Prada. Maybe if I sold my car, and didn't eat for the next six months I could swing them. And, I decided as I looked at myself in the mirror, it would almost be worth it. The soft tan leather felt as light and airy as silk against my legs and the soles were so finely crafted it felt like I was walking on clouds. Not to mention that the three inch heels made my calves look almost like Dana's. Tiny precision stitching, perfectly molded contours, and that shiny little Prada logo zipper. Ladies and gentlemen, this is what shoes were meant to be. I twirled in front of the mirror and did a little sigh.

Unfortunately my Visa won the argument when I did the math on how many pairs of kiddie shoes I'd have to design to afford one pair of boots. It was not pretty. Reluctantly I put my own emerald slingbacks back on. Dana and I left Prada at

Neiman's and she settled on a pair of white, vinyl go-go boots for her reinvention of Mod Squad Chic.

Purchases in hand, we walked down the street to Leon's where I ordered extra cheesy chili fries and Dana munched on a low fat cucumber and sprouts pita as I told her about my late night caller.

When I finished, Dana looked thoughtful, grazing on her sprouts. "So, who do you think it was?"

"I don't know. Bunny maybe? She was pretty pissed when I ran into her at Charlie Platt's."

"Uh-huh." Dana popped a cucumber into her mouth, chewing as she nodded.

"Or maybe Andi. She did sound like she had a vicious streak to her."

"You know," Dana said, licking her fingers, "I'm wondering, have you thought about the wife?"

"Celia?" I asked. "She's dead."

"No, I meant Richard's wife."

I froze, chili fry halfway to my mouth. "I thought we weren't mentioning his marital status."

"Sorry, sorry," she said, waving her napkin in the air. "It's just…" She trailed off, biting her lip.

I gave in. "What? What about Richard's wife?"

"Well, we've been going on the theory that the murders are tied to Greenway's infidelity. But what about Richard's infidelity?"

I cringed. "Go on?"

"Well, maybe his wife found out about you and was pissed. What if she used Greenway to frame Richard? Seeing your cheating ex on death row would be one hell of a revenge."

I popped a chili fry in my mouth as I chewed on this new angle. I had to admit, I liked it. "If she was planning on divorce, twenty million dollars *would* make a nice parting gift. And as Richard's wife, Cinderella could have easily gained access to his files."

"Right. And women do get a little crazy when they discover they've been lied to."

You're telling me.

Dana shrugged. "It's something to think about anyway."

It certainly was. The only question was, would Cinderella really kill two people in cold blood just to get revenge on Richard? I shuddered. I always knew there was something creepy about those Disney characters.

"Well," Dana said balling up her napkin, "this has been fun, but I've got to be in Hollywood in twenty minutes." She held up her go-go boots. "Wish me luck."

"Break a leg," I said as she gave me an air kiss and made her way back down Wilshire. As I watched her round the corner toward the parking structure, my mind was still digesting the Cinderella theory. I scooped up the last of the chili with a soggy French fry and popped it in my mouth. I had to admit, the more I thought about it, the more I really, really wanted the killer to be Cinderella. Why not? Ramirez said that the gun was hers in the first place. Who better to use it? And the blonde hairs in Greenway's room could have easily come from her. Heck, maybe Cinderella was even having an affair with Greenway? I mean, what did I really know about her anyway? Not much. Just that she drove a brand new roadster.

And was married to my boyfriend. The bitch.

I looked down at my watch. Two-ten. Visiting hours at the prison started ten minutes ago. No time like the present to drag a few answers out of Richard. I quickly threw away the remains of my calorie splurge lunch and headed for my Jeep.

* * *

The L.A. county lock-up was about the same as you'd see in any prison movie. Bleak and square, a series of cement blocks painted a dull orange sometime in 1976. The inside wasn't much better, lit by flickering fluorescent lights and smelling like Pine-Sol and cigarettes. An indefinable feeling of tension hung in the air and no one quite looked me in the eye.

I had to stop at the desk to have my purse examined inside and out for anything that could be used as a weapon (they held my nail file hostage) and was patted down twice by a woman who looked like John Goodman before being sent into the gymnasium like room full of tables and chairs where weepy women sat across from men in orange jumpsuits. All of them looking like they could use a good bath and a dose of antibacterial soap.

The stony faced guards flanking the room did little to soothe my nerves, so I took a place at a table near the door. Five minutes later Richard was led through the self locking door on the far end of the room. I almost felt pity for him as he sat down across from me. His eyes were rimmed in dark circles like he hadn't slept and his chin was covered in pale, blonde stubble. Only it didn't remind me of a Schick commercial. More Nick Nolte's mug shot.

"Thanks for coming," he said.

I nodded, not really sure what to say.

"Chesterton tell you I wouldn't make bail?"

I nodded again. "I'm sorry."

"Me too." He looked around himself as if still not believing he was here.

I admit, I was having a hard time believing it too. But, I tried to remind myself why I'd come here.

"Richard, I need to know about your wife."

He looked down at his hands, avoiding eye contact. "I'm sorry I didn't tell you about her, Maddie. I never meant to hurt you."

"You mean, you never meant for me to find out?"

"No. I…we're separated." He sighed, still not quite looking at me. "I've been living in the condo and she's got her life in Orange County. I just haven't filed for divorce yet because I don't want some lawyer of hers nosing through my assets right now."

I bit my lip. Did I believe him? I wasn't sure. "And what about the roadster?"

"God, how do you know about…" He trailed off, his eyes meeting mine. He shook his head, running a hand through his hair so it stood up in little tufts. I guess hair gel wasn't standard prison issue. "Look, I bought Amy the roadster to put her off for a while. She wanted to file now, but I couldn't risk it. Her lawyer would have wanted detailed accounts of every penny that ever went through my hands. With everything going on with Greenway…well, I didn't think that would be a good idea right now."

"So, she's after your money?" The Cinderella theory was looking better.

"No. No, Amy's not like that. She's not about money."

Yeah right.

He shook his head. "The roadster was my idea."

"Richard, did Amy know you were seeing me?"

He looked guiltily from side to side, his eyes looking everywhere but at mine. "No. I didn't tell her."

Which didn't mean she didn't find out on her own. And go completely postal over it. I wondered what Richard would think of Cinderella if she was the killer. Would he file for divorce then? Take back the roadster? Because it was kind of bothering me that he was defending her even as he talked about how they were separated. What did he mean Cinderella wasn't into money? Who wasn't into money?

I truly intended to continue grilling him about his possibly homicidal wife. I meant to be the unemotional fact finder, on a mission to nail her itty bitty butt to the wall. But the more I thought about perfect Cinderella and her perfect Z3, the more that other-woman insecurity got to me. I'd like to blame it on hormones that while I meant to ask, "Do you think your wife's capable of murder?" something entirely different popped out of my mouth instead.

"Are you still in love with her?" I bit my lip, loath to admit just how much his answer meant.

"No. God, no. Do you really think I would do that to you Maddie?" His blue eyes searched mine as he reached across the table and took one of my hands in his. He began to draw little circles on the inside of my wrist with his thumb as his eyes pleaded with me. "I swear, pumpkin, you're the only woman in my life."

I'll admit, I was starting to waver. He really did look sincere. "What about the condom wrapper on your desk?"

"What?" To his credit he looked genuinely confused.

"I searched through your office and found a used condom wrapper wedged beneath the calendar on your desk."

Richard's jaw dropped open, shocked that I'd have the audacity to search through his office.

I raised both eyebrows in a challenge, daring him to say something about it now. Go ahead punk, make my day.

"I don't know anything about that."

"You didn't have sex with your wife at work?"

"No." He shook his head, scrunching his nose like the idea really was repulsive. "Look, I know you have every reason not to believe me after what I've put you through, but I promise you, I don't know. Pumpkin, there hasn't been anyone but you. I swear it. Please, believe me. I need you."

I need you. Not I love you, I've missed you. I need you.

And I realized he really did need me. He was up poopoo creek, and I was the only one in the world who might lend a paddle.

Only—did I need him? I looked at the man across from me. He didn't seem like a Ken Doll now. He'd been stripped of his shiny veneer and I was getting a glimpse of the man inside. The man that might have taken me years of fancy dates to the Hollywood Bowl to uncover in any other circumstances. And under the lawyer veneer, I had a sinking feeling there wasn't much left.

I'd spent the last week desperately wanting to find Richard. Thinking that if Richard was here, then suddenly I wouldn't be going through this whole possible pregnancy thing alone. That if I saw that pink line and freaked out, at least I'd have Richard to fall back on. Only I had the idea now as I sat here looking at the man I'd spent the last five months of my life with, that even if he tried, Richard might not be strong enough to catch me. Instead of falling back on him, would I be the one holding the both of us up?

Suddenly all I wanted to do was let him have it. To scream and yell and take out all my frustrations on the man that was single handedly ruining my life. I wanted to let loose and have a crying, girly breakdown to end all breakdowns right here in the prison visiting room.

He was still waiting for me to say something. "I need you to believe me." He lifted my hand to his lips and gently kissed the back of my knuckles. "Please, pumpkin, you're all I have."

Ugh. If I ever contemplated getting involved with a man again, I made a mental note to shoot myself first.

"Fine. I believe you." Maybe.

Richard did a little half smile, his hand still covering mine. "Thanks, pumpkin. I knew I could count on you."

I walked out with an odd feeling in my stomach. Hollow. Nauseating. Painful. I think it was that damn pride again.

* * *

After my brush with prison life, I stopped in at a Taco Bell and ordered a big greasy plate of nachos, smothered in gooey cheese and jalapeños. Comfort food. I ate the entire thing before going back to my apartment.

I tried not to think about my conversation with Richard as I pulled up to my studio. The awful thing was, I really kind of did believe him. I didn't think Richard was capable of leading a double life, and I could see him buying Cinderella off with a car only too well. In fact, when I'd wanted him to come with me to my cousin Shannon's confirmation last month, he'd put me off with a sparkly pair of 24 karat earrings. His story fit with his MO. Which left me where? With a boyfriend? Without? I wasn't sure. I wasn't even sure it was about me anymore. I glanced down at my belly. I made a mental note to go out and buy a new pregnancy test in the morning.

I slowly trudged up the stairs, so lost in my thoughts that I didn't even notice anything was wrong until I reached the top step.

And saw my front door gaping open.

Cold fear prickled up my spine, my feet freezing in place. Maybe it was just Dana. Maybe she'd had a fight with Sasha and had come over looking for a shoulder to cry on. Maybe Ramirez was back. Maybe he'd just let himself in.

Only I didn't see a black SUV or Dana's tan Saturn on the street.

I slowly crept forward, one step at a time, my ears pricked for any sound. All I heard was the slight hum of my neighbor's TV and the street traffic from Venice. Gingerly I pushed the front door open on its hinges.

"Hello? Dana?"

I stifled a gasp when I saw my apartment. It looked like the Big One had hit. Every cupboard was open, the meager contents of my kitchen in a broken pile on the tile floor. My futon was on its side, cushions tossed across the room. My pens were scattered across the floor mingling with shoes, clothes, and makeup into one big mess.

Fearing the worst, I took a few steps toward my drawing table. I sucked in a quick breath, biting back tears. Someone had taken a big black marker and written across my Strawberry Shortcake shoe design. "Back off bitch."

The words swam before my eyes and I felt dizzy. I was still staring at the ruined designs, realizing I had to start all over on the damn thing now, when I heard a noise behind me.

I spun around.

But not quickly enough. Before I could see what had pricked my ears, I felt an explosion behind my temple. Then the drawing table, the ruined designs, and the entire mess that was my life faded and everything went black.

CHAPTER NINTEEN

———

Slowly I blinked one eye open. Then the other. My vision was fuzzy but as I continued the painful practice of blinking, objects slowly came into focus. One emerald slingback. The Purple People Eater across the room. My pens, lipstick, purse. Slowly the room materialized in front of me. I moved my head and felt carpet beneath my cheek. What was I doing on the floor? I slowly sat up, putting one hand to my head as a jackhammer began to pound at my temple.

Then it all came back to me. My open front door, the ruined designs. The whack on the head. My eyes whipped wildly around for a sign of my attacker. None.

I grabbed my purse where it had fallen beside me and quickly dialed 9-1-1. I stood up shakily and half ran, half fell out the front door with one slingback on, down the stairs to my Jeep, where I locked myself in until I heard the police sirens approaching.

Two uniformed cops were the first to arrive. It only took them a couple minutes, but it was long enough for me to work myself up into a state of unhinged hysteria. I was crying and babbling and I'm not entirely sure the bump on the head hadn't knocked what little sanity I had left right out of my brain. One called for an ambulance and pretty soon my block was full of flashing sirens. I was impressed. Usually we didn't get this kind of law enforcement turnout unless there was a gang shooting.

The police officers searched my apartment and, predictably, found no one. The paramedic gave me a pack of ice and wrapped me in one of those ugly green blankets even though it was nearing ninety outside. He said I was in shock. I didn't disagree.

By the time the black SUV pulled up to my building, I'm happy to say I almost had myself under control again. My breathing had slowed to a near normal pace, the nice officer had retrieved a pair of fuzzy pink slippers from my closet, and my nose had almost stopped running. Almost.

I sniffed as Ramirez got out of the car, his poker face in place. He was wearing those worn-in-the-right-spots jeans again with a navy T-shirt that highlighted his dedication to the gym. I hugged the green blanket around me to keep from throwing myself into his arms.

Ramirez sat down beside me on the steps, blowing out a long breath as if I'd just tried his last nerve. "Are you okay?"

"I think so."

He reached his hand to the back of my head and carefully felt the lump. His hands were warm and gentle and I resisted the urge to lean in to his touch.

"That's quite a lump."

"Thanks."

The corner of his mouth quirked. "That wasn't exactly a compliment."

I bit my lip. "Right."

His hand moved lower, caressing the back of my neck. I think I let out a little happy groan.

"So what happened?" he asked.

I drew a shaky breath and proceeded to relive what were quite possibly the scariest moments of my entire life. Something about the idea of being attacked in my own home, a place I'd always associated with coziness and safety, shook me harder than a 7.2. When I finished my eyes were getting watery again, and I was sniffling like the guy in the Allegra commercials.

Ramirez stared at me, his hand still gently kneading my neck.

"Just say it," I said.

One eyebrow quirked. "Say what?"

"I know you're dying to say, 'I told you so.' To tell me that I should have listened to you and left this whole thing alone. That I have no idea what I'm doing and I'm only going to get myself hurt. Just say it. I know you'll feel better if you do, so just get it over with, and—"

Ramirez silenced me with his finger on my lips.

I froze. His touch soft. The look in his eyes dark. Oh God, was he going to kiss me? Here? *Now?*

But he didn't. Instead he said, "Just promise me you'll leave it alone now."

I swallowed hard as Ramirez brushed his fingertips over my lips before drawing them back into his lap. I was trying really hard not to think inappropriate thoughts.

"But isn't the fact that someone broke in proof that Richard's innocent?" I protested. "That the real killer is out there somewhere?" I was aware I sounded frighteningly like O.J.

Ramirez just shook his head. "No, Maddie, it proves you've pissed someone off. And I'm frankly not surprised. You go nosing into people's private lives and someone's bound to get upset."

I hated to admit he had a point. Any one of the loony Los Angelinos I'd encountered in the last week could have found out where I lived. I wasn't exactly the world's best undercover agent.

"I don't want to hear your name on the police scanner anymore. Promise me you'll leave it alone?"

I nodded meekly. Even though I was crossing my fingers under the green blanket.

"Good." He paused. "The medic says you might have a slight concussion. You shouldn't be alone." His dark eyes met mine. "Do you have somewhere you can stay tonight?"

I gulped. The smoky look in his eyes hung in the air between us. I'd like to attribute it to the shock that my mind instantly began undressing Ramirez right there on my front steps.

I swallowed hard. "I'll, um, I'll call Dana."

I thought I saw a flicker of disappointment in his eyes, too, but it was so quick I might have imagined it.

"Good." Ramirez got up and spoke to the uniformed officer who'd first encountered me. The uniform did a lot of wild hand gestures, pointing at me, then miming hysteria. Great. Now Ramirez was really going to think I was girly. One bump on the head and I turned into Cybil.

I pulled my cell out of my purse and dialed Dana's number, praying she picked up. She did, and I quickly explained the situation. She said she'd be right there and I hung up.

Ten minutes later her tan Saturn screeched to a halt behind the black and whites, and Mod Squad Girl came running at me. She was wearing the go-go boots and a bright pink and lime green dress that just barely covered her derrière. Especially since she was running full tilt toward me. I saw two of the uniformed officers staring after her, their tongues dragging on the asphalt as they caught the rear view.

"Ohmigod, ohmigod, are you okaaaaay?" Dana reached me and wrapped her arms around my middle, hugging me so tightly I thought my eyes might bulge out.

"I can't breathe."

"Sorry." She backed away. "What happened?"

"Somebody broke in. They trashed my place and then hit me on the head."

"Oooohhh, honey," she wailed, hugging me again.

"I'm okay," I protested, wriggling from her iron grip. "I just need somewhere else to stay tonight. Can I come home with you?"

"Of course! I'll pull the sofa bed out. And we'll make cocktails, it will be like a sleepover."

"No cocktails." Ramirez came up behind us. To his credit, his eyes didn't even linger on Dana's peek-a-boo hemline. Much.

"She's got a possible concussion. So no alcohol."

"Right. Got it." Dana nodded, as if taking notes. "No booze."

"And she shouldn't go to sleep for more than two hours at a time. She needs to be woken up to make sure she's not nauseated or disoriented."

"Right. No sleep."

Ramirez slid me a sideways glance. "And no more sticking her nose in other people's business."

I resisted the urge to stick my tongue out at him. Under the circumstances, I thought it was very mature of me.

"Right. No nosing," Dana repeated.

"I'll make sure they lock up when they're done." Ramirez gestured up toward my studio door, still standing ajar. "Let me know where you're staying and I'll have someone drop the keys off."

Dana gave him her address and phone number, which Ramirez wrote down in his little notebook. Then Ramirez got back into his SUV and drove away, leaving Dana and me both fanning ourselves as we stared after his denim clad butt worthy of a GAP commercial.

"That man is Alabama in August hot," Dana said. "Did you see those glutes?"

I sighed. "I know."

"You sure you don't want to make him *your* detective?"

No. I wasn't sure. Just like I wasn't sure if I was experiencing actual morning sickness or just reacting to the nauseating state of my love life in general. All I knew was concussion equaled whopper of a headache and my brain hurt all the way to my ash blonde roots.

"Dana, please tell me you have some Advil in your purse?"

Dana reached into her Spade knockoff while eyeing my temple, where I could feel a goose egg slowly rising. "You know, I hate to say it," she said, "but maybe Ramirez is right. Maybe you should just leave this all to the cops."

Et tu, Dana?

Only I kind of agreed with her. I had tons of suspects, motives galore, and more outrageous theories than an *X-Files* fan. But what I didn't have was any real evidence that anyone other than Richard had actually killed Greenway and his wife. And I was beginning to think that maybe Chesterton was right, that Richard's best bet at that get out of jail free was an undotted "i" or misscrossed "t" in the legal system. Maybe I *was* just making things worse. Maybe it was time to consider a career in cheerleading after all.

Trying not to feel deflated, I downed two Advil, shrugged off the green blanket, and got into Dana's Saturn. I spent most of the ride into Studio City with my eyes closed, trying not to think about how my life had suddenly become something out of a B-movie.

When we pulled up to the Actor's Duplex I flickered them open to see a blue Trans Am parked outside the building.

Dana parked behind it. "Uh-oh."

"Uh-oh? What uh-oh?"

She bit her lip and turned to me. "You're not going to like this."

Great. "Then you better tell me quickly while my head still hurts too badly to strangle you."

Dana looked from the Trans Am to me. "I kind of told Sasha and Micha to meet us here for our double date tonight."

"Dana! I told you 'no.'"

"I know, I know. But I thought you'd change your mind. I mean your boyfriend *is* in prison."

Like I needed reminding.

"I'm sorry. I was so freaked when you called I totally forgot to call Sasha and cancel."

"Dana, I'm so not in an Energizer Bunny place right now."

"Look, let's go in, and I'll explain that you're not feeling well and we'll have to double date another time."

I gave her a dirty look.

"Okay, okay. No double date. Geez. You know, I've only got your best interests at heart here. When was the last time you even had sex?"

I did not dignify this with an answer. Mostly because I couldn't remember.

When we walked in the door, Sasha and another dark haired man were seated on the living room sofa. No Neck sat in the La-Z-Boy across from them, his arms crossed over his chest, glaring.

"Sorry we're late," Dana trilled, plopping her purse down on the kitchen counter. She gave No Neck a cursory glance, then deposited a kiss on Sasha's cheek.

No Neck's eyes narrowed.

"We are waiting with roommate. He let us in. We wait a long time for you," Sasha chided. Then he looked down at Dana's higher-than-a-kite hemline. "But is worth the wait."

No Neck's eyes narrowed further.

"Sorry, we had a little emergency. Maddie," she said, dragging me into the room by the hand. "This is Micha, Sasha's friend."

Micha stood up to shake my hand. I felt a bubble of laughter escape my lips. The top of his head only came to my chin.

Micha stuck out his hand, and smiled until his face was all teeth. "I do it on top."

I blinked. Okay, way too much information for a first date. I looked from Dana to the overly friendly midget. "Please tell me he didn't just say what I think he said."

"Micha's the top of the pyramid," Dana quickly explained.

"Yes." Micha nodded. "I do it on top."

Uhn. Mental forehead smacking.

Micha sat back down, patting the sofa beside him. I sat down, sliding as far to the other end as possible.

"I like new dress you wear," Sasha said, still eyeing Dana's outfit like an Atkins dieter with a Krispy Kreme.

"Oh, thanks, honey." She glanced in No Neck's direction. "The old *ball and chain* dresses up pretty nice, doesn't she?"

Sasha nodded, his neck getting all veiny again. "Is good. Make boob look very curvy."

No Neck's eyes became tiny slits.

"So, Micha, Maddie's a shoe designer," Dana said, still obviously trying to play matchmaker to my underfed libido.

Micha looked down at my fuzzy slippers.

"Not these," I clarified. "Children's shoes."

"Ah." He nodded.

"Only the Strawberry Shortcake high tops I was working on say 'bitch' all over them now, because Greenway's mistress broke into my apartment and hit me on the head, so they're not really child friendly anymore." For future reference, I apparently tend to babble both when I'm nervous *and* when I've suffered a concussion.

Micha gave me a concerned look. Then scooted further toward his end of the sofa.

"Dana," I prodded. "Didn't you have something to tell them?" I gestured to the pyramid twins.

"Right." She cleared her throat. "Guys, Maddie's not really feeling well tonight, so we're going to have cancel. Sorry."

Sasha's face fell. Micha looked a little relieved, still glancing at my fuzzy slippers.

"When I see you again?" Sasha asked. "You come out tomorrow night? We have date then? Go very fancy restaurant?"

"Aw, isn't that sweet," Dana said. "I love how some men," she glanced in No Neck's direction again, "aren't afraid to *commit* to a relationship."

"Sasha a fear of nothing," Sasha said and I swear he was about to thump his chest like Tarzan. "Sasha love date with Dana. Love my little curvy boob."

"All right that's it!" No Neck stood up, his sudden break from silence shocking us all into immobility. "Dana, you can't possibly be serious about this guy? Did he just call you curvy boob?"

Dana did a hands-on-hips pose. "It's better than ball and chain."

"He's a meathead!"

"You're a commitmentphobe!"

"Shhhh," I pleaded, "concussion."

Unfortunately, no one paid me any attention.

"Me?" No Neck countered. "You're the one who jumps into bed with anything that happens to cross your path. And I may not see the point of freezing a bunch of damn flowers from some damn wedding, but at least I have the decency to wait until we're in bed to talk about your boobs."

Sasha stood up. "You go to bed with roommate?" he asked, looking from Dana to No Neck.

I put a hand to my temple. I think it was going to explode.

Dana looked from one testosterone machine to the other. "Um, no. Yes. I mean, maybe once. Or twice."

"Five times," No Neck corrected. "Five times in one night. Beat that, Pyramid Boy."

"You challenge Sasha?" He balled his fists, taking a step toward No Neck.

No Neck narrowed his eyes. "Maybe I am."

Dana glanced from one pair of flared nostrils to the other. Then gave me a pleading look. "Maddie?"

I sighed, standing up and positioning myself behind Sasha. "Maybe we should all just calm down a little," I said.

Of course, being that they had already engaged their instinctive male combat modes, I was completely ignored. Sasha took a step towards No Neck. No Neck balled his hand into a fist, cocking it backwards. I watched in slow motion as Micha jumped off the sofa, Dana screamed, Sasha ducked and No Neck's fist came into contact with my right eye.

"Uhn." I groaned and fell backwards into the midget.

"Ohmigod! Look what you did, you...you...Neanderthal!" Dana yelled, rushing to my aid as she and Micha half lifted, half dragged me onto the sofa.

My vision was going fuzzy but I think I saw No Neck blinking rapidly as he stood with his mouth hanging open. "He ducked. I didn't mean to hit her. Hell, I wouldn't hit a girl."

"Very bad hitting girl. You no honor." Sasha clucked his tongue and shook his head at No Neck.

"It's your fault!" No Neck shouted. "You ducked."

"Shut up, both of you," Dana yelled, throwing them both the death look.

"Would somebody please get the girl some ice?" I croaked out, feeling my eye start to swell. With any luck it would swell shut and I wouldn't have to look at myself in the mirror tomorrow. Because I had a sinking feeling it wasn't going to be pretty.

No Neck grabbed a bag of frozen edamame from the freezer and Dana stuck it on my eye. I cringed, wishing I was on something stronger than Advil. Like Vicodin. Or tequila.

Dana banished No Neck to his room, then ushered the Russian duo out the door. Sasha looked reluctantly at Dana's skirt (or lack thereof) but conceded as she none too gently slammed the door behind them.

I closed my eyes and leaned my head back on the sofa, wondering what exactly I'd done to deserve this. Was it because I hadn't gone to mass since Easter? Because I was lusting after Ramirez? Was my mother right? Did God have it in for me now?

Dana sat down on the sofa beside me and blew out a long breath. "How's your eye?"

"I'm afraid to look."

Dana pulled the edamame away and inspected. She cringed. "It's not *that* bad."

"Dana, you're a terrible liar." I covered it with the frozen soy again, wondering if maybe I could just hibernate in Dana's bedroom for the rest of the summer.

"I'm so sorry about that," Dana said. "Men suck."

"No kidding."

"That's it, I'm off men. The whole lot of them. I've got my Rabbit Pearl, what do I need a man for anyway?"

At the moment I had to agree. A battery powered rabbit seemed like a far less complicated way to live. At least rabbits didn't slug you.

*　*　*

Dana diligently woke me every two hours throughout the night. Which was a great way to make sure I didn't fall into a coma but a lousy way to get a good night's sleep. By the time I finally felt semi-rested the events of the previous evening had turned into a dull ache behind my eye and the morning had already slipped into afternoon. I sat up with an acute sense of disorientation. I had no idea where I was. This wasn't my blanket, my pillow. Hell, I didn't even think this was my T-shirt.

Then it all came flooding back to me as I saw No Neck in his boxers pouring orange juice. Dana stood with her back rigid across the kitchen, making toast. Neither speaking to each other.

I slowly got up and showered, cringing as I caught a glimpse of my eye in the mirror. It was bluer than my mother's eye shadow and, dare I say, not nearly as attractive. I gave up on the whole make-up thing, figuring I was a lost cause today, and instead borrowed a pair of jeans and a fresh tank from Dana's closet. Unfortunately the only shoes Dana had in my size were a pair of spike heeled stilettos that looked like they belonged on the feet of Bunny Hoffenmeyer, but beggars can't be choosers. By the time I came out the Actors' Standoff was still on, Dana sipping coffee and reading Variety while No Neck ate cereal from the box and glared.

"'Morning," Dana said as I walked in. Then looked up at the clock. "Almost."

"Coffee?" I croaked out.

"In the pot."

"Bless you." I navigated around the stoic No Neck and poured a generous helping into an "Aerobics instructors do it until it hurts" mug.

"Ramirez dropped off the keys to your apartment," Dana said, setting aside her paper. "They're on the counter."

"He was here?" I had a vision of him watching as I snored and drooled on the sofa bed.

"Just for a minute. Man, that guy is hot enough to fry bacon."

No Neck crunched down hard on a bite of cereal.

Dana pretended to ignore him, sipping her coffee.

"Did he say anything else?" I asked. Like maybe how he'd caught the Murderous Mistress so I could go back to my studio without feeling like there was a big target on my head?

"No. Sorry. Just the keys."

Drat.

"Anyway, I've got to get to the gym. I have a spinning class at one. You want to come with me or hang out here?"

Hmmm...take my throbbing head through an hour and a half of sweaty bicycling to nowhere or sit on Dana's sofa watching daytime TV?

"Thanks, I think I'll be fine here. You go."

Dana nodded, finishing her coffee and grabbing her gym bag. She gave me a quick hug, then gave No Neck another death glance out of the corner of her eye before she left. No Neck grunted, then stalked off to his room again.

I poured myself a second cup of coffee and took it into the living room.

Well, now what?

Contrary to my decision to become an official cheerleader last night, the idea of sitting back and doing nothing while waiting for Ramirez to give me the "all clear" signal to go back to my life didn't appeal to me. And I was more convinced than ever that the real killer was not only on the loose, but that I was getting close enough to make her nervous.

The only problem was, where to go from here? I'd pretty much exhausted Greenway's supply of playmates. I closed my eyes, mentally going down my list again.

It was possible Carol Carter had hired someone to kill Greenway, but I seriously doubted she'd even know where to find him if she really had been in Canada all week. Ditto Andi Jameson. After the pencil dick incident, I didn't see Greenway inviting her over to the Moonlight for a reconciliation.

That left Bunny. I only had her word for it that she and Greenway had split at all. And let's not forget Cinderella. If she had been toying with Greenway on the side, she had just as much opportunity as Bunny to get rid of him.

The question was, which one of them had hacked into the phony accounts and funneled out the twenty mil? Who'd had access to Richard's computer? As I'd already proven, getting past Jasmine didn't take the skills of a CIA trained spy, any blonde with half a brain could have slipped into Richard's office while she was out at lunch. And luckily, my one ally in the Richard's Innocent Campaign, was the person who'd know the comings and goings of Richard's office better than anyone. Althea.

I looked up at the clock. It was too late to coincide my inquiry with Jasmine's lunch break, so I decided to wait until five. If I knew Jasmine, she'd be the first to leave when quitting time rolled around. If I was quick, I could probably catch Althea before she left for the day without having my conversation overheard by Gossip Barbie.

Feeling pretty pleased with my plan, I settled back onto the sofa and watched trashy daytime TV for the rest of the afternoon. Unfortunately, the first thing I flipped on was Maury Povich doing a segment on surprise paternity results. I looked down at my belly. Were there any surprises in there?

I contemplated going out to buy a new pregnancy test, but considering my Jeep was still at my place, it was at least a two mile hike in the rapidly climbing heat to the nearest drug store, and I looked like I'd just gone two rounds with Oscar De La Hoya, I decided that might not be such a hot idea.

Though, I seemed to remember Dana saying something about an emergency just-in-case test...

I muted Maury and went into the bathroom, rummaging through Dana's medicine cabinet until I hit upon that familiar EPT pink stashed behind a bag of cotton balls. I stared at the box. Well, I figured things couldn't very well get much worse in my life. I might as well face the music sooner rather than later.

I ripped open the box, skimming over the instructions again for good measure, then did the whole five second urine test thing. I sat down on the rim of the bathtub to wait, gnawing my fingernails so badly Marco was sure to shriek in horror when I came in for my next manicure. Seconds crawled as I watched Dana's Betty Boop shower clock tick off the three minutes until I saw lines. Or line—singular. God I hoped it was line. Finally Betty's little red second hand did three full rotations and I jumped up as if I was sitting on springs. Resisting the urge to cover one eye, I peeked at the little windows. Nothing. Huh?

I picked up the instructions again, re-reading them. Pee on the cotton swab, leave stick on flat surface, check for lines. I did all that. I stared at the empty windows again. What the hell? I picked up the box, turning it over to look at the expiration date. January 15, 2008. Ugh. Mental forehead smacking.

I threw the useless test in the trash, too emotionally drained to even curse Dana for keeping an expired test around and flopped myself back onto the sofa, wishing Dana had something more comforting than low-carb Newton's and Diet Snapple Iced Tea to gorge myself on. I so needed a box of double stuffed Oreos right now. Instead, I settled for *Judge Judy* reruns.

By four I knew how to stuff a game hen, six signs you need a sexy makeover, and that Bo's brother was really Hope's secret lover. I was sufficiently vegged out. Flipping off the TV, I decided Jasmine was probably packing it in for the day and it was safe to resume the next phase of operation Free Richard. I grabbed my purse and called a cab, hoping I timed my trip downtown so I'd miss Jasmine.

Unfortunately, the 101 was clear of accidents and my cab driver was an eager little beaver in a blue turban, so the first face I saw as I walked into Dewy, Cheatum & Howe was, predictably, Jasmine's.

She looked up as I walked through the front doors, her eyes narrowing like a cat's. "What do you want?"

"Are you always this friendly?"

She scrunched up her nose, squinting at my face. "What happened to your eye?"

"Some receptionist gave me lip. We tussled."

She took a hand on hip stance. "Listen, you, I don't have time for this. I have a date. Why don't you just go home and make an appointment to see Chesterton tomorrow."

"I'm actually here to see Althea."

Jasmine's eyes narrowed again beneath her drawn in brows. "Althea? What do you want with her?"

"Well, I think that's between Althea and me, don't you?" I gave her my best fake smile, showing teeth and everything.

She scowled. Well, tried to scowl. It was more like a lopsided squint. That Botox was really working. "Fine. I'll get her. Wait here." She walked around the reception desk, her lipo-shrunk butt wiggling in her barely-there skirt. I didn't know how she got away with wearing that kind of stuff to work. Honestly it was the kind of outfit I'd have to borrow to make another midnight run to the Moonlight Inn. The only decent thing about it were her knock off Prada boots, the perfect made in Taiwan replicas of the pair I'd tried on yesterday. Cute, but, like everything else about Jasmine, fake.

A few minutes later Jasmine came back through the frosted doors, Althea in tow. Althea was dressed in a striped jumper that reminded me of a private school uniform. Boxy and shapeless. She shuffled toward me, talking in hushed tones.

"Maddie, what's wrong? Has something happened to Richard?" she asked, genuine concern lacing her voice. Then she paused. "What happened to your eye?"

"Nothing. Bar fight. Tripped. Whatever." I waved the question away. "Anyway, Richard's fine. I actually just want to ask you…" I paused, glancing behind me at Jasmine.

I'd hoped she'd leave for her date, but she suddenly seemed in no hurry, picking up a nail file and trying to look like she wasn't listening in.

I sighed, resigned to her eavesdropping, and pulled the newspaper photos of Bunny and Andi Jameson out of my purse. "I wanted to know if you've seen either of these women come into the office."

Althea took the photos, pursing her thin lips together as she studied them. I could feel Jasmine leaning over the desk to get a better look.

"No," Althea shook her head. "Sorry, I don't recognize either of them. Who are they?"

I tried not to sound too disappointed. "Women Greenway dated. I thought maybe one of them could have slipped in and gained access to Richard's files."

Althea gave me an apologetic look. "I really wish there was something I could do to help Mr. Howe. We all miss him around here." She bit her lip, then turned awkwardly and shuffled back through the frosted doors.

I put the photos back in my purse, trying not to feel defeated. I mean, just because Althea hadn't seen anyone, didn't mean no one had snuck in. I looked up at Jasmine, still tying to appear uninterested behind her desk. Did I dare ask her?

I watched her for a second, filing her nails, her legs crossed so one Prada knockoff stuck out from behind the desk. They were pretty good knockoffs actually. I resisted the urge to ask her where she'd bought them. I looked closely, taking in the details. Unlike most knockoffs, the metal zippers were clearly embossed with the Prada logo and the stitching was tiny and precise, not puckered. And, as Jasmine uncrossed her legs, I noticed they had that soft ease of movement unlike the usual stiff imitations. In fact…I took a step closer, openly staring at her shoes now.

Oh my God. Those weren't knockoffs. Those were a genuine pair of five hundred dollar Prada boots.

And suddenly it hit me. Where did Jasmine get the money for Prada?

CHAPTER TWENTY

———

I stared, my gaze riveted to the imported calfskin. I felt like a Jeopardy contestant, suddenly faced with all the answers if only my brain would catch up quickly enough to find the right questions to ask. The blonde hairs in the motel room. Access to Richard's files. One expensive cosmetic surgery after another on a salary that made mine look decadent. Ohmigod. Jasmine was mistress number four.

I swallowed hard, realizing I was still staring. Then looked up to find Jasmine watching me. Our eyes locked and I felt my blood turn cold.

"Are you still here?" she asked, her voice oddly flat.

"Me?" I squeaked out. "Nope. No, I'm done. I'm gone. I mean, I'm leaving now. See, here I go."

She cocked her head to one side, looking at me funny as I turned and all but ran out the door. I didn't wait for the elevator, instead taking the stairs two at a time, hoping I didn't fall and break my neck as theories swirled through my brain at an alarming pace. Had Greenway met Jasmine on one of his visits to Richard's office? What if he'd had an affair with her? With Jasmine's eavesdropping habit, she was sure to have overheard something of Richard and Greenway's less than legal money shuffling. And she had easy access to all Richard's files. Including bank account numbers. Jasmine had shot Greenway, I was sure of it.

Breathing heavily, I ran outside into the heat and got halfway to the parking garage before I remembered I didn't have my Jeep. Crap.

I paused on the sidewalk between Bernie's Pawn Shop and Starbucks. I pulled my cell phone out, poised to call Ramirez and tell him what I'd learned. But I hesitated. As sure as I was that Jasmine had done it, I didn't have a shred of proof. And I had a feeling that when Ramirez heard about my latest shoe clue, he'd have a good chuckle and I'd get the Big Boy speech again. Add to that my promise to leave the whole thing alone (never mind I'd had my fingers crossed) and I wasn't really excited about facing Bad Cop again.

What I needed was proof. Anything that definitively tied Jasmine to Greenway. Something more than a designer shoe. I had to get to her computer. It hadn't escaped my notice that her computer screen closed with lightning speed whenever I walked into the reception room. I'd bet my favorite slingbacks that the numbers to an offshore account, recently twenty million dollars richer, were buried somewhere between her solitaire games. Ramirez and his crew had no doubt torn Richard's hard drive inside and out, but who would have bothered with the receptionist's computer?

I looked down at my watch. Five-fifteen. In another couple hours the office would be empty. One thing I'd learned dating Richard was that if lawyers were going to work late, they were damn well going to charge their clients for a steak dinner while doing it. After eight the offices would be deserted. And Jasmine's computer unmanned.

I ducked into the Starbucks and ordered a mocha frappuccino, which I took to a seat by a window with a good view of Richard's building. I hadn't been there two minutes when Jasmine exited the building, her Prada boots calling to me as she walked the two blocks to the garage. I sipped my drink and waited, watching one law clerk after another leave the building. Althea came out a few minutes later, a patchwork bag with a picture of a cat on it slung over her shoulder as she made her way to the Metro Rail. Finally Donaldson left the building, getting into his Mercedes and pulling away from the curb just as it was beginning to get dark.

I forced myself to wait another half hour, just in case an important file or brief had been left behind. The after dinner crowd began to arrive, filling the coffee house with hand-holding couples. I ordered another frappuccino, watching the theater goers and homeless converge on the downtown streets. After my butt became numb and my pupils were fully dilated from caffeine overload, I finally grabbed my purse and made my way back across the street to the offices.

The building was eerily quiet as I rode the elevator up to the fourth floor. I knew the doors stood unlocked for the cleaning crew, but the only noise I heard as I got off the elevator was the steady hum of abandoned computers.

Slowly, I pushed through the frosted doors of Dewy, Cheatum & Howe, my limbs buzzing with nervous energy. Not to mention two grande frappuccinos. I tiptoed through the dark office, the plush carpet swallowing up the sound of my heels as the light from Jasmine's idle monitor guided my way.

I quickly tiptoed to Jasmine's desk, slipping behind the mahogany behemoth. Luckily, like everyone else, she kept her computer on when she left for the day. She'd logged out of the system, but I entered her back in easily enough with Richard's password. Briefs. How original. I did a mental eye roll.

Once in, I wasn't really sure what to look for. I knew I wouldn't be lucky enough to find a file marked "Swiss bank account number" but I was at a loss for where to look. I'll admit, I'm not a computer genius. I can do AOL and iTunes, but beyond that I'm kind of clueless. I began opening random files, hoping to stumble upon something useful. I could feel the clock ticking behind me and I knew it was only a matter of time before a man with a vacuum came in and asked what I was doing here.

I opened her Internet Explorer and checked her online history. Yestheyrefake dot com, a plastic surgery site came up. No big surprise. I clicked around a little more and stumbled across a pay per play cybersex site. Livelovelyladies dot com. Ugh. At least Jasmine was keeping busy at work.

I'd almost given up, deciding Ramirez was right, I was grasping at straws, when I noticed a group of files that were numbered instead of named. I'd seen files like this on Richard's computer before. Usually these numbers indicated a case number, and contained Richard's typed trial notes. I clicked, opening the files one by one. As expected, most held snippets of information about witnesses, motions, and various legal citings. But as I went down the list, opening file after file, I ran across one that was blank. I looked closely at the numbers of the other files. They all had six. This one had ten. I felt my adrenalin kick in. Did Swiss bank accounts have ten numbers? I grabbed a Post-it note from Jasmine's desk, jotting down the number. Ramirez was so going to eat crow over this.

I was so completely wrapped up in my own total genius at suspecting Jasmine, that I didn't even hear it until it was too late.

The sound of a gun cocking.

I froze, pen hovering over the post-it, hoping maybe it was just my overactive imagination.

"Bravo, Sherlock."

Nope. My imagination didn't say that.

Quickly I spun around to find myself looking straight down the barrel of a .22. I willed myself not to pee in my pants as I raised my eyes to meet…Althea?

Huh?

"Althea, what are you doing here?" Which in hindsight was an abysmally stupid question considering the gun leveled at my head pretty well explained what she was doing here.

"You couldn't just leave it alone, could you? Nosey bitch." Gone was the meek frump. In her place a crazed pair of hazel eyes blazed behind her thick lenses. The gun in her hand was surprisingly steady, the confidence in her stance unnerving.

I swallowed the sudden lump of fear in my throat. The realization of my own error hitting me with the force of a low heeled loafer in the gut. I should have known Jasmine couldn't pull off a scheme like this. Jasmine had the brain of a turnip. Althea, on the other hand, I now realized was smarter than I'd given her credit for.

"This isn't Jasmine's file, is it?" I asked, pointing to the blank page on the screen. "It's yours. You're the one who took the money. And," I added, amazed at how level my voice sounded, even as my legs had turned into Jell-O, "you're the one who broke into my apartment."

Althea did a slow smile, her lips drawing back to bare a set of slightly crooked teeth. "And here I'd figured you for just another blonde bimbo in heels."

I looked down at the gun aimed for my chest and swallowed. "Is that the gun that killed Greenway?" I asked.

Althea smiled again. Only it didn't reach to her wild eyes, still leveled at me with a barely contained energy. "Greenway was an egotistical idiot," she spat out.

"Is that why you killed him?" Okay, I was asking more out of fear of being killed than curiosity. Honestly, I couldn't care less what Crazy Lady with Gun thought about Greenway. What I cared about was stalling for time until the cleaning crew came by.

"He deserved to die. Any man who makes love to a woman like he did then leaves them deserves to die."

"Greenway had an affair with you?" I think my voice betrayed my disbelief. I was having a hard time picturing Althea in a leopard print thong.

Althea narrowed her eyes, her unplucked brows drawing together. "What, you don't think Greenway would be interested in someone like me? You think he's too good for me? Who would ever love dowdy little Althea?" Her voice was rising, growing into a shrill screech. I took a step backward, coming up against Jasmine's desk chair.

"No, no. I-I'm sure you were just his type."

Althea let out a short bark of laughter. "Of course I was his type. I had a pulse. The man thought that just because he had a penis, women should fall at his feet. That he could charm the pants off anything. One night I forgot my purse and came back to the office after everyone had gone. Devon was here, in Mr. Howe's office. He asked me to come in and help him get into Richard's system. I said I shouldn't do it. Then he told me how clever I was. How I was much too smart to be a junior clerk. How pretty I was, how sweet. I gave him the code and he seduced me, right there on Mr. Howe's desk."

I cringed. That explained the condom wrapper.

Althea's eyes were growing wider as she talked, glazing over and unblinking like someone with a high fever. Only the gun stayed steadily pointed at me. I took another step back, sliding my hand in my purse, looking for anything that could be used as a weapon. Lipstick, cash, tampon. Crap.

"When we got dressed I asked when I would see him again," Althea continued, a far away look in her eyes. "And do you know what he did?"

I was afraid to answer. I shook my head.

Althea leaned in closer so I could smell the Pert Plus on her frizzy hair. "He laughed. He said he didn't need me anymore and he laughed at me. Do you know what it's like to have the person you love laugh at you?"

I shook my head again, my fingers clenching around a long sharp object. My nail file!

"So, I got even. I found out what he and Mr. Howe were up to and tipped off a clerk at the Securities and Exchange. I drained Devon's accounts. I strangled his perfect, thin, model of a wife. And," she said, her eyes snapping back to mine as she wrapped both her hands around the trigger. "I killed him. But not right away. I made him beg first. Plead on his hands and knees for his life. And you know what I did then?"

I shook my head, wrapping my fingers around the nail file.

She leaned in, her voice low. "I laughed."

I think I was going to be sick. She had become seriously unglued. I don't know why I didn't see it sooner. Anyone who paired checked cardigans with corduroy skirts had to be touched. And this chick was way beyond touched. Her mouth was smiling while her eyes held a dull, open stare as if she was actually seeing Greenway beg in front of her.

Then a realization hit me as I stared into her vacant eyes. "I led you right to him."

Althea smiled. "Thanks for that. I knew he was still in town but it wasn't until you came waltzing in here that I knew he was at the Moonlight. The conceited ass actually thought I wanted to sleep with him again. He actually thought he was going to get laid. I played along. I dressed up in painful heels and a tight little skirt." Her eyes took on that hollow look again. "And then I shot him. Twice."

I looked down at the .22. "With Richard's gun?"

She nodded. "I found it in his desk while he was in court last week. It seemed the easiest way to kill two birds with one stone. I wasn't about to share my hard earned cash with a philandering jerk like Mr. Howe. And don't pretend otherwise, 'cause I know he was married."

I shrugged. Okay, so maybe I'd give her that point. "So, what now?" I hesitated to ask.

All traces of smile left her face. "Now, I get rid of the last loose end, drive to LAX and disappear with twenty million in retirement. I think it almost compensates for having slept with Greenway."

I swallowed hard as she leveled the gun at me. I heard blood pounding in my ears, not at all enjoying being called a loose end. My fingers tightened around the nail file in my purse. I took a deep breath as Althea leveled the gun at me.

"Goodbye," she whispered.

If I waited another second, I knew I'd be sleeping in the Dumpsters. I ducked my head down and lunged at her, nail file first, cringing as I felt it jab into her flesh.

I heard her scream as the gun went off, a shot hitting Jasmine's computer monitor with a shattering crash. I felt warm liquid ooze over my hand and I think I screamed too.

Only when I looked down, it wasn't red but clear. I looked up at Althea. One side of her chest was all wet. And smaller than the other.

"You bitch! You busted my implant!" she yelled.

Mental forehead smack. Even Althea had implants? Were mine the smallest boobs in L.A.?

Althea stood there, the gun dangling from her hand as she deflated on one side. I decided running was a good plan now. I turned and bolted across the small reception room. I almost made it to the doors, when I heard the crack of the gun and frosted glass shattered in front of me. I dove for the carpet and I heard another crack as fire seared through my arm. I clasped my hand to the pain and this time my fingers did come up red.

Yep, I was definitely going to be sick.

I lost one of Dana's stilettos as I crawled on my knees behind a potted palm. I heard three more shots embed themselves in the tastefully papered walls of Dewy, Cheatum & Howe. Then I heard a sound which was music to my ears. The clicking of an empty chamber.

"No!" Althea screamed. She was out of bullets.

I jumped up and made a run for the elevator. Only I didn't get far. My feet crunched on the shattered glass of the front doors as I felt myself being jerked backwards by my hair.

I spun around, trying to remember anything from that Tae Bo class Dana dragged me to last year. Lunge, spin, punch? Or was it spin, punch, lunge? Crap. If only I'd been paying more attention to the moves and less to the teacher's sculpted buns. Instead, I flailed with kicks, screams, and slaps. I was fighting so girly, but I didn't care.

Althea easily wrestled me to the ground. Man, she was strong for a woman. Under all those dowdy clothes she'd been hiding a body builder's physique.

I sunk my nails into her skin, digging until I heard her scream. But she didn't stop. Her hands circled around my throat and I began to see stars. I grasped around on the floor wildly for anything to smack her with. The room started to go fuzzy, all I could see were Althea's eyes, crazed and intent on me. Her glasses must have been knocked off somewhere along the way. Her bushy eyebrows drew together, her lips curled back in a creepy smile that belonged in a Wes Craven movie. I felt like crying that my last vision would be of unplucked eyebrows and frizzy hair. It just wasn't fair.

And then my hands came up against something. The fallen stiletto. I reached my fingers out as far as they would stretch, wrapping my hand around the shoe. The room was fading from my vision, my lungs gasping for air as I wiggled beneath Althea's bulk. I channeled all the strength I had left into my arm as I swung Dana's hooker footwear in the direction of Althea's neck.

I heard a scream. In all honesty, I think it might have been mine. As the hands left my throat I blinked, sucking in welcomed breaths of air. I looked down. Althea had fallen off of me. The side of her neck was covered in gooey red, Karo syrup. The stiletto heel was sticking out at an odd angle and Althea's eyes looked kind of glazed over, her mouth making gurgling sounds.

This time I'm sure the scream came from me.

I was still screaming when Ramirez burst through the shattered front doors, a handful of uniformed officers right behind him. One of them started doing some mouth to mouth on Althea and yelling for a paramedic. They came, attaching tubes and masks to her prone form, while one cop after another arrived, talking loudly into their radios. It was all so surreal and I couldn't tear my gaze from the pool of red forming around Althea's body.

At some point I stopped screaming and realized Ramirez was holding me. Close. Tight. His arms wrapped around me. He whispered into my hair.

"Are you okay?"

I gulped. Was I?

"I, I think she shot me. Is she..." I trailed off, willing myself to take a deep breath before I screamed again.

"No. She's alive. For now." Ramirez pulled away, inspecting my left arm where the fire had dulled into an aching pain like a bikini wax that wouldn't stop. "It looks like a flesh wound," he said, carefully pulling my torn shirt away. He flagged a paramedic down from the group huddled around Althea, who confirmed Ramirez's diagnosis. He said I needed stitches and Ramirez packed me into his SUV and took me to the emergency room.

Three hours later my arm looked like it belonged to Frankenstein and my neck was the same color as the Purple People Eater. I knew that I'd be wearing turtlenecks for the next few days, but at least it matched my eye. Ramirez drove me to the police station where I gave a statement in triplicate amidst barely concealed laughter as I relayed how I'd popped Althea's saline implant. By the time we were finished, the adrenalin high of the attack had worn off and left me crashing into a new low. The only thing holding me up was Ramirez, who hadn't left my side the whole night.

The sun was just starting to peek over the horizon when Ramirez finally drove me back to my studio. As he parked in the drive and shut off the engine, I voiced a thought that had been nagging at the back of my mind ever since I saw Althea wielding Richard's gun.

"If Althea was the one who took the twenty million, where did Jasmine get the money for all the Botox and Prada?"

Ramirez cocked his head, as if he didn't quite get the Prada reference, but answered anyway. "They're still processing Jasmine's computer, but from what they've found so far, someone that went by the username of SexyJas was working at a cyber sex chatting site."

Mental forehead slap. LiveLovelyLadies dot com.

"She was having cyber sex at work?"

"The way the site works is men log on and pay $3.99 a minute to chat with these women over the internet. The technologically evolved 900 number."

I rolled my eyes, doubting evolution had much to do with it.

"Apparently," Ramirez went on, "SexyJas had logged over a thousand hours in the last few months."

I mentally did the math. $3.99 times a thousand equaled...a whole lotta Prada. I made a mental note to become more computer savvy.

"So", Ramirez said, turning in his seat to face me. "You've had quite a night." He brushed the back of his hand along my cheek, tucking a strand of hair behind my ears.

"Go ahead," he said softly. "Say it."

"Huh?"

He smiled. "I know you're dying to say, 'I told you so.'"

I couldn't help it. I smiled back. "I told you so."

He grinned until that dimple flashed in his cheek. And then he leaned over the console and kissed me. Softly, gently. His lips moving over mine as if he was afraid he might break me. And the way I felt, he just might. I melted right there into his leather seats.

He pulled away, and I think I kind of fell toward him.

"Do you want me to come up?" he asked. His eyes as dark and dangerous as the panther tattooed on his arm.

Yes, yes, yes! I took a deep breath. "No." My God, was I as crazy as Althea? What did I mean 'no'?

The disappointment was clear in his eyes this time. "Right. It's been a long night. I'm sure you're tired."

Right. Tired. What I was, was confused. I'd finally found the answers to Greenway's murder, but I realized with a sinking feeling, they didn't provide me with any answers about my own mixed up life.

Ramirez walked me to my door. Then kissed me gently on the top of my head. His eyes held mine and there was no mistaking the thoughts running through his mind. I felt my resolve weaken. "Rain check," he whispered. Then got back into his SUV and left.

I stood on my darkened porch watching him. Okay, so here's the thing: More than anything I wanted Ramirez to come up. I admit, I was seriously in lust with the man. He did things to my body with one look that I didn't even think were possible.

But then there was Richard. I had kind of told him I was on his side. And even though we were both sort of ambiguous about what that meant, I'm pretty sure it didn't include me sleeping with sexy cops. Until I decided what to do about Mr. White-Collar Criminal and my inability to get a clear result out of a pregnancy test, I somehow didn't feel right letting Ramirez spend the night. Especially after the up close and personal look I'd gotten tonight at how crazy infidelity can make people.

As my libido and my better judgment mentally duked it out, I unlocked the door to my studio.

Then let out a little yelp.

Sitting on my futon in the midst of my scattered possessions was Richard.

"How did you get here?" I asked blinking rapidly.

Richard stood up. He was once again dressed in his trademark slacks and button down shirt. He'd shaven since I last saw him, and his hair was gelled back into Ken doll position again. Actually, he looked good. Really good. Like the familiar Richard I'd fallen for in the first place.

"You gave me a key," he answered.

I shook my head. "No. I mean, aren't you in jail? Oh God. Did you break out?"

Richard smiled. "No I didn't break out. The DA dropped the murder charges after they arrested Althea and I made bail."

I shook my head. Mr. Chesterton didn't waste any time.

I picked my way carefully over the piles of broken dishes and scattered clothing and sat down hard on my futon. Richard sat down beside me.

"What happened to your arm?" he asked, his voice genuinely filled with concern.

"Your secretary shot me."

"Oh, pumpkin, I'm so sorry." He put an arm around me. I was too tired to protest. Even when he started doing little kissing things on my cheek.

"I missed you so much," he whispered.

I sighed. While it would be so much easier just to hate him, I had to admit, I'd missed him a little too.

"Maddie, look, I know a lot has happened between us," Richard said, taking my hand in his. "But, I just want you to know how much I appreciate everything you've done for me. Chesterton told me how it was you that figured Althea out. I—" He choked up, his eyes misting. "No one else believed me, but you had faith in me."

I bit my lip, refraining from pointing out it wasn't so much faith as fear of having a felon's baby.

"Maddie, I know in the past I've done some stupid things."

Correction—colossally idiotic things.

"But, I want to make it up to you. Chesterton said he thinks he may be able to get me off with just probation if I agree to testify against Althea. It could take a while for the trial, but once this is all over, I want to make it up to you. I want you to move in with me. Being apart like this has shown me just how much I need you in my life and I don't want to be away from you again."

I held up my hands. "Wait, move in with you? This is all moving too fast."

"Too fast?" His puppy dog eyes looked up at me.

"Richard, you're married!"

"I had the divorce papers drawn up today."

Ouch. Poor Cinderella.

"Maddie, I know things have been crazy. But, believe me, you're the only one for me."

I shook my head, a migraine brewing behind my eyes. "Richard, I...I need time to think about this."

His shoulders sagged, but he nodded. "Of course. Take all the time you need."

I stood and walked him to the door, careful not to trip over my abused slingbacks, as he said goodnight and slipped out into the predawn light. I locked the door behind him, leaning against it with a sigh.

Bad Cop or Ken Doll?

Richard had happily ever after stamped all over his designer slacks. Once the trial passed and the divorce went through, I could easily see a house in the suburbs in Richard's future. Ramirez, on the other hand, had instant gratification tattooed across his muscular biceps. The look in his eyes tonight promised a night that could easily top Dana's four times. But then what?

And there was another aspect to consider in all this.

I looked down at my belly. Was there really someone in there? Even if there was, was that enough reason to stay with Richard?

"Well," I asked my flat belly, "what do you think I should do?"

No answer. Damn. If I hadn't just spent the night getting shot at I'd like to think I would have had the energy to go out and buy a new test then and there. As it was, I promised myself that tomorrow was The Day. Hell, I'd faced the homicidal frizz ball, I could face one little pink line. Or two

Firm in my resolve, I pulled out my futon and curled up in my blankets, and fell asleep the second my head hit the pillow.

* * *

I awoke to the sounds of a school bus dropping kids off at the end of the block and my neighbor's steamy soaps from downstairs. I cracked one eye open. 3 p.m. Yikes. I got up and took the longest shower on record, letting the scorching water sooth my over abused muscles. I put on a denim skirt and mock turtleneck to cover the purple necklace gracing my skin and added a pair of very high heels to compensate for the big ugly bandage on my arm. There wasn't much I could do about the black eye, but I gunked blue eye-shadow over the other one to try and even things out.

I made a pot of strong coffee and checked my messages. The first was Tot Trots threatening to cancel my check if they didn't see a design by Thursday. Then Marco called saying he saw me on the news last night and everyone at Fernando's was demanding details now. Mrs. Rosenblatt called and said Albert saw a black panther in my future and I should come in for an aura cleansing soon. Dana left a hysterical message, the gist of which was that she and No Neck had decided to kiss and make up, and, in the midst of the kissing part, she'd seen me on the news, and ohmigod was I okay?

I called Dana back first, and she answered on the first ring with a breathless, "Hello?"

"Hi. It's me."

"Ohmigod! Are you okaaaaaay?!"

I held the phone away from my ear, cringing at Dana's dog-whistle pitch. "Yes, I'm fine." Relatively speaking. I quickly filled her in about the Prada clue, the files on Jasmine's computer and my run-in with the Frumpty Dumpty. When I finished I could almost hear Dana vibrating with excitement on the other end.

"Ohmigod, Maddie, you totally kick butt, girl."

I couldn't help a little smile. I kinda did, didn't I?

"This is so cool," Dana continued. "You're all over the news, you know. You're like a hero now."

"Well, I don't know about that—"

"Oh, honey, don't be so modest. You single handedly solved *two* murders."

I bit my lip, refraining from mentioning I'd actually suspected the wrong blonde. "Well, I got lucky."

"I'll say. Honey, you could have been killed."

I looked down at the bandage on my arm. Like I needed a reminder.

"Well, I didn't. I'm fine."

"For now. But what about next time?"

"Next time?" I'm sorry, but I wasn't exactly chomping at the bit to come face to face with another gun wielding psycho. "Trust me, I'm a one trick pony. There will be no next time."

"How can you be sure? Maddie, this is a wake-up call. Crazies are everywhere!"

I rolled my eyes at the phone. "I'm fine, Dana."

"This guy at the gym does these self defense classes for women. We should totally sign up. He has one starting next week called Urban Combat for the Modern Woman. What do you think?"

"I think I'm hanging up now, Dana."

"Well, what about carrying a gun for protection? Or pepper spray. At least think about getting some pepper spray."

I rolled my eyes so far I think I saw blonde roots. "Goodbye, Dana." I hit the end button, leaving my best friend making a shopping list of deadly weapons.

Crossing my fingers they were in a good mood, I dialed the next number on my call back list, Tot Trots. I explained the situation and asked for an extension on the Strawberry Shortcake designs. They weren't too thrilled with one of their employees being affiliated with embezzlement and murder, but they agreed to give me until the end of July. Next I called Marco back and promised to come in for a long pedi soak and gossip session tomorrow. Then I called Mrs. Rosenblatt and promised to let her do an aura cleansing for me next week.

Then I didn't have any other calls to make except for the one I'd been dreading since I saw Richard sitting on my futon last night.

I made another cup of coffee.

I scrolled through my speed dial numbers. Ramirez's was right next to Richard's. God, I hated decisions. I closed my eyes and did a little *eenie-meenie-miney-moe*. I didn't like the outcome, so I did it again. I took a deep breath and dialed.

"Hello?" he answered.

"Hi, it's Maddie. Listen, do you want to meet for a drink tonight? Say, seven at Casa Madera on Wilshire?"

I could hear the eagerness in his voice. "I can't wait."

I admit, as I hung up I was eager too. For the first time in days, I knew I had the right answer.

CHAPTER TWENTY-ONE

———

I threw on a black, silky dress with a high neckline, high hem, and low back. I put on my Gucci two-inch heels, black mascara, and fire engine red lipstick. After giving my hair a good mousse and blow dry, I think I was looking damn sexy. Which was good. Because I needed all the confidence I could get if I was really going to do this.

I jumped in my Jeep and took the PCH up to Wilshire. The only parking spot I could find was two blocks down from the restaurant so I used the short walk to summon up my nerve. Butterflies were doing the mambo in my belly, but I told myself this was what I really wanted.

I spied him as soon as I walked in the doors. Sitting at the bar with his back to the door. I took a deep breath and held my chin up high as I made my way toward him.

He must have sensed my presence as he turned around just as I approached. His face breaking into a slow grin as he took in my outfit. I had the briefest moment of doubt at his appreciative stare, but it was all washed away as he leaned in and planted a kiss on my cheek with a, "You look gorgeous, pumpkin."

Pumpkin. Ugh. I forced a smile back. "Hi, Richard."

"Can I order you a drink?" he asked, as I slid onto the stool beside him.

"Uh…" I looked down at Richard's scotch and soda. "Just a Diet Coke, thanks."

He signaled the waiter, who quickly deposited the cool drink in front of me. I took a long sip, hoping to settle the over active butterflies.

"Maddie, I'm so glad you called," he said, taking my hand in his.

I took a deep breath. "Listen, Richard, I've thought about what you said last night."

"You have? I'm really glad to hear that. Because while I was in prison I had a lot of time to think about us and—"

"Richard it's over."

He looked up. "What?"

"Us. It's over." I let out a long breath. Wow, it felt good to say that.

"But, I..." Richard trailed off, his eyes pleading with me. "I thought we had a good thing, pumpkin. What happened?"

I snorted. "What happened? You lied to me about everything, Richard."

"But I thought you understood why." His perfectly waxed eyebrows drew together in confusion.

"I understand that when things got rough, you lied, cheated, stole, and then ran off. You're weak, Richard. And I'm way too strong to be sucked down by a guy like you. I can hold my own, but I can't hold us both up. I'm sorry."

I downed the rest of my Diet Coke in one gulp as Richard sputtered beside me. I took his bewildered face in both my hands and deposited a quick kiss on his cheek. "Good luck, Richard. I hope you don't go back to prison."

With that, I collected my purse and walked as quickly as I could through the restaurant and out the front door. I knew he was watching as I left, but I didn't even feel his eyes on me. All I felt was an enormous sense of freedom.

As soon as I got out the door I flipped my cell phone open and hit the speed dial. Ramirez answered on the second ring.

"Hello?"

"What are you doing tonight?" I asked.

He paused. "Why?"

I grinned from ear to ear. "'Cause I'd like to cash in that rain check."

I felt him smile through the phone and could almost see that sexy dimple denting his cheek. "I'll clear my schedule."

Heat wrapped around my spine, clear down to my panties. Which were so *not* grannies tonight. "There's one thing I have to do first. Meet me at my place in half an hour?"

"I'll be there."

* * *

I almost ran the rest of the way back to my Jeep. I hopped back on the PCH, pulling off at Pico for a quick duck into Rite Aid before heading home. I bought a new EPT. And this time I made sure it had a splashguard *and* an expiration date that was eighteen months into the future. I was determined to conquer the test this time.

As soon as I got home I took it into the bathroom, carefully leaving my Diet Coke in the kitchen this time. Then I sat down on my futon, trying not to look at the clock as I waited out the three minutes. You'd think I was a pro at this by now, but it was honestly the longest three minutes of my life. I chewed on a stubby nail. Rearranged my drawing pencils. Paced back and forth the four steps from one end of my living room to the next about fifteen times.

Then I heard a knock at the door. I looked up at the clock. Two minutes fifty-five seconds.

"Just a second," I called. I closed my eyes. I counted to five. Then looked down at the readout.

One line. Negative.

I let out a long breath, feeling something like a mix of disappointment and relief. Okay maybe just a little higher on the relief side. I glanced down at my belly. Maybe someday. But, tonight I had other plans…

I quickly threw the test in the wastebasket under the sink and opened the door.

Ramirez leaned against the doorframe, dressed in his usual black T-shirt and worn jeans. The panther flirted with me from beneath the hem of his sleeve and his dark eyes swept me from head to toe.

There went that panty heat again.

"Hi," I said, trying for sexy seductress but falling closer to Minnie Mouse territory again. "I'm sorry I didn't invite you up last night. I wanted to, but everything was just too confusing, and I didn't know where things stood with Richard, or what to do about the pregnancy tests, which just kept breaking, but I got a new one, and I just took it and it's—"

Ramirez silenced me with his finger on my lips. "Enough talk," he said, his voice low and smooth.

And this time he did kiss me. *Oh boy* did he kiss me.

ABOUT THE AUTHOR

Gemma Halliday is the #1 Amazon, *New York Times* & *USA Today* bestselling author of several mystery series. Gemma's books have received numerous awards, including a Golden Heart, two National Reader's Choice awards, three RITA nominations, a RONE award for best mystery, and two Killer Nashville Silver Falchion Awards for best cozy mystery and readers' choice. She currently lives in the San Francisco Bay Area with her large, loud, and loving family.

To learn more about Gemma, visit her online at
http://www.gemmahalliday.com

Series in print now from Gemma Halliday...

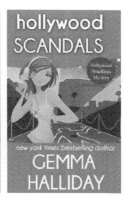

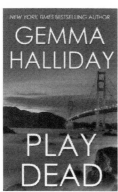
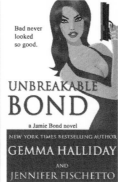

Want to get an email alert when the next High Heels Mystery is available? Sign up for my newsletter today and as a bonus receive a FREE ebook!

www.GemmaHalliday.com